# AVENGING ANGEL

## ALAN DEL MONTE

AVENGING ANGEL

Published by:
Fishing Pole Publishing
Milford, CT

ISBN: 978-1-7326886-0-5 (pbk)
ISBN: 978-1-7326886-1-2 (digital)

Printed in the United States of America

For my lovely wife Jan: Always standing by my side and in my corner.

# CHAPTER ONE

Tiny ghosts and goblins scurried merrily along the streets as a clear star filled night quickly descended on the Borough of Manhattan. Just days before, the clocks had been rolled back, making the hour of 7:00 p.m. much darker than weeks past. Carmine Cogiulo expertly maneuvered the Lincoln limousine he was driving through the heavy traffic along 97th Street E. through Central Park. He made a right-hand turn onto Fifth Avenue, then carefully worked his way onto the left lane before easing his way down Embassy Row, before coming to a stop at a vacant space in front of the Japanese Embassy. He had been in no hurry. Carmine had planned the route perfectly, allowing himself plenty of time for any unexpected snafus. His attention to detail and his excellent work habits made him a valued soldier in the Trumenta crime family. Follow-through guys had a high priority placed on them. Carmine's two passengers this evening were about to finalize business dealings that were of the utmost importance to the Trumenta and Po organizations. He was well aware that the safety and security of his passengers were to be taken seriously.

Joon Ho Lee, a trusted business associate of the Pos, shifted nervously in his seat as the large black limo sat idling, waiting for the arrival of a second passenger. The thought of sharing the same space with a Japanese diplomat, even one in league with the Pos, made him uneasy. For centuries, the Chinese and Japanese nations had been at war with one another. The assumption that these two great nations shared a mutual distaste for each other was correct. But huge sums of money have a unique way of overcoming any lack of trust that exists between even the bitterest of enemies, and desperation has a funny way of breaking down the most formidable of barriers, especially in the 90's. Soon, a small, impeccably dressed middle-aged gentleman emerged from the embassy and made a direct path to the rear door of the limousine. He was right on time. Hiso Yamagachi, an attaché to the Japanese ambassador slid into the seat alongside Joon Ho. Token greetings were exchanged. Then Joon Ho instructed Carmine to proceed. Carmine obliged, guiding the large car into the traffic and moving steadily down Fifth Avenue towards 51st Street and their destination. His two passengers wasted little time. They opened their briefcases and began to sign and exchange documents. No words were spoken.

Carmine had no interest in the activities of the two Asians in his back seat and soon he became lost in thoughts of his young wife Carla with whom he had shared a bed just hours before.

The entrance to the parking garage on West 51st Street between Sixth and Seventh Avenues appeared, snapping Carmine out of his reverie. He slowed down and turned into the building, gave a knowing wave to the attendant who motioned him forward and drove six levels up to the top floor. Carmine noticed that his two passengers were now sitting with closed cases on their laps. He assumed that their business was completed. His instructions were to pull the car over to the northwest exit and wait for a courier to appear.

They waited about five minutes before the exit door opened and a young Japanese male, this one in his late twenties, walked over to the car, opened the door and placed his head inside. The sight of the young man startled Yamagachi. Before anyone knew what happened, the young man pulled an automatic weapon and emptied the clip into both the Asians. Their hysterical screaming almost matched the deafening noise level of the exploding gun. Carmine acted instinctively and reached for his weapon, but a hot pain in his shoulder stopped him. The glass of the driver side door shattered all around him as he took a full clip from a shooter who had approached from another direction. Carmine was not prepared for anything like this. He had paid only casual attention to anyone who ventured nearby. The Trumentas told him to be on the lookout for photographers. The concern was that photos of this meeting could be very hard to explain and would surely prove detrimental, even fatal, to their plans. It would be embarrassing for the Japanese and Pos if news of this meeting leaked out. For weeks the underworld was experiencing rumblings that the Japs and Chinks were cooking something up. It was a foregone conclusion that the Chinese involved must be the Pos. They were the only organization large enough to pull off something big like this. But no one could figure out the identity of the other group. And then there was another matter of great concern. If the Pos were involved, wouldn't the Trumentas be right there with them?

But no one could have foreseen a massacre. Who would that benefit? That was sure to take some time to figure out. Meanwhile, the first shooter snatched both briefcases and he and the other man ran two levels down the back stairwell to a waiting Mercedes with dark tinted windows. The car roared down the final four levels and exploded out onto the 52nd Street side. The driver yanked the car to the right and up 52nd towards Sixth Avenue and the East side. The lights and traffic were obliging so the getaway car easily made its way to the F.D.R. Drive and quickly disappeared downtown.

Two attendants who had been on the fifth floor ran up to the top level to see what had happened. The barrage of gunfire and all the screaming startled them. When they got to the car they saw the grisly scene of three bullet filled bodies. Blood seemed to be everywhere. All they could do was to call the police.

Detectives Lucy and Bobby Ferrigno were grabbing an early dinner at a restaurant on the corner of 52nd and Sixth. Bobby had gotten tickets to a Knicks game so he and Lucy had decided to make a night of it. The blaring police sirens roaring around the corner of Sixth Avenue onto 51st Street and into the parking lot shattered the ambience of the restaurant. A young man who was on his way up 51st Street to meet friends at a local bar rushed into the restaurant yelling, "There's been a shooting across the street at the parking garage." Instantly the restaurant became chaotic as people strained to see what was going on. Lucy and Bobby jumped up, flashed their badges to their waiter and ran out of the restaurant and over to the garage trailing the emergency vehicles up to the top level. The scene was pure bedlam. At One Police Plaza, in the financial district, Chief of Detectives Marv Levy was getting ready to call it a night when the phone rang. He lifted the receiver to his ear and was pleasantly surprised to hear the voice of his old friend Bobby Ferrigno.

"Hey Pal, how are you?" Marv asked.

"Great," said Bobby. "How are things with you?"

"Couldn't be better," said Marv. "Man, it's good to hear your voice. What's up?"

"I just thought you should know, two Asians just got gunned down in their limousine at a parking garage on 56th between Sixth and Seventh. It appears that one is an attaché to the Japanese consulate."

"I'll be right there," said Marv, who slammed the receiver down before waiting for Ferrigno's response. Marv called for his car and wasted little time making it to the elevator that would carry him down to the garage level. Within moments, officer Cal Munroe pulled the standard issue Crown Victoria sedan to the waiting area to pick up an anxious Marv Levy.

Munroe was the perfect fit for the demanding Levy; he didn't say much, he just went about his job quietly and efficiently. He was also a decorated officer. On an insufferably hot August night, while the city found itself choked by a prolonged heat wave, two rival Hispanic gangs decided to stage a turf war shootout on Avenue A on the lower East side of Manhattan. An unsuspecting Capt. Levy had the misfortune to be there at the same time. Suddenly, Marv's car was taking fire from all directions. Without a moment's hesitation, Munroe drove into the area of heaviest gunfire. He managed to run down and kill three of the assailants emerging safely on the other side of the war zone. Two of his tires had been flattened in the barrage, but that had little effect on the outcome. Munroe drove like a man possessed. He managed to save Marv's life and get himself decorated in the process.

At the time Munroe was only on temporary assignment with Marv's unit. Marv decided right then and there he would become a permanent part of the team. From that day forward Munroe became a son to Marv and Maris Levy, the son they never had. Munroe steered the Chief's car up to the fourth level of the garage. The glut of official vehicles and media vans made it impossible to go any further. Marv and his driver got out and walked up the remaining two levels joining Bobby and Lucy at the scene. The media people were beginning to get in everybody's way and on everyone's nerves. Orders had come down that nothing was to be moved until Marv got there. The growing crowd was making it more difficult with each passing moment.

Marv greeted Lucy and Bobby with a hug. That raised a few eyebrows from some of the badges who were unaware of the trio's history. It wasn't exactly standard operating procedure for New York City police detectives to exchange hugs at a crime scene. The confused looks on their faces were understandable, if not comical.

Marv walked over to the crime scene boss who gave him the details of what he had, then went on over to get a look at the vehicle. He looked inside to see for himself the carnage that had taken place. Suddenly, he had a bad feeling. He straightened up and asked the crime scene boss for the names of the three victims. He was informed that one was Chinese, one Japanese and the one in the front was definitely Italian- American. Hearing their names only confirmed what Marv suspected. For one of the few times in his long career, Marv wished he was wrong about what he was thinking. With an air of reluctant resignation, he stepped slowly back, plunged his hands deep into his coat pockets and exhaled deeply as his shoulders collapsed. He knew exactly what had gone down. Lucy and Bobby were taken aback at his words.

'Dammit," he said. "Here we go again."

# CHAPTER TWO

**Previously:**

Carmine could never believe his good fortune that Carla De Maio, a hot little 23-year-old waitress at Sally B's on Avenue U in Brooklyn, could be attracted to a 42-year-old "old man" as he referred to himself. After all, there were so many young Turks prowling the streets of the neighborhood.

Carmine's first wife, Jenny, had died of cancer at 36 years of age and for three long years, Carmine took it one day at a time. It all seemed innocent enough when Carla would come over to his solitary booth at the diner and make small talk. Carmine never allowed himself to read anything into it. He assumed that she was being kind to the neighborhood's lost soul. Then Carmine noticed that the usually animated Carla began to act strangely, even distant towards everyone. She seemed to have lost her cheery personality. She was still a top-flight waitress, but there was no bounce in her step, no music in her voice. Carmine began to become concerned. When he questioned her about it, she just put him off. She told him it was nothing and that she didn't want to bother him with her little problems. But Carmine asked around and found that the young girl had an admirer whom she did not care for, one who would not take no for an answer. It seems the guy was bothering her at home and Carla was beginning to become frightened by him. As usual, Carmine let a little time pass to assess the situation and formulate a plan. He needed to know if this guy was connected to anybody. If he were, then Carmine would have to go through channels. But the troublemaker was a nobody, so Carmine was free to take action. On a very cold December night, a week before Christmas, the unwanted suitor got an early Christmas present, courtesy of Carmine Cogiulo. Four large boys from the neighborhood waited until the young man emerged from his favorite tavern at about 1:30 a.m. They proceeded to give him a thorough beating and dumped him clothed only in his cotton briefs in front of the bar. Tucked in his drawers was a note telling him to go away for good if he valued his life. The neighborhood never saw or heard from him again. Carla had an idea that Carmine had a hand in this. A friend to the friendless and known as the "neighborhood fixer," anyone in need knew to go to Carmine when all else failed. Carmine nearly fell off his stool when Carla invited him to dinner one night.

"Come on, Carmine," she pleaded. "Neither of us seems to be breaking any dating records. Besides, I bet we could have a good time if we tried."

"People might think you're out with your father," said Carmine. He was half kidding, but soberly called attention to the embarrassment they might feel from the strange looks they were sure to experience out in public.

"That wouldn't be so bad," she countered with a playful look in her eyes.

They both shared a good laugh and when Carla's shift was over, they headed down Flatbush Avenue to Vincent's, a restaurant specializing in veal dishes.

The unlikely couple talked for hours. The conversation was effortless on both sides, as the time seemed to fly by. Carmine couldn't believe that this was their first in-depth conversation. They laughed and joked as if they had known each other for years. Finally, it was time to leave. Most of the restaurant's lights were turned off and the wait-staff all left at once. Carmine and Carla took this as a sign. Carmine grew nervous because he wasn't sure what to do next. It seemed like a thousand years since he had gone on a first date. He didn't want to break the spell, but it really was time to call it a night. He took Carla home and walked her to her door. He thanked her for a great time and suddenly felt awkward. He calmly leaned towards her to kiss her good-night. Carla accepted his kiss. As Carmine started to back away Carla gently took hold of his coat collar, smiled and then pressed her voluptuous young body up against his. The warmth of her mouth and the crush of her firm body felt so good to a man who had been without a woman of his own for such a long time. Carmine put his arms around her and pulled her even tighter. Carla released his lips, looked into his half believing eyes and said, "I want to be yours. Do you know what I'm saying ?"

Carmine wasn't sure. He didn't know what to think.

"Come on, Carmine," Carla continued, "you must have known I've been digging you for months. I could not wait for you to come into the diner every night. I looked forward to that every day."

Her words stunned Carmine.

"I want to be your girl and then I want to be much more. But right now, I want everyone to know that I am your woman."

She paused for a moment to allow her words to take hold and then she went on.

"I want to take care of you in every way."

Carmine stumbled for words. "You sure about this?" was all he was able to offer.

"Why don't you give me a shot?" she said with a smile that took away all his defenses.

Three months later they were married and this afternoon, Carla was determined to send her man off satisfied. She cooked for him, made love to him and sent him on his way to meet the Asians with a smile on his face.

The massacre at the garage on 54th Street put a very unhappy ending to that story.

# CHAPTER THREE

The top floor of the Puck building on Houston and Lafayette was magically transformed into Sleepy Hollow. Hundreds of branches connected by hanging moss and floating draperies and a room illuminated by thousands of tiny white lights produced an eerie atmosphere reminiscent of a time when Hendrick Hudson and his Dutch brethren ruled the areas north of the city. Nicholas Thor Hewett and his family, descendents of the original Knickerbocker ruling class of New York society, were throwing their annual gala. The finest and wealthiest of the city had turned out as usual to see and be seen. Halloween night with the Hewetts was the social event of the Fall season and omission from the guest list was social homicide. Political bigwigs, local dignitaries, the couture elect, even the coiffeur of the moment came as guests of New York City's true aristocracy. Hewett's only daughter, Katherine, a thirty-something knockout, acted as hostess for the family bash. Strikingly tall and beautiful with a bountiful mane of shoulder length blonde hair, Katherine Hewett more than held her own among the galaxy of models and assorted lovelies escorting the well-heeled power players, very much in attendance. Katherine's mother had died when she was quite young, and though an only child, she and her father maintained, at best, a strained relationship. The elder Hewett had little to no chance controlling his independent daughter through financial means. Two of Katherine's paternal aunts had passed on and bequeathed Katherine their considerable fortunes. Katherine's holdings rivaled those of her father's, which would make her fabulously wealthy when he passed on and left everything to his rebellious, but deeply loved daughter. The problem was that Nicholas Hewett was too steeped in tradition to have a clue as to understanding his daughter's free spirit. Katherine loved her father, but refused to live a life according to the dictates of family. That air of rebellion she carried with such flair simply made her skin glow. Her every move, every gesture was the epitome of elegance of one who belongs to that lofty group still referred to as the beautiful people.

Nirigama Nagoto and his girlfriend, Holly Tanaka, were the head chefs for one of New York City's most popular and expensive caterers, Rising Sun Caterers. Everything at the affair was going well, but Nagoto was a mass of nerves. His brother Maso, the first gunman at the 51st Street execution was coming there to drop off the contents of the two stolen briefcases to pass along to people who would be coming to collect them. Maso would simply pass as a helper until delivery could successfully be completed. Maso showed up on schedule, but after an hour passed and no one at the party made contact with him, he began to get panicky. He assumed that something had gone wrong. He had been told that the transfer would occur shortly after his arrival. He began to look for a place to hide his package and get out of there to make some calls to try to find out what happened and what to do next. He was too scared to take the package with him so he brazenly approached the hostess and told her that he had something that needed to be placed in a safe place until he could return. Katherine was caught off guard, but the young man seemed so sincere and concerned that she agreed to help him. She told him to seek out her best friend, MaryAnn Vanooster, and give her whatever he had with instructions to place them with the rest of the Hewett belongings. Maso thanked her and set out to find the Vanooster woman. The lady had temporarily left and Maso was becoming increasingly nervous. He found a box with the Hewett's name on it and placed the documents at the bottom of its contents. He then found his brother and instructed him that should anything happen to him, he should retrieve the package from Ms. Hewett and hold onto it until he was contacted. Nirigama was not thrilled by his brother's request, but seeing how upset his younger brother was, he agreed to do as he was asked. He embraced his brother and wished him well.

Maso made a hasty exit to seek some answers. His quest and his life ended one minute and 20 paces from the front of the Puck building. His body was discovered the next morning by two workmen having a smoke in the side alley.

The festivities went on until 1:00 a.m. The Hewett party took their leave to catch Bobby Short's special late show at the Carlyle Hotel. The Hewetts never required a reservation. After the crowd left, MaryAnn Vanooster placed the Hewett package along with some other odds and ends in the back of her Jeep Cherokee. She was heading up to Hyde Park to spend the rest of the week with her family. The Vanoosters were from the same moneyed class as the Hewetts. She and Katherine were childhood friends. For Katherine, MaryAnn was the only true friend she would ever allow herself. Katherine trusted her with her life. Both grew up knowing the loneliness of an only child; their friendship bore nearly spiritual bonds.

Holly Tanaka and Nirigama returned to the Rising Sun warehouse, stored everything away, dismissed the staff and prepared to leave, satisfied with a job well done. The Hewetts had expressed their profound gratitude for their excellent work. The evening had been a smashing success. Now they were free to head home for a well-deserved good night's sleep. But they had visitors.

Nirigama was startled by the appearance of three Chinese men who had quietly entered the building after the others had left.
"Is there something I can do for you gentlemen?" he asked

The men just smiled at one another.

This made the young couple nervous. Their apprehension was

not unfounded. Two of the men slowly pulled out large 9 millimeter handguns and pointed them at Holly.

"For your friend's sake, I sincerely hope you can," said the older man, obviously the one in charge.

"What is it that you believe I can tell you?" asked a now frightened Nirigama.

"I believe that you have in your possession a package that belongs to us. It would be wise to give it to us now. That is all we want from you. Simply give it to us and we will be on our way. Then you could be on yours," the older man assured.

Nirigama realized that he and his companion were in grave danger. "I do not have your package, but I can tell you where it is. I only know what my brother told me. Surely he could tell you," reasoned Nirigama.

"We cannot find your brother," the man lied, "but we were informed that he came to you for aid earlier this evening."

"That is true," Nirigama offered. "He was alarmed when someone did not come to collect it at the affair at the Puck building, so he gave it to Miss Hewett for safekeeping. I was to go to her if anything were to happen to him. Those were his instructions."

"Are you saying this Hewett woman has our package?" The leader inquired. "Why would your brother do such a thing? Did he know this woman?"

"I honestly do not know. Maybe he just took a chance. Listen, my brother and I do not have much contact. Our lives have taken different paths. You must believe me. We had no part in this," said Nirigama.

"I know that," said the leader. "Our only concern is for the safe recovery of our package. But I must be sure that you are telling us the truth."

"I am telling you the truth. You must believe me." The young man pleaded.

The leader paused for a moment to consider the caterer's story. It seemed plausible. He reasoned that the two people standing in front of them were merely two working stiffs. He felt confident that the couple was too scared to do anything but tell the truth.

"I do believe you," he said, finally. And then he ordered, "kill them!"

The two gunmen opened fire on the defenseless couple, hitting them many times and leaving them dead on the office floor.

"Come, we must find this Hewett woman and take control of those documents," he informed his companions.

# CHAPTER FOUR

It was 10:00 p.m. and night was in full bloom in Manhattan. In Hong Kong, it was 11:00 a.m. the next morning. Victor Chen, head of operations in the Far East, was just settling into his office at number 13 Desveaux Street, in the business district. Luckily for him he had just set his cup of European roast coffee on its saucer when he received his uncle's disturbing call. Victor quickly took his phone off its conference call setting so that only he could hear Han Li's words. He waved his staff out and proceeded to process the disastrous news from America. The two leaders spent a few more moments formalizing a plan of action then agreed to talk again in a few hours. For Han Li, it would be a long night.

Victor took another sip of his coffee and leaned back in his huge leather chair. His outward demeanor appeared calm, more pensive than upset. It only served to mask a mind racing at warp speed. Most leaders in his position would be trying to figure out what happened and how to avoid panic among the ranks. Victor's thoughts were leaning more towards retribution; that was typical of Victor. Someone in New York was going to pay dearly for what had happened. The way Victor saw it, the worst case scenario was all out global warfare with rival factions. He was confident that the Pos could win such a conflict. But, the cost would be mind-boggling. He reasoned that few would have the stomach to take part in such a struggle, given the power and the allies of the Pos. He further reasoned that there would not be enough enemies left to be punished properly afterwards for causing such a fruitless war. The best case scenario, he reasoned, would be that a deal worth $1 billion had just gone sour due to the untimely intervention of a meddlesome third party. Whatever the case, Victor was not happy. That would not be good news for anyone in the near vicinity of wrongdoing.

A meeting of the Asian brain trust convened in very short order at 2:00 p.m. Hong Kong time. Family members from Malaysia, the Mainland, Tai Pei and Taiwan had settled into their seats, preparing themselves for the worst. Back in New York, a tired and agitated Han Li was waiting deep into the night to hear the outcome of that meeting.

Like the joint chiefs of staff, all the powerful heads of Po interests in the far east sat around the massive conference table at Great Wall headquarters. Many of these men were much older than Victor, but it was obvious who they considered the "chairman of the board." Victor was a brilliant tactician, knowing who to trust and who to listen to. He would carefully consider their advice and make his conclusions, all the while being careful to uphold their honor. He knew all too well the magnitude of that.

An historic deal had been made with Masotoma Electronics, the giant of the Japanese hi tech community. Never before had a Japanese company done the unthinkable, and come to the Chinese, of all people, for money. Of course, the Pos were not just any Chinese group. And let us not forget that the Trumentas had some cash as well. But the business and financial atmosphere in Japan was deteriorating amidst stock market and corporate scandal, something never before seen in Japan's long and honor-bound history. Honor was taking a backseat to economic greed and trust from the international community was evaporating. Enter the Pos and their banking connections. By a sheer twist of fate, Li Xsing Po had befriended Hiakama Masotoma many years ago, and now an older Masotoma was coming to the family of his deceased friend for assistance.

The Pos would loan Masotoma E. thirty million dollars American to see them through a cash flow problem. In return, Great Wall would be issued stocks in the company which would be worth considerably more to them in the future. This was a deal of epic proportions, given the changing economics of the Pacific rim and the history of these two unfriendly nations. The development of China's fledgling hi tech industries would surely be a problem for Japan in the future. But, Masotoma had a problem right now, and if not addressed, there was a very real chance that Masotoma E. might not have a future. So, first things first. A deal had to be worked out and each side would have to trust the other to honor it in every way.

It appeared as though a time of testing was at hand. It would now be up to the principals to hang tough and see this through. This was going to prove most interesting. After two hours of debate and one very long conversation with Hiakama Masotoma, a decision was reached. Victor immediately sent word to Michael on the island and then placed a call to his uncle waiting anxiously in New York. Victor's message was clear and direct. "No one in Asia knew what to expect." This was really uncharted territory. But it was agreed upon that, for now, the Pos would have to go forward on faith and sheer determination. This was all made necessary because Masotoma still wanted the cash and the quicker the better.

# CHAPTER FIVE

Michael DeAngelo sat peacefully in front of the gravestones of his late wife and father. Two years had come and gone, but nothing seemed to diminish the hollowness Michael felt for his loss. He had become a cult-like figure in lower Manhattan, moving easily in all circles. Even the mayor, thanks to Walter Larkin, now counted Michael a trusted ally. In Chinatown, he was reverently called Master Po. He succeeded in attaining the same warmth and good will of the people of Chinatown as he had enjoyed in Brooklyn years ago. Dinner at Rosa's, every Sunday, was a must for Michael and Wee. And Michael loved entertaining his momma Rosa over in Manhattan whenever he could coax her into joining him for the opera or just spending an enjoyable afternoon walking in Central Park. He loved taking her to dinner, even though Rosa complained that he spoiled her and spent too much money. It took a while, but Rosa began to realize the position of importance Michael now held in his new community. She also came to understand that her Mikola was among the wealthy. Exposure to constant tabloid articles about him convinced her of that.

Michael sensed the presence of someone quietly approaching. The islanders always allowed him his time of solitude, paying his respects to his late loved ones. To Michael, it was as if they were here with him, if only for a few precious moments. His visits were so infrequent that he was allowed all the space he needed. He didn't come often, but each visit was special to him and the people of the island.

Michael felt the gentle touch of Quan Tsi's hand on his shoulder.

"I am very sorry to disturb you, Master, but we have just received an urgent message from Victor in Hong Kong," he reported.

Michael quickly rose to his feet and faced the man.

"What is it, old friend?" he asked.

"There is trouble in America. Victor will be going there, soon, from Hong Kong and you are requested to leave as soon as you can. A helicopter is on its way from the mainland to take you to Kai Tak."

"Do you have any idea what this is all about ?" Michael asked.

The look on Quan Tsi's face was all Michael needed to remind him that Quan would never have any knowledge of the business of the inner circle. That would only serve to place his life in jeopardy.

"I am very sorry, old friend. I should have remembered. Please do not take offense at my short memory," begged Michael.

Quan Tsi simply laughed. "Oh master, you are so serious. But, come, please prepare to leave. I do know that it is important that you return to your family as soon as possible. I can assure you of one thing; no one in your family has been harmed. If that had occurred, surely, I would have been told." Michael was greatly relieved by Quan Tsi's assurance.

The scene was pure bedlam the following morning at Complex Four at the World Financial Center at the base of Manhattan Island. Lee Chow and members of the inner circle, including Susan Lee's husband, Quan Yee, who had steadily risen through the ranks, were all trying to be heard above the constant clamor. Han Li had just received his much anticipated call from Victor and he and Sung Mae were trying to calm the frayed nerves of their business associates.

"How could such a terrible thing occur?" appeared to be the question on everyone's mind. Surely, there must have been a loose tongue on the part of the Japanese. How foolish it had been to believe that they could be trusted. The Japanese were known for their grandstanding, and now their treachery would bring much calamity on the Pos and their allies.

Han Li instinctively looked to his wife. Sung Mae was busy working her side of the room while constantly pausing to look in her husband's direction to see if she was needed. Their eyes met and he motioned for her to join him. He knew that the fear in the room was justified. Should the truth concerning the reason for a meeting between the two Asian victims become known, there would be far-reaching repercussions and plenty of hell to pay. There were many who disliked the Pos. They were one of the most dominant criminal organizations in the world and many had suffered at their expense during their ruthless rise to power. Once they joined forces with the influential Trumenta family, they managed to gain even more enemies. Sure, it was lonely at the top. But for the Pos, the top was the only place to take up residence.

Han Li and his family had no doubts concerning their rightful place on the world stage. They considered themselves conquerors and as such, they were well aware of the risks involved. Characteristic of mighty nations that had come before them, those whom they likened themselves to, they knew there would not be many times of real peace. There would always be a new "pretender to the throne". That is why the Pos were always battle ready. There was no such thing as a peacetime army where these people were concerned. Every member of their organization was expected to be prepared when such an occasion reared its ugly head. Now it was time for Han Li to bring the group to order.

"I have just received word from Victor in Hong Kong. We have decided that he wait a few days before coming here. We do not want to send up any red flags," he began.

Silence fell over the group. Everyone was anxious to learn what Victor and Han Li had decided.

"We feel it wise to wait and see what the media makes of this. Everyone is on 24 hour alert until we can formulate a response to their stories. Remember, we cannot assume that the truth is known to any but us and those who have conspired against us. Michael will be returning shortly and I will be meeting with our Italian friends in an hour. Let us not panic. It only makes sense to wait and see if those who came against us are out to expose us or simply hold us for ransom."

The room erupted anew. Somehow, the thought of ransom being a motivator brought a sense of relief to the gathering. No one had even considered the possibility of a ransom. There was a definite sense of relief in the crowd, if only temporarily. But it would buy Han Li a little time to ease the minds of his associates until Victor and Michael returned and for the truth to finally surface. Han Li knew that it was imperative that he give his people a sense of hope. Many of the old-timers were weary of the constant fighting. These men had proven their value and loyalty over the years, but in their collective minds this situation, if not properly checked, might precipitate a full scale war with rival Chinese, Japanese, Italians and who knows who else. Even the government might be persuaded to get in on the action as they would assuredly be pressured by the Japanese government, upset that one of their officials had been so brutally killed on American soil. The possibilities were endless and the spin doctors of the Pos and Trumentas would be working overtime to stem the tide of the endless blubbering's of the media. All would have to be prepared to deal with whatever spin the media chose to come up with. For the time being, it was their ballgame. It promised to be another long night.

Han Li walked over to talk to Quan Yee. He asked the young man to stay with him after everyone else had left. Han Li had decided that he would accompany him to meet the Trumentas in Michael's place. Lee Chow voiced his concern. He reasoned that Quan was not a proven warrior and that might compromise Han Li's safety. No one really knew who to trust at this point and Han Li had to agree with him. But Han Li was forced to go on instinct. Lee Chow protested that this would be more of a meeting of strategy than one of force and that he, being a senior adviser, should be the one to go.

Han Li acknowledged his old friend's concerns, but reminded him, "If something should happen to me, who else could be counted on to hold things together until Victor and Michael return?"

Lee Chow was flattered, but he knew that what Han Li said was true. The unenviable task of avoiding total collapse, should anything happen to Han Li, would fall squarely on his shoulders. It was a monstrous task. Han Li reminded him that it would also be his responsibility to look after Sung Mae's welfare. The Queen must be protected at all costs. Lee Chow acknowledged his responsibility. He and Han Li bowed in agreement.

# CHAPTER SIX

Big Al Trumenta was furious. After all these years of doing business with the Pos, how could he allow himself to be so naïve as to think that there would be no real danger? His trusted right hand man, Pat Figamo, knew that his boss needed to vent and get beyond the moment. Right now, Big Al was totally disgusted with himself. First of all, he had dropped the ball. He knew how important this meeting was for his friend and business associate, Han Li. The financial and global consequences were huge and far reaching. It stood to reason that someone would be threatened to the point of taking drastic action. He should have anticipated that. Secondly, he had let his partner down. It was his responsibility to provide sufficient security. He had grossly underestimated the potential for danger. Lastly, he was experiencing incredible guilt over sending one of his own to be slaughtered. It would be his responsibility to take care of Carmine's widow. But there was more here than met the eye. Obviously, he could not admit negligence to his troops. Someone was going to pay for Carmine's death. The Trumentas took care of their own, especially the survivors of their fallen warriors who died doing family business. Carla Cogiulo would be well taken care of. Big Al would see to that. This would be a good thing for all to see. Let's face it, even though a tragedy had occurred, big Al couldn't be blamed for a little image building, given the circumstances. Great leaders always know how to take advantage of misfortune.

"We meet with Han in 45 minutes," Al said. "What the hell can I say to him?"

Patty knew his boss was not looking for a response. He was just thinking out loud. Patty said nothing. He knew his boss well. That was the fabric of which their friendship was woven. Big Al knew how smart Patty was, smart enough to wait him out and friend enough to allow him moments of quiet understanding when there was no answer. All that was required was a brief passage of time.

"Po is going to meet us in the bar at the Marriott Marquis midtown. That will ensure everyone's safety. He's bringing one member of his inner circle and four bodyguards. We have agreed to do the same. Only you, Po and I know the location of the meeting. There is one small problem. Michael is still in China so he will not be there. That means we better make sure nothing happens to Po. If something goes wrong, you stay near me and instruct our people to cover Han Li's butt. Let's get going. We don't want Po to be there without us. None of this stuff makes any sense. Obviously someone in Po's camp has turned. Let's not have anything happen to him on our watch. This meeting must be very important for him to be willing to expose himself without Michael or Victor at his side," said a very apprehensive Albert Trumenta.

Patty went downstairs to the recreation room to gather the four soldiers that would be going with them. Knowing that Michael and Victor were not here did not sit very well with him. No one could foresee what had just occurred, but in retrospect, someone had picked the perfect time to come against Han Li. Patty's brain was racing. He knew exactly what his boss was thinking. Big Al knew how to handle a pistol, he didn't get to the top being a Boy Scout. He knew that he and Patty could take care of themselves. But no one was sure of what Han Li was carrying. That piece of information had never been divulged. Han Li was a man of extreme honor. Carrying a knife would be more his style. But a knife would not be too helpful at the O.K.Corral.

Patty instructed his men to bring two cars around. Two of the men would ride in the front seats in the car with him and big Al, while the other two brought up the rear. He and his boss would be covered front and back. It would take a good 30 minutes to get from Big Al's home in the Mill Basin section of Brooklyn, to midtown Manhattan. Mill Basin was a mafioso enclave at the far reaches of Brooklyn, off Flatbush Avenue towards the Rockaway's. There was only one road in and out. That road breaks off into a maze of streets where members of the Italian and Russian mafias built their castles. And heaven help anyone who didn't belong or ventured in and didn't have sense enough to make a hasty retreat. Such a person might find himself going for a little swim, face down, in one of the many water inlets in the area which produced a modern version of the blind canyons of the old West. It had been twelve years since the gunfight on Bayard Street in Chinatown, and once again, big Al was going to a meeting he was dreading all the way.

# CHAPTER SEVEN

At 9:00 a.m. sharp, the old team met at Chief of Detectives Marv Levy's office at One Police Plaza in lower Manhattan. Marv had requested the attendance of his old crew, but let no one know why. Walter was the first member he contacted. Walter was only too happy to drop by. Lucy and Bobby came together. Both had established themselves as first-rate captains of their own ships. They had purchased the apartment adjoining theirs when the owner decided to sell and move out of the city. The expansion helped to furnish accommodations for Bobby's two daughters who were finding more and more excuses to spend time with Lucy and their dad. Life was good, and two high-grade paychecks in one household helped ensure that. The Ferrignos were a shining example of the positive side of marriage on the force.

Walter was the darling of the upper echelon. It was remarkable how many times his name made it into print in the local newspapers. Of course, that was only exceeded by the number of luncheon and dinner invitations he managed to procure. At any major event, especially one that included food, there stood Walter, smiling and glad handing the powers that be. For a cop, Walter moved remarkably well in society. He was a gifted performer.

Marv and his three old friends settled into the plush furnishings of his stately office. He was enjoying the moment. It had been far too long since the gang had been together. The camaraderie they had enjoyed as a team was sorely missing in Marv's life. Life as Chief of Detectives had proven to be a lonely deal. If not for Cal Munroe's spectacular entry into his life, he probably would have opted for early retirement and obligatory residence in Florida, the birthplace of the "early bird special." Homicide was a filthy business. New York seemed to have joyfully adopted the mantle of the home of scandal, rape, insider trading, kidnapping, incest and an ever increasing promise of disgusting criminal possibilities. Ah, life in the big city: it had all served to dull his soul. Somehow, the three bright but curious police officers seated in front of him had managed to bring joy to the job. Since their departure, it was pure doom and gloom.

"Well, people," he began, "it sure has been a while."

Everyone agreed.

"I hear good things about all of you. Especially you ,Walter. Come to think of it, it seems I am always hearing your name."

Walter wasn't sure where this was going. He was about to find out.

"It appears that you have taken your new position very seriously. I understand that you are about to be given an award."

Walter was taken aback. Lucy and Bobby looked to Marv with anticipation.

"What gives, Chief?" Walter asked.

"The higher- ups have been enormously impressed by your diligence, Walter. It seems that everyone is curious to find out how an officer can work as hard as you do and never miss a meal, especially a free one."

Bobby and Lucy exploded in laughter. Even Walter joined in. He had been had, but managed to be a good sport over the laughter at his expense.

"Very good, Chief," he said. "And you two," he said, pointing to the Ferrignos, "you laugh at the expense of your old comrade. Shame on both of you," he scolded.

Marv had successfully broken the ice. It was important for him to set the right atmosphere to make his pitch. He was satisfied that it was achieved.

"Come on, Chief," said Bobby. "There've been a lot of rumors going around with your name attached to them. What's all the hush, hush about?"

A smile of acknowledgment spread across Marv's weathered face. "As usual you are right, my friend. Well, here is the story, and this comes straight from Gracie Mansion. It appears that the powers that be are going to bring us back to those heady days when John Lindsay ran our fair city. A 'super group' of cops is about to be assembled and yours truly has been asked to head them up. Now let me finish before you all jump in. The mayor and the city council agreed that the police department's hands are tied due to lack of funding. So some genius up there discovered a way to get money to fund the whole shebang. All the funding comes under a new federal crime budget. The poor bastards on the beat can't get a freekin' cost of living increase, but the city is about to get millions and millions of dollars to start up yet another agency. Well I'm here to tell you that as long as I am in charge, they are going to get their money's worth," declared Marv.

"What in the world makes them think that this is such a great idea?" Walter wanted to know.

"Maybe they're hoping all this money will produce a few Frank Serpicos," Lucy quipped, referring to the decorated officer of the 60's who gained national attention by being a clean cop in a corrupt department. The city and the force took a real beating over that little episode.

That comment momentarily stopped everyone in their tracks. Marv started to ask Lucy where she was coming from, but thought better of it and let it pass.

"I met with some of the 'big boys' last night and after I shared my feelings concerning yesterday's incident in midtown, they decided that the new agency should go into effect immediately. That's why I called you so late last night. I needed you to be here this morning. What I am trying to say is that I want you three to be in this with me. I know that you are all department heads, but I need you. This may look like a step backwards, but believe me, this is no demotion. You all know how much you guys mean to me. I would never be part of anything that denied you the respect you deserve," Marv said.

It didn't take long for Lucy to break the silence that followed Marv's revelation. "How would this affect our grades and pay scale?" Lucy blurted out.

Bobby could not believe the boldness of his wife's question. He always held Marv in the highest regard. Lucy's question left him mortified. Marv could see Bobby's look of disbelief. Walter was also caught completely off guard. Marv was enjoying this more than he had anticipated.

"Well, gentlemen," he began, "it appears that there is one set of gonads in this group and the lady here is the one who owns them."

Bobby looked over at his wife and tried to speak, but Lucy cut him off.

"Look guys," she began, "it's not for me that I asked. It's for Bobby. Ever since I introduced him to shopping at Barney's, his spending has been out of control."

Bobby was aghast; he was speechless.

"I'm telling you, things have gotten way out of hand. He thinks he's Kojak, for goodness sake. I had to ban him from those damn reruns before he puts us in the poor house trying to keep up with Telly Savalas's wardrobe," she continued.

Kojak was a popular television police, crime drama series starring the celebrated movie actor Telly Savalas as the slick talking, wisecracking lead detective of a Police Headquarters in lower Manhattan. Besides displaying a penchant for having a lollypop in his mouth on many occasions, Theo Kojak was an impeccable dresser, constantly appearing in a wardrobe that could never bear the title, *off the rack*. His constant use of the phrase, "Hey, who loves ya?" became part of the American culture.

Marv and Walter exploded in laughter.

"Gees, Bobby," exclaimed Marv, "just who did you marry?"

"Deep throat," Walter chimed in as they really started to give Bobby a royal going over.

"Alright, alright you savages," Lucy scolded. "That's quite enough. You've had your fun, now settle down. How can you guys gang up on my Bobby like that?" as she put her arms around her totally embarrassed husband.

Marv and Walter feigned being wounded. Both shared a good laugh and then attempted to compose themselves so that Marv could continue his pitch.

"First, let me assure you that your grades and pay scales will stay intact. In fact, I wouldn't be surprised to see raises across the board once we prove that this thing can work."

Everyone liked the sound of that.

"I've got to know if you people are interested. If so, I'll answer all your questions. Okay, Lucy?" he said with a wink. "But, first things first." Marv paused for a moment and then decided to alter his approach. He chose to do something he intended to do later in the presentation. He took the group down the hall to view the suite of offices that was being prepared for them. To a person, they were impressed. Marv brought them back to his office and for the next hour, laid out the whole operation while answering every one of their questions. It did not take long for them to see how serious the mayor was about reducing crime in the city. There was to be a major focus on crime prevention and the team led by Marv would be at the front as far as the media was concerned. Being the most celebrated team of detectives in New York City's municipal history was a sure bet to fuel the fires of a salivating press ravenous for circulation. Not since the days of John Lindsay had the term "super cop'" been visited. Now the mantle would be brought out, dusted, polished and placed squarely on the heads and shoulders of Marv's new team.

The group broke for lunch, just like the old days. Marv's treat, of course. Well, in reality, the city of New York was footing the bill. Cal Munroe joined them so it was five for dim sum at the Golden Unicorn on Broadway East.

Back in the office, Marv wasted little time getting down to business. What he wanted to know was if anyone was ready to make a commitment. He offered to leave the room to allow them some time to talk it over amongst themselves. He reasoned that since Bobby and Lucy were a married couple, they might want a few moments alone. A move like this would most assuredly impact their relationship. If they agreed, they would be working together again on a daily basis. Marv was not sure how they would react to that. He did not have to wait very long.

Surprisingly, it was Bobby who was first to speak. "Chief," he began, "I really appreciate my job and the fact that it came on your recommendation. But, I have to say that I have never been able to assemble a team like the one we had. Things aren't getting any better in Chinatown, especially as it just keeps growing. The way it looks to me, it won't be long before our station house will resemble Fort Apache the Bronx. Little Italy has gotten so small. The old days are gone. Cops and Wops found a way to coexist with some form of civility. Now, the cops are considered an intrusion. The new people seem to want to handle things themselves and some of their solutions are downright bloody. The gangs and opposing factions are becoming overwhelming. Let's face it, we're never going to be embraced down there. The only time these people talk to us is when they want something. Other than that, they treat us like we don't exist. Speaking for myself and not to influence Lucy, it wouldn't take too much for me to make the move. I kind of like the idea of working with my wife again, but I don't want to put any pressure on her. If she decides not to do it, that's okay with me. It would be special to work with you again, Chief, and Walter, if he's in. So I guess I'm saying I'm in."

"Make that two," said Lucy without any hesitation. "You know that I'm really grateful for the position you gave me, sir. At first it was a challenge. But, to be honest, I miss the rush. I miss working with you guys and I really miss working with Bobby."

Everyone smiled at Lucy's tender words. Lucy made sure the mood was short lived. She was not through. "I have to admit I do have a selfish motive," she continued. "I feel that if I can spend more time with Bobby, I can help him overcome his spending problems."

The group once again shared an old-fashioned laugh. This time, even Bobby joined in.

Walter made it unanimous. He shared how he loved being able to play with the bigwigs, but spending so much time around these people had created an addiction to Gas-X. Once again the room erupted in laughter.

"Poor Walter," said Lucy. "I think he needs his old friends to help navigate him through these troubled waters."

"Thank God for Lucy," Walter answered. "Walter needs some love and understanding."

Satisfied that the old crew would be mounting up and riding together again, Marv decided to bring the group up to snuff. "Bobby," he began, "here is the answer to your question. For some time now, I have suspected the Pos and the Trumentas have been brokering a deal with a Japanese business group. Nobody has a clue as to what business group that would be or even why and how such a deal has come about. Given the age-old climate between the Chinese and the Japanese communities, I would imagine that a whole lot of people, on both sides, would be unhappy with the possibility of such a union. Any number of groups would do whatever they could to stop them or even destroy them if they could come up with some proof. My guess is someone close to the deal decided either to try to stop it or, quite possibly, use whatever information they had to extort money from the highest bidder. My guess is that whoever these people are, they have no loyalty to either party. We live in a whole new climate, and I suspect that when Hong Kong goes back to China, it will cause many in that region to choose between fiscal survival and ancient traditions. Anyone want to venture a guess which one they will choose?" he finished.

"That's assuming your first assumption is correct," Walter spoke up.

"Exactly," said Marv. "Carmine Cogiulo was no flunky driver. He was a made man, highly respected by the Trumentas. Carmine had 'balls' for days. He was a tough guy and an honorable one. My guess is that big Al thought Carmine was just the guy to taxi the two Asian businessmen to a safe place where they could exchange letters of intent and to have these papers brought by a trusted courier to whoever set this thing up. For your information, the Trumentas own that garage. Carmine's job was to provide protection.

"He did a great job of that," Lucy quipped.

"Now wait a minute, Lucy," said Marv. "I'm guessing that no one in the Po or Trumenta camp suspected the possibility of a shooting. They'd never send just one man with no backup. No, at this point, I got to believe that these people were probably more concerned with exposure than bullets."

"There is something you've not told us," said Bobby, who probably knew Marv better than anyone else.

Marv smiled and agreed. "Patience, my learned friend," Marv responded. "Bobby, have a little patience. But, you are right. This is what we've learned since the shooting. A man of Japanese descent was found dead yesterday evening at his home on West 94th Street His family came home early from a trip upstate and wanted to surprise him. The surprise was on them. The name of the deceased is Joseph Sito. Sito ran one of the most prestigious courier services in the city. Many of his clients are the foreign embassies. His family discovered his body at around 6:00 p.m.. While our people were going over the place, Sito's wife told the detectives that the only thing missing was her husband's courier case. It seems the case was unique, one of a kind; very expensive, made by some famous designer of leather goods in Japan. She said he never let it out of his sight. A look at his appointment book revealed that he had an appointment scheduled for the time of the shooting. No details, but, it did say midtown. I think we can assume that he was the one who was supposed to make the pickup. Obviously he would not have anything specific written down. The deal was very hush, hush. I also think it's safe to assume that someone killed him and took his place at the garage. The Japanese attaché must have realized a switch was made. That would explain all the mayhem. If the switch had gone as planned, we might be looking at a burglary and lots of irate barking from some very embarrassed members of the Asian business community, instead of a triple homicide.

Next, we have the venerable Jun Ho Lee, a member of the Po inner circle. That makes things easy. The Trumentas sent a trusted soldier to assist their partners. Now, a Japanese attaché, that's where it gets tricky. We need to connect Yamagachi to some big time Japanese organization. That is critical. Without that, we got real problems."

"Lucy," he barked, "that's going to be your baby." Lucy nodded in agreement

"Bobby," I want you to give Yamagachi's family a real going over. Check on his closest associates and any known enemies that are close to the surface."

"Sure, Chief," responded Bobby.

"Walter, I have two jobs for you. I want you to investigate everyone who is employed by Sito's company. Let's see if there is any opportunist lurking nearby. But first I want to contact Michael DeAngelo. I know it's a long shot, thinking we will get any real help from him, but maybe you could appeal to his civic sense of duty. At the very least, you might be able to get a rise out of him. Word is he is on his way here from China. Coincidentally, Victor Chen is also coming, real soon. You think Victor is coming for "Don Giovanni" at the Met? One more thing. Neither of the two Asian victims at the garage had their briefcases on them when our people showed up. It shouldn't be too hard to figure out what that means. Whoever has those two briefcases now has in their possession the plans these people were cooking up. The flame is going to get turned up real high, people. Sources tell us that the Pos are pouring in from all directions. Looks like a  war party is about to begin. The Pos get real pissed when one of their own goes down. Let's not forget the last time something like this occurred. The Trumentas are honor bound to back the Pos. The body count could get scary. We don't know who did this and it's a good bet neither do the Pos. That won't stop them from whacking a few people just to send the message. It won't matter if the victims are innocent or not. Somebody is going down and a clear message is about to be sent. Walter, DeAngelo's body language is all we're going to have to go on. No way he gives up his family. Who knows, he may even get to kill somebody for them. It won't be the first time for him, and the word is he would do anything for Han Li; I mean anything.

Now listen up, everybody. You've got till noon tomorrow to clean out your desks, say your goodbyes and start punching the time clock here. Your offices will be ready and waiting for you when you get here. Now scoot."

It was 4:00 p.m. when the meeting broke up. Bobby and Lucy went over to Dean & DeLuca's on Broadway in Soho, the favorite marketplace for Manhattan's upward mobility set. They picked up some steaks and vegetables for dinner. Lucy put on a Windham Hill CD. She and Bobby shared a candlelight dinner. Bobby helped her clear away the dishes and then they retired to the living room for a little wine and Dave Koz. They spoke about how great it was that they were working together again and how exciting the work was going to be. Lucy told Bobby just how excited she was, period. The whole idea really turned her on. They turned in very early that night.

# CHAPTER EIGHT

As expected, the meeting between Han Li and Big Al was more ceremonial then fact producing. Both sides needed assurances that their allegiances were intact and that they would go to the wall for each other. Both needed a little soothing, and who better to apply the balm than the principals themselves? Han Li could see that Big Al was visibly embarrassed. He took the lead and pointed out that it was his side who should have had a greater understanding of the possibility of danger. It was he who knew, only too well, the centuries of animosity that existed between these two great cultures. What is more, it was his responsibility and his alone to anticipate every possibility. Han Li made it clear that the needless loss of life of one of his dear friend's soldiers was a heavy burden for which he accepted full blame and pledged to make restitution.

Big Al and Patty were impressed by the generous words of Han Li; they were also relieved. But it was Quan Yee who sat and marveled at the eloquent words from his boss. Quan had never been granted the opportunity to see Han Li Po up close where his greatness could be observed. Now he could only stand in awe of him. Few were ever privy to what Quan was witnessing, and it was at that moment that he came to understand how Han Li's men could pledge dying allegiance to such a man.

For his part, Big Al promised the full weight and cooperation of his family to his partners. He made it clear that the Trumentas could be counted on to stand side-by-side with them. Both men knew the enormous cost this affair could exact on both sides. Han Li knew Big Al well enough to believe he meant every word he said. He also knew that someone of lesser honor might have chosen discretion over valor. The Pos were a huge and powerful organization, fully capable of fighting on their own. It was most comforting to know that when the time came for your friends to step up to the plate, Big Al and the Trumentas never flinched.

# CHAPTER NINE

The lunch crowd at Anthony's on Mulberry Street, just off the corner of Grand, was a raucous blend of local business types and wide-eyed tourists. Walter dropped a few names and secured a window table. He had just taken his seat when Michael came through the door. Michael was always on time. It was not easy not to notice him. Some of the patrons looked up from their meals to observe him as the headwaiter escorted him over to Walter's table. Tall, elegantly dressed and with a majestic grace of movement, Michael looked important; that's why people always took notice of him. It was that simple.

"Hey, pal," came Walter's greeting. "Thanks for coming on such short notice."

"Your treat, right?" was Michael's reply.

"Absolutely," Walter assured.

"No problem," Michael said with a smile. His answer let Walter know that he was there as a friend. This allowed Walter the freedom to conduct whatever business he needed to. Both men knew why this meeting was arranged. The waiter appeared with a bottle of Merlot. It was the best of the house, moderate in price and a good year. Restaurants in Little Italy were not known for $500 bottles of wine. In the old days, many served Uncle Viduch's neighborhood cellar brand: aged about six days. Walter's selection was sufficient for the occasion.

38

Besides, neither man was much of a drinker. The gesture was satisfactory and correct.

They ordered and waited for the waiter to be out of hearing range.

"Walter, my friend, you look a little worried," Michael said. He knew Walter would be.

Walter possessed great people skills. Those skills made his life easier. He was known as a man who believed in a win-win approach in all his dealings. Even as a child, Walter was a gifted politician. He knew the correct way to address his approach to Michael. He wasn't expecting much to come of their meeting. It was more important to be mindful of their ongoing relationship then on one random fact-finding mission.

"Yeah, Michael, I am," said Walter." We're all worried over at Police Plaza. Nobody seems to have any idea why three men are gunned down gangland style in a midtown garage. But some things are hard to dismiss. First off, a Chinese businessman known to be connected to the Pos, and the Japanese attaché from the Japanese embassy are found dead in each other's arms. Ironic wouldn't you say?" He expected no reply. "A fairly high- ranking member of the Trumenta family is a chauffeur? Now that is extraordinary. Neither of the Asian victims has a briefcase and the driver's gun is still holstered. Three other homicides happened that evening and we're fairly certain that they have some connection to the one at the garage. All the victims were Japanese. Two were related, but killed in different locations. One of them had a record. He also had a history of violence. Oh, one other little piece that may be part of the puzzle. A well-known Japanese courier, highly trusted in the diplomatic community, was also killed that evening. His courier case is also missing. Nobody knows much right now, but nobody is in the market for a bloodbath either. You know, like the one we had some years ago when you left town, suddenly. I am not expecting you to compromise your family, Michael, but I really don't want to see innocent people die just to carry out some s.o.p. scenario for their advantage either. I guess I came to appeal to your sense of decency. One thing I know about you, friend, is that you are a decent human being."

"What is it you think I can do to help?" Michael asked.

"It's starting to feel like Little Big Horn around here. The Trumentas and your people seem to be gathering for a storm. The arrival of your cousin, Victor Chen, makes everyone nervous. Victor ain't exactly Mr. Congeniality. He has a habit of conveniently forgetting that the laws here are just a little more limiting than back home."

Michael knew what Walter meant about Victor. Victor liked to scare people: scare them to death. And Victor took everything personally. Michael knew that Victor's credo was, you come against a Po, you come against all the Pos and all the Pos can do, which is considerable. Victor always made sure that he was the one who saw to that. Michael moved forward in his chair and leaned across the table so that no one could hear what he was about to say.

"I am only now learning the whole story, myself. You must understand that I am never privy to the inner workings of my family business. My father never was either. Those were his wishes. They are also mine. I choose to carry on that tradition to honor his name. He chose a life separate from empire building. But make no mistake, he and I share a common bond: we would die for our family. Whoever comes against them comes against us. However, you are right. It is not my desire to see innocent people suffer. I will do all I can to prevent that. I will strongly advise the council against the shedding of innocent blood. Do not forget, I am a family head. As such, I have a vote in all our dealings. I will voice my opinion and cast my vote. I can be outvoted, however, and probably will be. My family will know exactly where I stand and will, I am sure, do all they can to respect my wishes. If I can be of assistance to you without compromising them, I will be more than happy to do so. On that you have my word, the word of a Po which needs nothing more than to be offered."

The last part of Michael's words were partially drowned out by a great clamor coming from the street. A large group of Chinese

40

youths was marching in protest and obstructing traffic. Walter and Michael rose to their feet just in time to observe Lucy Ferragamo making her way towards the group. She was attempting to affix her shield as she drew near the main group. In one beautiful motion, a young Asian woman in the group swung her right leg straight up over her head while circling clockwise before bringing it crashing down on Lucy's right shoulder. The blow sent Lucy tumbling towards a large Cadillac sedan, crashing headlong into the fender.

"Are you insane?" One of her male companions yelled. "Can't you see she is a cop, you fool? Quickly, help me get her to her feet."

The young woman merely laughed at her friend's fear. "It was an innocent mistake," she said. "I'm sure she will understand. After all, how was I to know?"

Walter and Michael came running out of the restaurant and began to make their way over to where the couple was attempting to help Lucy to her feet. Michael came to an abrupt stop and prevented Walter from going any further. Police were beginning to show up and form a perimeter around the mob.

"What is it?" Walter wanted to know.

"Watch," was all Michael offered.

"Stand back, weasel," instructed the woman, in perfect Mandarin. "I will do it myself."

As Lucy started to get to her feet, she rolled up her fist and landed a powerful punch deep into the pit of the woman's midsection. The woman yelled out in pain as a wave of nausea began to sweep over her. Lucy was not through. Once again she landed a thunderous blow to the same spot: the girls eyes began to roll back into her head. From her crouching position, Lucy began to straighten up and in one continuous motion, landed an uppercut to the girl's jaw, sending her flying up onto the hood of the Cadillac. Lucy pointed to the young man who was frozen in his tracks.

"Don't move," she commanded. "We're not through here." She needn't have worried. His feet were sucked into the pavement.

She walked over to the stricken girl who was out cold. She

grabbed the girl's hair with both hands and began to read her Miranda. Each sentence was punctuated by the slamming of the girl's head onto the hood.

"You have the right to remain silent." Slam. "Anything you say may be used against you in a court of law." Slam. She carried on the same way till the end. It really didn't matter. The girl was unconscious through it all.

Walter made his way over to where Lucy was standing. He looked back at Michael and asked, "How on earth did you know?"

Michael only smiled back. Then he walked over to talk to Lucy. "I would love to train you, Captain. You are a very powerful woman. If you could harness that power, it might be of great value to you."

Lucy was slowly catching her breath. "I might just take you up on that," she responded.

"The pleasure would be all mine. Please do not hesitate to call on me," said Michael. He handed Lucy his business card.

The police had pretty much dispersed the crowd. Only a few arrests were made. The young woman was among them. She offered no resistance. She was still in dreamland.

"We'll talk again, Captain." Michael said to Walter. Then he turned and walked up Mulberry Street.

Walter just stood there and watched him go. He was still totally amazed by Michael's actions. If he had not been there to witness it with his own eyes, he would not have believed it. He only had one question. "How could he know?"

# CHAPTER TEN

Wee Fong met Michael at the entrance to his apartment with news from Victor. "Victor wishes you to meet him at the Four Seasons at 2:00 p.m.. He says that it is important."

Michael had been anticipating Victor's call. He knew that the Pos were about to make plans of action and Victor would be the one who would fill him in. Whatever the family decided, Michael was pretty sure that tight security would be a major part of that. There was another reason why Michael was glad to hear from Victor; he never had a chance to eat with Walter and he was really hungry. Where better to satisfy his cravings than with his cousin at the Four Seasons?

The first person Michael saw upon entering the hotel lobby was Victor. Michael fully expected as much. They embraced warmly.

"Let's take a minute to go up to my room," said Victor. "A decision has just been made and I need to fill you in. It won't take long. Then we can relax and enjoy our meal."

Michael acknowledged Victor's ever-present bodyguards. They in turn bowed to him. The two men knew Michael well. Michael had trained them, and was so impressed with them that he recommended they become Victor's personal bodyguards. The position was as high as one could go for men of their station. Both were most appreciative and their bow displayed a reverence that was unmistakable. Once inside Victor's suite, Victor explained the family's plan for action.

"We will all be making a trip up to Hyde Park to a safe place where we can spend a few days sorting things out. Mr. Masotoma is coming in from Japan and it will be your responsibility to personally escort him. Michael, I cannot tell you how important it is that we guarantee his safety. Whoever has our documents knows that Masotoma is with us."

Victor's words had crystal clear meaning to Michael. The two great Asian families were about to be united and the disgrace of harm befalling someone in the Po's care would bear a worldwide stench.

"I am ready," was Michael's immediate reply.

Victor smiled a knowing smile. He never expected anything else from his cousin.

Katherine Hewett and MaryAnn Vanooster were hardly touching their salads. Their animated conversation left little room for that. "These people have been bothering me for days. MaryAnn, are you sure a young man didn't give you something for me at the Puck?" Katherine asked.

"I am absolutely positive, Katherine. How on earth could I forget something like that? I assure you, I never saw that person," said MaryAnn. "It was just that he was so insistent, almost scared. I can't imagine what could have happened. To the best of my knowledge there were no incidents at the event, nothing out of the ordinary."

"Maybe he just left," said MaryAnn.

"No, I'm sure I saw him later. There has to be a simple explanation, but I'll be damned if I know what it is."

"Well, I never saw any of your belongings. I just took my things and brought them up to my parents' home. So, how are you going to get these people to believe you and leave you alone? " MaryAnn asked.

"Good question," said Katherine. "Got any ideas?"

Michael was having difficulty paying attention to his conversation with Victor. There, across the room, was a beautiful blonde woman he had seen the day he was leaving to go to the island. He had just come out of his bank on Madison Avenue when he noticed a tall, striking blonde walking in his direction. She was with the other woman at her table. It was an unusually warm day for late October. The woman wore a light flowing blouse and skirt that seemed to flow with her movements. Michael assumed they were expensive. He also noticed that she had a most unusual gait to her walk. She seemed to bounce and glide at the same time. She walked with authority. Her hair kept brushing across a face that Michael could not take his eyes from. It had been a long time since any woman had such an impact on him. She and the other woman walked right past where he was standing without ever taking notice of him. Even on the island, he could not get her out of his thoughts. And, now, here she was, sitting right across the room from him and Victor. Once again, he could not help but stare at her.

"What's wrong?" MaryAnn asked her friend.

"I don't believe this," said Katherine. "There is a man over there who keeps staring at me. And his companion is Asian."

" Do you think he could be one of the people harassing you?" MaryAnn inquired.

"I don't know but I am about to find out," said Katherine as she pushed her chair away from the table and sprang to her feet.

"Katherine, calm down," pleaded an alarmed MaryAnn. "Wait a minute."

Her words fell on deaf ears. Katherine was already under a full tailwind storming across the restaurant. She came to an abrupt halt at Michael and Victor's table.

"Is there something I can do for you gentlemen?" she blurted out.

. The men were taken by surprise. Almost magically, Victor's two bodyguards appeared. Victor waved them off.

"Well, you have been staring at me for quite some time," she said, looking directly at Michael." Is there something that you want?"

Michael attempted to get to his feet, but was met by a pointing finger and some harsh words. "Don't you dare get up. I've had just about all I am going to take from you people. I want you to stop bothering me," she declared.

Michael was horrified. Victor seemed slightly amused.

"Well, say something," she demanded of Michael. "Why are you staring at me?"

Michael looked directly into her eyes and said, "I think you're one of the most beautiful women I have ever seen. I am sorry, but the truth is, I just could not take my eyes off you. I must confess, your attitude towards my attraction to you has me puzzled." Michael's words defused Katherine's anger just enough for her to realize that many of the patrons were staring at her. Now, slightly embarrassed, she abruptly turned and headed straight for the exit. MaryAnn quickly got up and trailed her out.

"Well, Michael," said Victor. "That was most interesting."

"I saw that woman on Madison Avenue just before I left to go to the island," Michael attempted to explain. "I could not get her out of my mind, but I never thought I would see her again. The odds are so great. I only hoped," he paused. "Now she's gone again. I guess that's that," Michael sighed resignedly.

"Judging from what we just witnessed," said Victor, "I would have to caution my cousin to be careful what you wish for."

Michael smiled weakly and asked, "What on earth do you think she was talking about? I mean, 'You people,' 'bothering her;' I've never even met her."

"I'm afraid I am as much in the dark as you," was Victor's response.

Just then their food was served. Victor devoured his steak. Michael hardly picked at his lemon sole. This was turning out not to be a good food day for Michael.

# CHAPTER ELEVEN

Michael and Victor went over to Han Li's residence on Fifth Avenue. The three men spent a few hours strategizing all the scenarios and preparations for Masotoma's safe arrival and stay in their care. They all agreed that things would be a lot simpler if the meetings were held in China. Michael was not the least bit surprised to learn that the Trumentas would certainly be visible during all this. They had a big stake in the deal and a few days spent with all the principals gathered together could go a long way towards easing tensions, to say nothing of tightening bonds. By far, this was to be the largest undertaking for the Po and Trumenta partnership. There would be much to consider and discuss. And everyone wanted to meet the man from Japan who wanted to do business with the Chinese.

Kennedy Airport, at the far reaches of Brooklyn, was its usual lively state of organized chaos. No airport in the world was quite like it. The fact that it was in Brooklyn never escaped Michael. Today, he was taking no chances. No fewer than twenty trusted soldiers were stationed throughout the British Airways in-coming flight terminal. Tashiro Masotoma arrived on the Concorde with four trusted aides. His people were all short and stout, looking very much Bushido.

Each looked as though they could take on a full regiment. Sizing them up quickly, in a fight, Michael's money would have been riding on Masotoma's four. Michael had one of his men dressed as a chauffeur. The man held a sign that read "Mr. Meeting." Victor really liked that touch. If anyone had any ideas about interfering, they would have difficulty adjusting swiftly enough to recover and mount any problems. By then, Michael and his men would have quickly gathered their valuable guests and made their exit, unfettered. Michael was giving nothing away, allowing no margin for error to the other side if they showed up.

The pickup went flawlessly. Two limousines bearing the diplomatic plates, graciously provided by Capt. Walter Larkin, and two Chevrolet 6200 Tahoe SUVs raced to the terminal exit and swiftly gathered up twenty-five passengers. The four vehicles exited the airport and were immediately joined front and rear, by two Mercedes sedans carrying four more soldiers each, all carrying assault weapons. The caravan headed out towards the Throgs Neck Bridge that connects with Westchester County, then continued north up I 95 to Port Chester and Route 287, the Cross Westchester Expressway. They drove the width of Westchester County then grabbed the Route 9 cut-off, just before the Tappan Zee Bridge that links New York to New Jersey. Their destination was Duchess County and the town of Hyde Park, the hometown of Franklin Delano Roosevelt and the stately and legendary residences known as the Castles on the Hudson.

The planned two-day affair was to be held in the manor home of Woodruff Yeng, the president of Bank of China New York. His twenty six-room home with two outbuildings would provide the perfect venue for the summit meeting. The property was gated, and fairly hidden from sight. It just happened to adjoin Val-Kil, the 180 acre estate of the late Eleanor Roosevelt, now a national park. Val-Kil formed a perfect barrier for half of Yeng's property. The other side was mainly preserved wetlands. The large group would not attract any unwanted attention. It was not unusual to see activity on Yeng's estate, even a group this size; he was known to entertain the rich and famous. He was a good neighbor. The locals had no quarrel with him. Basically, he kept a pretty low profile. Yeng would not be attending this gathering. His ignorance would help to ensure his continued good health. The Pos put him and Mrs. Yeng up in a suite at the New York Palace, a $3000 a night show of gratitude.

Michael and his group finally arrived. Han Li was waiting in the grand entrance foyer to greet Masotoma. Han Li was determined that everything would go smoothly. Wee Fong and the Po household staff would see to the cooking and everyone's needs.

Han Li and Masotoma exchanged greetings and then made their way to the dining room where a great table had been set to accommodate all the dignitaries. The subordinates were seated directly behind their superiors in chairs made available to them. No one was to stand during these proceedings.

Han Li introduced his associates to their honored guest. Lee Chow and Quan Yee were first. Next, he introduced Albert Trumenta and his trusted associate, Pat Figamo. Then Victor was introduced; the sequence was his idea, along with the two associates who accompanied him from Hong Kong. Obviously, Michael needed no introduction.

Masotoma had informed Han Li that he would prefer to begin the meeting as soon as possible. He waved any need to rest from his long journey. He was more concerned with addressing the problem at hand. Everyone was grateful for that. The threat of a war was hanging ominously over the group and the sooner they got everything out on the table the better.

Drinks and finger foods were served during the first round of discussions which consisted of airing all possible scenarios and speculation of problems that might arise. Everyone had to be assured that all participants were in total agreement. There was no time for hedging now. The dye had been cast, meaning it was sink or swim as one. There simply was no other way. The first round of meetings broke up around 5:00 p.m.. It was agreed that everyone would take some time to freshen up and convene back for dinner to be served at 6:30 p.m. under the supervision of Madam Po.

A masterful mix of Chinese, Japanese and Italian food was enthusiastically consumed by all in attendance. All saluted Wee Fong and his group for a job well done. Everyone expressed their agreement as Michael looked on with pleasure at his friend's triumph. The sumptuous meal aided the easing of any tensions that may have existed.

Everyone retired to the great parlor for after-dinner cordials and fine Cuban cigars. Han Li was biding his time to ask Masotoma to share the story of his friendship with Li Xsing. He was the only one present who knew that story. Even Victor had no knowledge of it. Han Li concluded that the timing was right for everyone to find out what connected Masotoma to the Pos. Han Li asked, and the room fell silent with anticipation. Masotoma took a brief moment then soberly began his tale.

"What I am about to tell you gentlemen and Madame Po is very painful for me and for my family. My story begins at one of the most disgraceful periods for my country. In 1937, China and Japan were embroiled in a great conflict, the Sino-Japanese War. At that time, I was a sixteen-year-old soldier in the famous 6th Battalion. But more importantly, I was Bushido, a member of the Samurai class. My father, Hyakamo Masotoma, was the general responsible for the defeat of Shanghai in November of 1937. By December of that year, we had secured the neighboring city of Nanjing. What happened next was the most sickening thing I've ever witnessed in all of my long life. Almost 15,000 Chinese soldiers lay down their arms and surrendered. That should have been the end of the story, but it was not. Orders came down from the high command, eager to demonstrate their mastery to the people of Japan, that all the prisoners were to be executed. Many of us in the ranks could not believe what we were hearing. Such an action would be completely without honor. It was, simply, unthinkable. The high command thought otherwise. My father never hesitated. He ordered all the captives to have their hands bound behind their backs, a task that consumed a great part of the day. And when that task had been completed, he had all the prisoners marched down to a nearby river and began having them executed with machine guns. For nearly one whole hour the firing never stopped. When it did finally stop, my father gave orders to bayonet everybody to make sure all were dead. This took most of the night to accomplish. There were so many corpses that the river and neighboring ponds were nearly covered up by all the flesh piled on top of each other. One of my fellow soldiers informed our commander who immediately informed my father that I had never drawn my sword and had refused to take even one life.

My father was disgraced in front of his own army. He had me marched up before the troops and slapped my face. Then he tore all the buttons from my uniform. Had he not been pressed for time, I really do believe he would have had me shot on the spot. He might have completed the action himself. Instead, he had me taken back in chains to Japan to stand trial as a traitor. Fortunately for me, I was spared the 'Nanjing Datusha', the massacre of Nanjing, one of the most deplorable episodes of these or any other times in history. Rape, murder, and torture of the most heinous methods possible was carried out on 300,000 Chinese women, children and old men; it made no difference to my father. Some were burned alive, others were mutilated and cut to pieces. Every female, regardless of age, was raped repeatedly and then murdered. And my father was the one in charge of it all. To this day, their faces still haunt me.

When I returned to Japan, I fully expected to be executed. My father was a very important general. Surely his wishes would be carried out. But fortune smiled on me. My father's brother, Tashiro, whose name I have taken as my own, was a statesman and industrialist of enormous stature. He had been sickened by the glorification of these atrocities being celebrated daily by the government-controlled media. He was deeply disgraced by the man responsible for such unthinkable horrors: his own brother. My uncle was most cunning. He knew that he must not openly oppose the popular climate of the day.

He would need to exercise patience. Through influential friends, he took me as his charge and had my ancestral lineage changed to his. It was a great honor, to say nothing of the relief it brought me. My father was informed, but offered no resistance. I'm sure that he was grateful for such an annoyance as me to be removed from his life. My uncle proved to be as compassionate and caring a human being as my birth father was a ruthless madman. Because he was an industrialist of great vision, he was able to align himself with MacArthur after the war. The great general recognized how valuable an aid he could be for his plans to rebuild Japan. Tashiro Masotoma became a valued friend and member of MacArthur's inner circle. Such a position led to great wealth and stature over the years.

My uncle made only one request of the general. He wished to rid the world of his brother who had secured an executive pardon for war crimes. As far as my uncle was concerned, allowing Hiakama Masotoma to have a place in any part of the new Japan was totally unacceptable. At my uncle's request, a private duel was arranged between the brothers. I was one of the few who attended. My uncle was a peerless samurai. My father knew he was going to his death. He did so defiantly and very painfully. He suffered many wounds and much pain before my uncle put an end to his vulgar life. Then my uncle did something I have never seen repeated to this day. He took my father's sword and broke it in a sign of sheer contempt. It was the highest of insults. Years later he told me that his one regret was that he was not able to inflict more pain and disgrace upon him to make atonement to all those who had suffered at his hands."

Then Masotoma stopped talking. Tears had begun to well up in his eyes. The group, sitting in stunned silence brought on by the story they had just heard, waited for him to continue.

"It was at the World Congress of Martial Arts in Taiwan in 1960, that I had the good fortune to meet the great Li Xsing Po. Our mutual interest brought us together. I was astonished to learn that Li Xsing knew all about my past. We dined alone one evening and revisited that awful period. Li Xsing implored me to forgive myself for he knew that I had no part in my father's crimes. My old friend greatly flattered me by telling me he considered me one of the most courageous men he had the good fortune to befriend. Naturally, I was taken aback. Even then, Li Xsing was a legend. To have one of his stature acknowledge me was an honor far beyond my wildest dreams. Here I was, a mere industrialist who practiced Bushido, while Li Xsing was already acknowledged as the ultimate martial artist. Everyone in Asia knew him. All admired his many talents. But most of all, it was his understanding and compassion that truly demonstrated his greatness. It was a most sad day when I learned of his passing." Then, looking in Michael's direction he said, "I am confident that his son will be a worthy successor to his legacy. I feel very safe in his charge."

Masotoma paused to allow the mood in the room to lighten. Everyone was mesmerized by his story. These men were no strangers to death and war, but no one was prepared for what they had just heard. And certainly, the thought of one of Japan's greatest and most respected industrialists baring his soul to a room of complete strangers made for a brilliant icebreaking start for negotiations. The bonds between the Masotomas and the Pos were now obvious to all. Han Li's eyes scanned the room attempting to get a read on his guests. He was confident that the time remaining would produce the results he was hoping for.

# CHAPTER TWELVE

Michael leaned back in his seat and closed his eyes. His limo made a steady unobstructed path through the light traffic from Kennedy, along the Belt Parkway, through the Brooklyn Battery Tunnel and into Manhattan. It was the first chance he had to relax in days. Masotoma was safely on his way back to London where his people would be waiting to escort them back to Tokyo. The meeting had gone much better than anyone anticipated, helping Han Li and Victor to feel a lot more secure. The fact that no one had come forth with the stolen documents was puzzling, also a little encouraging. It just didn't make any sense to delay exposing the Po's plans, especially after so much blood was shed to get them. Three hundred million dollars American was being transferred to Masotoma E., and time had all but run out for those who had intentions of intervening. The merger was very close to completion. One more day and then any disclosures would simply be an annoyance, one that would have little impact.

Of course, the real problem, from Victor's perspective, was that nothing else made any sense other than there had to be a traitor in their ranks. Remember, pistol Pete was no longer available to be the scapegoat. Victor knew he would not find any peace until the guilty

party or parties were flushed out and made to suffer a proper punishment. And the longer that took the more scary it promised to get.
Whoever did this thing was fully aware of that. To know Victor was
to know the wrath of Victor. It definitely was not something one
would go courting.

Michael was anxious to get back to the apartment. He was so
pleased at Wee's culinary efforts and their positive effect on the
meetings that he could not wait to share his feelings of pride with his
friend. Everyone at the meeting had expressed a conviction that surely they had gained some weight, unable to control overindulging in
Wee's masterpieces. Michael assured Wee that his efforts went a long
way towards keeping the atmosphere at the meetings as loose as possible. Victor was well aware of Wee's culinary expertise, having dined
with his uncle and Michael during his trips to the island. Han Li and
Madame Po, however, found themselves in constant awe of his
amazing abilities. They vowed to reward him in the very near future.

Night was fast approaching and Michael had to hurry back to the
apartment. A very influential person at City Hall had requested he
lend assistance to a dear old friend who was experiencing some problems that would not go away. The official had assured his friend that
Michael would be the best person to aid him, given the circumstances. Michael had not a clue what these problems were or why someone was convinced  that he could be of assistance. His focus was on
getting a two-hour workout in before the visitor arrived. After
properly congratulating Wee, Michael made straight for the dojo. The
plan was for Wee to entertain the visitor until Michael could successfully complete his workout. Wee was riding a major high and both he
and Michael were confident he was up to the task.

All during the workout, Michael could sense the strange presence of Li Xsing. He made no attempt to ignore it; he so revered the
memory of his late father. He loved the old master and missed him
terribly. As he made his way through his routines, always mindful to
honor Li Xsing's instructions never to alter the patterns in any way,
he kept thinking about days long past when the master would in-

struct him and spur him on. Michael longed to be able to show him how far he had come. Li Xsing had taught him well. Michael was constantly amazed to find he was still progressing. The old master's methods were timeless, and Michael found himself appreciating them more and more as the years passed. If only he could tell him of his great affection for him and how proud he was to be the one to carry on his legacy, the *Dance of the Masters*. He was so thankful for the time they had together, a time Michael felt was far too short. Michael brushed away the tears that had welled up in his eyes and settled down on the floor for final meditation. The visitor would surely have arrived and must not be kept waiting. That would be an insult. Michael had no intention of doing that.

After an abbreviated meditation, Michael made his way to the living quarters. As he drew nearer, he was sure that the voice he heard along with Wee's was that of a female. He entered the living room to meet his guest.

"Oh, no," was all Katherine Hewett could muster as she buried her head in her hands. The site of Michael was just too much for her. "This can't be happening to me," she muttered.

Michael just stood there, not ready to believe his eyes. The very woman who had verbally accosted him at the Four Seasons was right there, sitting in his living room. "Could three times be a charm?" he wondered, not willing to believe it was just yet.

Wee looked confused.

"It's all right, Wee," Michael assured his friend."The lady and I have already met." Michael turned back to Katherine, then hesitantly asked, "What is it that I can do for you?"

"Do you happen to have a gun handy?" was Katherine's wry response. She took a moment to compose herself and then looked over at Michael. "My father arranged this appointment with you in an effort to help me with a serious problem I am having. My concern is that you may be part of the problem, so I confess I am a little confused at this point."

"I cannot imagine my master being a problem for you or anyone else," Wee protested.

"Thank you, Wee," said Michael. Turning back to Katherine he asked, "Why don't we start at the beginning? It's obvious someone felt that I could be of some assistance to you. As of right now, I am totally in the dark. Why don't you tell me what this is all about."

Katherine agreed and began to tell Michael and Wee all that took place at the Puck Building on Halloween evening and how she was constantly being harassed ever since. Michael realized that she was speaking about the family's stolen documents, but could not let on. Wee played along.

"It seems you were supposed to be given something important, but never received it. Had you ever seen the young man you spoke of before that night?" Michael asked, knowing full well what the answer was.

"Never," was Katherine's immediate response. "Evidently, his plans did not work out so he sought my help. My only guess is that he informed someone else there what his intentions were, but it never happened. My closest friend in the world, MaryAnn, assures me that she never had any contact with them. She's the only one who could have involved me, but didn't. Of that I am sure. I didn't realize it at the time, but many people were murdered that evening. It appears they are all somehow connected. My family has close friends in the mayor's office. Our information comes directly from them and what we read in the Times, of course."

Michael was paying close attention to Katherine's story. He was hoping to learn as much as possible. Han Li would be most interested in what he had just learned.

"I came to you with the hope that you can get word to whoever is involved in this and make them understand that I have no part in it. My father received information concerning an occidental who lives among the people in Chinatown, a man who is highly regarded in the Chinese community. He called a trusted friend to set up this appointment. I understand that most of the individuals who died that evening were Japanese, but, honestly, I would not know the difference. I am not even sure that you can help me, but where else can I turn?"

Michael took a moment to think, then asked, "Are you hungry?"

His question surprised Katherine. Yet she found herself quite amused by it, coming completely out of the blue. "Actually, I am," she found herself responding.

"Good," said Michael. "I'd love to take you on a little walk through my neighborhood to a wonderful restaurant. We can talk further. How does that sound?" Michael asked.

"Hopefully, things will turn out better than the last time we were in the same restaurant," Katherine countered.

Michael liked her answer. He found he also liked Katherine, very much. He was not sure how much assistance he could provide, but he was not going to let her get away so quickly this time. "Please give me a few moments. I need to change into some dry clothes. I promise I won't be long and I'm sure you have discovered Wee is a wonderful conversationalist."

Wee flushed with embarrassment, but did his best to entertain the guest until Michael's return. He knew that Michael's first order of business would be to call his uncle. Han Li listened intently as Michael relayed all that Katherine had shared with him. He was grateful for the call. Every piece of information, no matter how small it appeared, served to provide him with a clearer understanding of how the whole series of events took place. Finally, he had a first-person account of what went down on that fateful evening. He would alert Victor who was still at the Four Seasons.

Michael escorted Katherine down Mott Street through what was left of Little Italy on a street rapidly becoming part of Chinatown. Their destination was Chin Wah, the favorite restaurant of the Pos. As they walked, Katherine noticed that many people acknowledged her escort. Indeed, many even bowed. She found herself becoming strangely fascinated by this occidental who lived among the Chinese. They shared subgum house soup for two and lively conversation. Nothing could have prepared Katherine to meet this man who was quite obviously very intelligent and self-assured. Yet through it all, he exhibited a humble grace she found very appealing. She had not taken the time at the Four Seasons to notice how handsome he was. Now it was her turn to return the compliment; it was she who could not take her eyes from him. Katherine was accustomed to men paying all of the attention to her. Michael was doing just that. But, Katherine realized rather self-consciously, that she was paying it right back. And, actually, it felt rather good. This was new territory for Katherine Hewett. She made a conscious decision right then and there to make no attempt to stop herself. She realized she probably could not, even if she tried. This man had really caught her attention.

When dinner was completed, Michael escorted Katherine up Mulberry Street to Café Biondo for some espresso.

"I am Italian," emphasized Michael, answering Katherine's questioning eyes.

"Was I that obvious? she asked with a laugh.

"I get that a lot when people first meet me," Michael informed her. "It's funny, but New York Italians love to eat Chinese food. I just wish that I could introduce my Chinese brethren to espresso. Maybe I'll make that my life's work."

They shared a good laugh and New York cheesecake topped with fresh strawberries and fresh made whipped cream. Michael excused himself to make a phone call, then returned to the table to finish his third espresso. After a short time, he stood up.

"I believe it's time to take you home, Miss Hewett," he said. He paid the bill and bade goodnight to the waitress and counterman who obviously knew him. Michael led Katherine out to the street to a large Mercedes sedan, waiting to take her home.

"Just tell Lee where you wish to go and he'll take you. I want to make sure you get home safely," he said. Then, as an afterthought, "I'd also like to know where you live."

Katherine was pleased. She handed him a card. On it was her address and three telephone numbers where she could be reached. She used the time Michael had excused himself to accomplish the task. Then, looking into his eyes she said, "I'm not sure if you can help me or not, Mr. DeAngelo, but, at the moment, I'm not really thinking of you in that context." Then she asked, "Do you have any plans tomorrow?"

"What time?" Michael asked.

"All day," Katherine answered. She smiled, then turned her attention to the driver.

"Ninety-sixth and Riverside," she said as she entered the auto. The large car raced up Mulberry. Michael just stood there, speechless.

# CHAPTER THIRTEEN

The sun was shining, the breezes were gentle, a perfect temperature prevailed and the balls were dropping in the hole. Marv Levy was playing the greatest round of golf in his life. There he was, standing on the 13th green at Hilton Head with a smile of invincibility spread across his well tanned face. But there was the matter of this annoying noise invading his reverie. He looked around but could not seem to locate its origin. Then he winced as something struck him in the side. When he opened his eyes he realized he was lying in his own bed on the upper West Side of Manhattan. Once again, he felt the pain in his side.

"Answer the damn phone Marv, it's killing me," came the annoyingly irritated voice of his wife, Maris.

"Ah, Maris," he thought to himself.

Marv grabbed the receiver. It was Bobby Ferrigno and it was 11:58 p.m..

"You've got my attention," said Marv.

Bobby informed him that there was a killing up in East Harlem at Luna, the famous Italian food Mecca for gangsters, actors who played gangsters, the glitterati and anyone who knew someone who could squeeze an invite into this hallowed Italian eatery which was nearly impossible to gain entrance to unless you were known. Bobby informed him that a fifty-five-year-old smalltime wise guy wannabe, Johnnie Stonato, better known to all as Johnny Stoonod, (translation: stupid) just gunned down a made man from a New Jersey crime family in front of a packed house. The victim was shot in the back.

Bobby was the guest of an actor who was in town for talks with Martin Scorsese and Robert De Niro concerning a role in an upcoming crime drama they were developing. De Niro got him in along with Bobby, who was a boyhood friend of the actor. It was Bobby who apprehended Johnny S. as he was attempting to leave. Obviously, all hell broke loose. Luna was a place where people fantasized about things like this happening, but it was the fantasy of such things that was Luna's lure. No one really expected anything like this to happen, not really, even if you choose to ignore the fact that a good sixty percent of the males in the place were packing.

Marv listened intently. There was only one word that could describe what was going through his head; "Oi!"

"Listen, Marv, I got this if you don't want to deal with this right now," said Bobby.

"Oh no, I wouldn't miss this for anything," said Marv as he threw off the covers, jumped out of bed and stood there waiting for his feet to get accustomed to the floor. "I'll be there as soon as I can."

Marv put in a call to Cal Munro, jumped in the shower, threw on yesterday's clothes and made his way down to the street. Within a few moments, Cal came with lights blazing to pick him up and take him up to East Harlem. Marv gave Cal the address then said not another word until they reached the crime scene. And then all he had to say was "wait here."

Marv exited the car and stared up at the front of Luna. Police vehicles were everywhere. The coroner's vehicle was just pulling away with the dead body. Johnny S. had been taken to the 137th precinct until Marv could get the lay of the land and decide what to do with him. Marv stood for a moment, staring up at the entrance. He knew the place well. Luna began as a neighborhood eatery that somehow became legendary. Along the way the Luchese crime family made it one of their own. Over the years, it attracted the Who's Who and the Who used to be Who from every walk of celebrity. They say Sinatra sang here once. He came as a guest of Tony Bennett who still came around every now and then and could be coaxed to belt out a song or two. And then there were the locals who could still gain a welcome entrance. Some of them had moved far away, but came around when they were back in town visiting the old haunts. Among the most notable were the cheese brothers, Tony Provolone and Louis Scamotz, known obviously for their love affair with cheese. The story goes that these guys even had cheese on their pancakes. Some thought that was a slight exaggeration. Others weren't so sure. The funny thing was, these guys really were brothers.

The owners, Nicky and Santino Luna were third-generation proprietors. Through the years, not one thing was changed from the original version.

Marv saw Bobby and motioned for him to join him.

"Whatcha got?" asked Marv.

It seems that Johnny S. was sitting at the bar and got into a heated discussion with one Frank Bonadeo from over in Jersey. According to Johnnie S., Bonadeo was bragging that he was with the Scalesie crime family out of Newark. When Johnny hinted that he was associated with the Luchese family, Bonodeo just laughed and informed him that if he wanted to whack somebody, it didn't matter what family they belonged to. Johnny took this as a direct threat. Bonadeo was in his late thirties and was all Gold's Gym. Johnny S. looked like he spent his life in a Gold's Delicatessen, which is why Bonadeo looked at him and figured he was no made man or any man of any significance. Johnny slowly let his hand slide over to the .38 caliber Smith and Wesson he had tucked into his belt. Bonodeo was obviously a little 'lit'; he never noticed. He said something else, began to laugh and turned away from Johnny. Johnny panicked. In his delusional mind, he feared the guy would turn back towards him and fire away, which is exactly what Johnny did, putting two slugs from his .38 into Bonadeo's back. Bonadeo staggered forward and fell onto a table of customers, sending the place into panic mode. Johnny immediately got up from his stool and headed for the door. He was met there by Bobby who pushed him outside and handcuffed him. Interestingly, the police discovered that Bonadeo was not carrying a weapon. He had been assured that it was safe and wise not to. Obviously, a sit-down was going to be necessary to soothe some pretty pissed-off feelings between the New York mob and the New Jersey mob. Marv was already getting a headache.

Marv made sure that the owners of Luna were given a police presence so that they could clean up the place and see that all their patrons were safely taken care of. Most restaurants would suffer from something like a murder taking place while filled with customers. Marv knew, from his years around this city that Luna just took another giant step on that road to priceless free advertisement and fabled existence. He and Bobby went over to the 137th to talk with Johnny S. Johnny's story, obviously scripted, resembled his statement at the scene. However, Johnny didn't get his infamous nickname by accident. The detectives at the 137th told Marv that Johnny had a history of coming up with stories that glorified his existence, whatever the situation. Unfortunately, Johnny really believed the self-aggrandizing tales he fabricated. The trouble was, he assumed everyone else did too. The stupid part was that his stories were usually so far removed from anything plausible, that there was no way anyone could take them seriously. Marv decided to send Johnny to *RIKER'S* Island until he could get things sorted out. He then headed home in the hopes of recapturing that dream of golfing magic.

# CHAPTER FOURTEEN

Lucy came into the squad room like she always did, bursting with energy, looking like she couldn't wait to take on the world. She stopped in her tracks and looked at Bobby and Walter slumped in their chairs looking like someone told them La Bella Ferrera's had just closed down.

"What?" Bobby asked, looking up at his wife like a man without a clue.

"You're kidding, right?" Lucy said. "What is this, the Night of the Living Dead? You and Walter look like……..." She didn't finish. She didn't have to. " It's only nine o'clock in the morning."

Walter just groaned. He knew better than to try and stop Lucy when she was in full throttle.

"So, what's up with you two? Why so happy?"

"It's two days and we got nothin' on Johnny 'Stoonod'. The DA is just thrilled with us. It seems his sister was at Luna that night with some people from the Met and now she won't leave her apartment. He's not happy," said Walter.

"Doesn't she live in New York?" Lucy asked.

"Upper East side," said Walter.

"You know her?" Lucy asked Walter.

"All too well," Walter said. "A real piece of work. You know,

Ms. Society. She is shocked to her core," said Walter, eyes wide with exaggeration.

"Yeah, well, where'd she grow up, Connecticut?" Lucy asked. She then took a moment to think. "I take that back. Is she from Mars or is she just another self-indulgent uptown pris?"

Walter said nothing but pointed his finger at her as if to say "right on".

Once again, Lucy stopped and got quiet. The wheels in her head were turning. "You know, I read something about this Bonadeo guy somewhere recently. Give me a few, but I'm sure what I read wasn't about him so much as someone involved with him.

A half hour later she exclaimed, "I have it!"

Lucy made her way over to Walter and Bobby to show them a clipping from the gossip pages in the Daily News. The report said that two women had to be physically removed from Steve Wynn's Hotel in Atlantic City. It seems they got into a screaming match and refused to quiet down. One of the women was thought to be the girl-friend of a reputed New Jersey mobster, Francis 'Frank' Bonadeo. Witnesses at the scene claimed that both women claimed their boy-friends were gangsters.

"And, right now I'm sure you two geniuses are asking, is this supposed to mean something? The answer is, you tell me. It seems the other female in this altercation is a Linda Calderone from Kew Gardens. You two do know where Kew Gardens is don't you?" Her words were dripping with sarcasm. What made it all the more comi-cal was that Lucy was Puerto Rican, so she had a funny way of pro-nouncing certain words which, when added to her delivery, made her two colleagues feel even more defenseless.

"Queens," said Walter, wishing he hadn't.

Lucy flashed Walter an 'I'm so proud of you' look. Then, she charged ahead.

"So, here's what I'm thinking. A New Jersey gangster comes to New York and goes to a restaurant he's never been to, one that is almost impossible to get into. Through the long arm of coincidence, he gets himself killed by a New York guy who fantasizes that he's a mobster. The girlfriend of the deceased is from New Jersey, the other lady is from New York. I know it's a stretch, but am I the only one here who can see that maybe there is a connection?"

At this point, the guys just looked at each other. Bobby, like his esteemed partner, Walter, knew better than to say anything else now that Lucy was on a roll. And Lucy was definitely on a Lucy roll.

"I'm going to find out where this Calderone woman lives and then you are coming with me, Bobby, to have a little talk with her."

"Of course," said Bobby. And nothing else. A decision had been made.

Linda Calderone's apartment was located just behind the court-house on Queens Boulevard at the intersection of Queens Boulevard and Union Turnpike. It was a nondescript three-story red brick building. But it did have an elevator. Linda Calderone lived on the third floor. The elevator was a good thing. Bobby knocked on the door and announced they were the police. A female answered the door. She was in her early fifties, just about the right age for Johnny Stonato. She was about 5 feet 4, with a head of straw-like blonde hair. She looked as though she just got up. It was noon. She also looked like she forgot to take last night's makeup off. Bobby's assessment was that she could be attractive. But it would take work.

They went inside and sat in the living room. Unlike its inhabit-ant, the apartment was immaculate and tastefully decorated. Lucy was impressed. She took the lead questioning Linda. It took a while but Linda finally told them that she and the other woman did get into an argument over a slot machine and their words were heated. She said the other woman said her boyfriend was some big-time mobster from Jersey. Linda laughed and said her boyfriend was connected to heavy people in New York City. And who was this mystery gangster? None other than Johnny Stonato.

"Bingo," said Lucy.

Marv had Stonato brought from Riker's to One Police Plaza for questioning. His lawyer was not happy. A few words from Marv changed his attitude. Marv reasoned with him that it would go much better for his client if the truth were told. The lawyer knew differently. Johnny's story and the truth were as far apart as downtown Brooklyn and Sheepshead Bay, out in the Rockaways.

"I have two words for you, Johnny, " said Marv. "Linda Calderone."

Johnny looked down at the table, then he looked sheepishly at his lawyer. "They know," Johnny said.

"What is it you want, Captain?" The attorney asked.

"The real story would be nice. From what I have been told, reality and your client are unknown to each other."

The attorney told Stonato to tell the true story of the events of the night of the shooting.

"I was sitting at the bar minding my own business," Stonato began. This young guy takes the stool next to me. I've been going to Luna for years, you know, I'm from the neighborhood."

Marv acknowledged him and motioned for him to continue his story.

"I try to make nice with this guy 'cause I figure he's somebody new to Luna and he appears to be alone, which is sort of suspicious. Anyway, we get to talking and after a while, he tells me his reason for being there is to try to find out who the guy is that's related to the woman his girlfriend had a beef with over in Atlantic City. He tells me his lady-friend won't give him any peace until he roughs that guy up. We're talkin' about a beatin' here. So I say 'hey, this is Luchese territory. No one comes in here and roughs anybody up without a sit down.' The guy laughs and tells me he could give a rat's rear end whose territory it is. If he feels like it, he'll whack the guy and nobody from no New York family can stop him. My first thought is, this guy is not showing any respect."

That got a collection of rolled eyes from the group. Yeah, like this "jabeep" is going to defend the family honor; a family he has no association with.

"Then I think, this guy looks head to toe muscles and I got at least fifteen years on him. He gets me alone and I'm done for. The guy was drinking pretty good, I figured he might be nervous. Whatever, I figured the booze was starting to get to him. No way I can tell if he really knows me or not, but one thing I know for sure; if I don't take care of him right now, he'll get me sooner or later. Maybe he'll get Linda too if she happens to be with me when he does. I got my honor and my lady to protect."

The room was silent. Walter and Bobby had a pretty good idea what Marv was thinking, but had all they could do to keep from laughing in this clown's face. Johnny looked at his lawyer. They were both waiting for Marv's response. All Marv could think about right now was the possibility that this bozo in front of him might just have set off fireworks between mobsters from New York and New Jersey. His stomach was beginning to react negatively.

"So what you're telling me is that in some way, you felt you were acting in self-defense," said Marv.

"Exactly," Johnny said.

"Shocking," was all Marv could offer.

"Well, what do you think, Captain?" The lawyer asked.

"I think I'm sending your client back to Riker's and the D.A. will be in touch. By the way, his sister was in Luna when you acted in self-defense. Word is, she hasn't left her apartment since. Good luck gentlemen," said Marv.

The lawyer had to help Johnny out of his seat. At that very moment, there were no positive scenarios rolling around in that head.

Marv brought the gang into his office. "Walter, you better reach out to the Trumentas and see what they think. Bobby, you get your people on the street on this. If something bad is going to happen, I'd like to know about it sooner than later. Lucy, what can I say? You really read that crap in the Daily News? God bless you, Lucy."

Walter was the only one to offer anything. "Listen, Captain, Michael DeAngelo is nowhere to be found right now and Patty Figamo and I are not exactly blood brothers. There is no reason he wants to share with the police."

Marv just stared at him. He said nothing.

"Right," said Walt, who got it. "I'll reach out to my old pal Patty and see what I can do," he said, backing out of the office behind Lucy and Bobby. Marv had made his point and any more conversation on the matter would be pointless.

Before Walter could even attempt to contact Patty, The Trumentas got word to him. There would be no repercussions over the Luna killing because Johnny S. was a nobody, and the best place for him would be in prison because the people in New York were not going to throw any parades in his honor. In fact, right now, prison was the safest place on earth for Johnny S. The fact that the New York people had to apologize to the New Jersey guys was not sitting very well with them. Other overtures and concessions had to be made to them, but it was best Walter didn't know the particulars. Nobody wanted the police nosing around anymore than necessary. So far as the murder at Luna was concerned, unnecessary bloodshed had been avoided. Case closed.

# CHAPTER FIFTEEN

It was the coldest November in years. No one could remember the last time it snowed on Thanksgiving Day, but snow it did. Manhattan found itself covered in a fresh blanket of the white stuff imparting a magical setting for Santa's float in Macy's annual homage to the season. The flaky intrusion did not seem to have any ill effects on the throngs who braved the weather to take part in the festivities. Included in those numbers were Michael and Katherine, who had spent every moment they could steal over the last three weeks in each other's company. The moments were few, but greatly treasured. They laughed and clung together for warmth as they made their way over to Rockefeller Center for hot chocolate and a warm vantage point to enjoy the skaters at the Center's magical rink.

Business was moving along nicely for the Pos and Trumentas. The time of peril had passed without further incident. Still, the Pos would not lower their guard until a name could be attached to the author of the Halloween murders. By now, Masotoma E. had fixed its cash flow problem to the astonishment of the Japanese business community and the investment world at large. This seemingly miraculous turnaround spurred Masotoma stocks to new heights. Just who bailed them out was still a mystery, but a gluttonous financial world was more concerned with the calculation of profits than the origin of someone's capital infusion. All indications pointed to a lovely green Christmas for the market. Once again, the movers and shakers had displayed a complete lack of concern for how, choosing rather, their avarice induced pursuit of how much. For Masotoma E. and its new partners, things could not have turned out better.

On the weekend, Michael would be clearing up some unfinished family business and heading out to Brooklyn for Sunday dinner with Rosa. Katherine would be dining in the city with her father and the newest potential Mrs. Nicholas Thor Hewett. As her father got older, Katherine observed that the potential candidates to fill the vacancy as his mate were becoming more numerous and considerably younger. She took solace in the knowledge that MaryAnn would be returning to the city to spend time with her. They would make the rounds of never-ending parties given by New York's privileged class. But Sunday evening was the night Katherine was most looking forward to. That was the night she would finally introduce her best friend to the mysterious Mr. DeAngelo. MaryAnn was most anxious to meet the man who appeared to have completely captivated the heart of her dearest friend. MaryAnn had never seen Katherine act this way towards any man and the anticipation of that meeting was "quite overwhelming" as MaryAnn put it.

Victor found that he could no longer delay his return to Hong Kong. There was always Po business that needed his personal attention. He was forced to overcome his reluctance to leave even though he was convinced that the seed of their problem was planted here in New York. He did not relish separating himself from his family and, let us not forget, the action. There is a saying that "the passage of time heals all wounds." However, where Victor is concerned, each day that passes without answers only serves to piss him off more. There is another saying, this one in Hong Kong. "It is not beneficial for one's health to keep Victor Chen waiting...for anything."

Victor made sure that he and Michael spoke daily by phone. His chief concern was for Han Li's safety. Just as he had held his uncle Li Xsing in the highest regard, so too was his love and admiration for his uncle Han Li. Victor was an enforcer and a keen businessman. His mastery of the game of chess had served him well. Han Li was the acknowledged brains of the Po's worldwide empire. Who else could have imagined a marriage between his family and the Italians? More importantly, who else could have made such a marriage a reality? It was to Han Li that Masotoma had come to propose their unlikely merger. And, again, it was Han Li who made it happen. The Chinese, the Italians and now, the Japanese; it was all mind-boggling. To Han Li, on the other hand, it was simply business as usual. Who knows what this man could have accomplished had he ever taken up the game of chess?

For the second time that weekend it was snowing. MaryAnn Vanooster had reached her party threshold and was now looking for Katherine to head back to the apartment. Her stomach was queasy, compliments of the massive amounts of holiday food and drink she had consumed on her rounds. All she could think of was the comfort of a warm bed and a good night's sleep. Katherine, being more a schmoozer than consumer, was not feeling MaryAnn's pain.

"Go back to the apartment and get some rest," Katherine instructed her weary friend. "I'm going to catch up on some gossip with old friends. She exchanged overcoats with MaryAnn assuring her, "It's warmer than yours. You'll need it if you are going to catch a cab. Don't worry about me, I'll be along shortly," she told her exit-minded friend. "I am sure there is someone here who will be just dying to give me a lift home," she quipped.

MaryAnn knew exactly what her friend meant. Men always seemed ready to brave the elements to please Katherine. They laughed, hugged and headed in opposite directions. MaryAnn was in luck. It took only a few moments for her to flag down an empty uptown-bound taxi. Considering it was a holiday weekend and the weather conditions, that was remarkable. It was also very fortunate as the temperature was plunging. A bitter cold was settling in. The cab was not very warm. MaryAnn was thankful the driver drove as though someone forgot to introduce him to the vehicle's braking system. She was relieved to exit and escape into the warmth of the lobby.

The doorman was nowhere in sight, but the large glass doors offered no resistance. All MaryAnn had on her mind was a quick hot shower and a warm featherbed. As she exited the elevator on the sixteenth floor, she witnessed the playful carryings-on of a young Asian couple, shamelessly kissing and groping, right there in the hallway. The two appeared to be heading in the same direction as MaryAnn who was making her way to apartment number 21. She exchanged warm smiles with the couple who seemed to be heading into the apartment right across the hall. As she opened the door, MaryAnn was knocked to the ground by the young man who then struck her in the face and dragged her into the living room. The young woman made sure that no one witnessed the attack and then entered the apartment, pulled out a short-barreled 38 Smith & Wesson and placed it up against MaryAnn's face.

"We have a few questions for you, Ms. Hewett," she said.

Katherine found the gossip less juicy and infinitely less interesting than anticipated. It appeared that her relationship with Michael was giving her a whole new perspective on things. The babblings of the spoiled-from-birth acquaintances who had inhabited her life until now seemed droll and mundane. She did, however, manage to convince a certain young man in attendance that he too was ready to leave and fetch his Grand Cherokee to give her a ride uptown. Katherine was very good at helping others identify what they wanted to do, for her, of course. And, so, a hopeful but disillusioned young man drove her uptown and reluctantly deposited her safely in front of her building.

A large crowd was gathering in the lobby. The group was quite concerned that the building entrance was not being monitored, and, of much more concern, the security of the building was being compromised. The management office had been contacted, and assured all that help was on the way. Katherine was confident that there were enough in attendance to ensure the proper amount of righteous indignation. She felt secure that her two cents would not be necessary. It had only been a little over a half hour since MaryAnn's departure.

It was about 10:00 p.m. and for most New Yorkers, the night was young. But two days and nights of festivities and cheer had suddenly caught up with her. A good night's sleep was beginning to take on a certain luster. She wearily made her way down the empty hallway to her apartment. Opening the door she was immediately made aware of broken and overturned furniture. Instinctively she wedged her coat and scarf in between the door and wall to prevent it from closing behind her. Suddenly gripped with fear she found she could not move.

She called out to her friend, but heard no reply. Finally, she gathered up enough nerve to enter the living room. She gasped at the blood soaked body of her friend, bound and gagged on the floor. She bent down to check her friend's condition. She nearly vomited at the sight of the woman's face, beaten beyond recognition. She looked around to see that the apartment was a shambles. Once again, seized with fear, she rose and backed clumsily towards the door. She opened the door to the hall closet frantically searching for her ski coat. Ripping it from its hangar, she took it and kicked the coat jamming the door back into the apartment, slammed the door behind her and ran headlong down the hallway to the elevator. A mixture of fear and sorrow warred back and forth in her head; her emotions were too strong to control. She suddenly found herself in the underground parking garage. She hurriedly made her way over to a dark green Range Rover, looking constantly around to make sure she wasn't followed. Luckily, the lock was remote controlled. Given her state of mind, gaining access to the vehicle by successfully placing a key in the lock might have proven difficult. As it was, it took three tries to get the key into the ignition. As soon as she heard the roar of the engine, she slammed the lever into drive and quite by accident, made it out to 96th Street without causing any damage. Going purely on instinct, she made her way over to the West Side Highway, then north heading towards Duchess County.

# CHAPTER SIXTEEN

The 11 o'clock weather forecast had just concluded promising an end to the snow, but a long siege of Arctic-like weather conditions.

"Please, please Ms. Hewett. You must calm yourself down. I can hardly understand you," Michael heard Wee exclaim from the living room. Wee had answered the ringing phone in the foyer just as Michael was turning off the late news. Michael made his way over to retrieve the phone from a perplexed Wee Fong.

"They killed her, Michael, they killed her," she blurted out. "They killed MaryAnn in my apartment. They killed her thinking she was me. I just know it, I just know it," she kept repeating.

"Where are you now?" he asked

"I am at a diner in Hyde Park. It's the only one. Can you come for me? Michael, I am so scared. Please come and get me," she pleaded.

"Of course," he assured her. "What's the address?"

"You can't miss it," she exclaimed. "It's the big diner on Route 9 in Hyde Park. It stays open 24 hours. You can't miss it, it's the only one."

"Sit in a front window and don't do anything until you see me. Do not leave, no matter what. Do you understand?"

"Yes, Michael," she said, her voice barely audible. "I'll wait right here. Please come for me."

"Don't worry. I'll be there before you know it. No one is going to hurt you. I will see to that," he promised, emphatically.

Michael told Wee to pack an overnight bag for him as quickly as he could. He had a call to make. Walter Larkin was surprised to hear Michael's voice at 11:30 on a Saturday night. "Does your social life suck that bad that you need to talk to me, kid?" Walter joked.

"Walter, listen." Michael instructed. "There has been a homicide at the apartment of Katherine Hewett."

"Dear God," Walter gasped, "did someone kill the Lady Kate?"

Walter's question momentarily confused Michael. "Come on, Michael," Walter demanded, "did somebody kill her?"

Suddenly Michael realized what Walter was saying. "No, Walter," he responded, "someone killed MaryAnn Vanooster. I believe they thought she was Katherine."

Michael interrupted Walter's barrage of questions. "Look, just get over there. Have the doorman let you in. I'm going to get Katherine now. I'll call you in the morning, I've got to make sure Katherine is safe, talk to you in the morning. Now just get over there."

The dead phone line was all Walter needed to confirm that this conversation was over and that he might as well follow up on Michael's information and do his job until Michael could get back to him.

Wee put in a call to Penn Station to check on the departure time of the last train to Duchess County. The 12:05 a.m. was the last train. Michael was sure he could make it. He grabbed his bag and headed out the door to Houston Street to hail a cab. It was 11:40 p.m.; he had just a little under a half hour. He made his way to the far side of Houston to westbound traffic. He and a taxi arrived at the same time. Michael jumped in and barked, "Penn Station and make it fast. I don't want to miss my train."

"Sure, man," came the cabby's reply. "Must be some fine young lady for such a fire to be burning, man."

At first, Michael barely acknowledged the cabby's words; all that was on his mind was making that train. The roads were cold and wet. There would be no racing up Eighth Avenue in this weather. But there was something familiar about the cab driver's voice. Michael inched closer to the dividing glass to get a look at his shield. "Could it be?" He wondered.

"Nikki, is that you?" He asked

"Sure it is man," came the reply. "How does the gentleman know Nikki Josef, man?" He asked

"It's been a few years, but you once picked me up at Kennedy and drove me and my friend to the Plaza."

Nikki had to think for a moment and then it came back to him. "Oh, man, it's you, Dickens, man. Nikki could never forget you, man. And how are you?"

"Great, up till now, but now I've got a bit of a problem," Michael informed him. "I've got to make this train and get up to Hyde Park fast. It's my last chance."

"Not to worry, man, northbound trains are all running late. Big problem; no need to hurry. You'll be lucky if they don't cancel them. Electric problems, man; frozen switches."

Michael fell silent. Katherine was counting on him. She was scared. He had to get to her.

"Nikki could take you, man," he said. "The roads are open. Piece of cake till Route 9. Even then, Nikki could beat the train. What do you say, man?" He asked.

"How much?" Michael wanted to know.

Nikki let out a laugh. "The way Dickens pays, Nikki would be wise to let Dickens set the price."

"How does $100 sound?" Michael asked

"Like sweet, sweet music to Nikki's ears," came his reply.

"Relax, man," Nikki said. "Nikki has plans for that $100. He intends to spend it on fine ladies and smooth drink."

"In that case, better make it $200," said Michael.

"Dickens is a gentleman of the highest quality," said Nikki who completed the distance in uncharacteristic silence.

Katherine was right. The Every Day Diner in Hyde Park was truly hard to miss. The mammoth diner was ablaze with enough light to illuminate a small airport runway. "Come in with me," Michael instructed. Nikki obliged and followed him up the steps into the diner. Katherine recognized Michael and ran to him. She dove into his arms and held on for all she was worth.

"Give me a second," Michael said to the driver.

"No problem, man," Nikki responded, sensing the lady's desperation.

"Kate, I have to pay the man," Michael told her.

Instinctively, Kate grabbed for her purse. Michael gently stopped her and led her and Nikki to an ATM machine in the entranceway. He collected $200 and handed it over to Nikki. He also gave Nikki his business card. "If you ever need me, friend, just call this number. I may be able to be of some assistance to you."

"Nikki knows who Dickens is, man." The cab driver assured him. "Nikki keeps up with the news. You were not exactly a mystery to Nikki. He appreciates the gesture, man."

Next, Nikki handed Michael one of his business cards. "Even Dickens can use a hand some time," he informed Michael. With that, he turned and was gone.

# CHAPTER SEVENTEEN

Michael led Katherine back to her booth. His presence definitely helped restore her composure. He ordered coffee and then began. "Tell me what happened," he instructed.

Katherine told Michael everything that happened from the time MaryAnn left her until now. "I never saw anyone at the apartment. By the time I got there, whoever did this thing was gone, and poor MaryAnn..." her voice trailed off. "What am I going to do?" She wanted to know. "She was my best friend, my only friend. I am the reason she is dead."

Michael had no answers. The silence that followed was deafening. All Michael could do was to reach across the table and take hold of Katherine's hands. "What now?" he asked.

"I need you to come with me," she said. "Please, just come with me. I'll explain when we get there."

"Alright," he said. "Let's go."

Katherine led the way to the Range Rover. They got in and she began driving north up Route 9.

"I didn't know you had a Range Rover," he said. "I always wanted one of these."

Katherine said nothing. She drove a few miles north and then made a sharp left turn off the main road onto a small country road. It was obvious she knew exactly where she was going. She easily navigated the winding road. Michael did not want to distract her with any questions because she was driving with reckless abandon. However, she made easy work of every challenging turn. Michael had to go on faith that she knew exactly what she was doing. He relaxed his hand from the door handle, realizing he was about to rip it from its frame. They crossed a major road and continued north for a few more miles. Once again, Katherine executed a sharp left turn off the road, a move that startled Michael as there was nothing to suggest the road or anything else.

"This is my uncle's estate," she offered. "We're on a road that is not in use anymore." Michael accepted her explanation

"Hang on, it gets a little rough," cautioned Katherine. She didn't lie. Michael held on tightly. Finally, Katherine eased off the accelerator and eased the vehicle slowly down a steep hill. Once again, she knew exactly where she was going. Michael was amazed. The snow was coming down at a fast clip. It had no effect on her driving. Just then, Michael caught sight of a small building about twenty yards directly ahead. Katherine made another left turn and headed down a small incline. She brought the vehicle to a stop and turned off the engine.

"It will be safe to leave it here," she said.

They got out and made their way to a small cottage. Katherine used her hands to wipe away the snow from a small space to the right of the slate porch. She removed a tile, reached in and pulled out a key. She replaced the tile, opened the door, and led Michael inside.

"This is the old caretaker's cottage. My uncle Max let me use it as a hideaway any time I needed to escape from my family. Give me a minute and I'll turn the power on," said Katherine. But she didn't move. Something made her pause. "What if they have a tracking device on my truck?" She said. "These people are very smart. They have electronic gadgets for everything. We won't even be able to start a fire. It will be a dead giveaway," she said. "Now what are we going to do? We'll freeze to death out here."

"We don't have to stay here," said Michael.

"Oh, please, Michael," she pleaded. "This is the only place I have ever felt safe. I can't leave, please don't make me leave."

Michael looked out the window. The snow was already covering the tire and foot tracks. "It looks as though the only way anyone can trace us here would be by some electronic device. Let's hope they didn't know you owned a vehicle. Most New Yorkers don't," said Michael. Michael opened the door to the bedroom. "Get every piece of bedding you can find," he ordered. He took the mattress off the bed and dragged it into the main room, and placed it on the floor up against the front door. Katherine emptied the drawers of all the bedding. Michael secured the one window in the bedroom and pulled all the furniture out of the room to barricade the bedroom door from inside the front room.

"Don't be afraid, we'll be alright," Michael assured her. Katherine smiled weakly. Right now, she wasn't too sure of anything. She was emotionally and physically exhausted. Her life was in the hands of someone she had known for three weeks. She realized how vulnerable she was. All the money and prestige in the world would be useless to guarantee her safety. It was not a good feeling.

Michael was satisfied that the cottage was secured. At least no one would be able to surprise them in their sleep. He instructed Katherine to get down on the mattress.

"Quickly, take your coat off and put it on backwards," he told her. "Get under the covers."

Katherine did as instructed. She got under the three blankets that were stored in the cottage. Michael opened his coat and joined her, gently turning her to the door as he pressed his chest up against her back. "Get some sleep," he said. "We'll leave at first light." His voice was so convincing that Katherine totally gave in. All of a sudden she had no fear. She closed her eyes and before long drifted off.

It seemed like only a few seconds had passed as Katherine felt herself being awakened. The sun was up and it was time for them to do the same. Michael took a few moments to survey the whole landscape: no tire tracks, no footprints, no intruders. He satisfied himself that they were safe. He pulled the mattress away from the door. Then he took the keys to the Range Rover and went to check it out and collect his overnight bag. All seemed safe. He made his way back to the cottage. Katherine was sitting up on the mattress, her coat turned back around and fastened. A look of satisfaction covered her face. Michael's control and obvious survival skills really impressed her.

Michael reached into his bag and pulled out a bottle of mouthwash. He took some, swished it around and spit it out into the dry sink. He handed the bottle to Katherine, who did the same. Katherine wiped her mouth and handed the bottle back to Michael. She took him by surprise as he was fastening the top back on. She put her arms around his neck and kissed him full on the lips, then pulled away. She seemed very pleased by what she had just done. It was hard for her to believe that they had not yet kissed in the three weeks, but she had been given sufficient notice that a man in Michael's position would not enter into frivolous dalliances. When he kissed her, it would be a sign of serious intent. It would then be up to her to acknowledge their movement towards a binding relationship that can have only one conclusion: marriage. She knew full well the terms and was comfortable with Michael's vow of celibacy. At this point in her life, Katherine wanted much more than a "roll in the hay."

"You hungry?" Michael asked.

"Always." Katherine answered.

"Take me back to that diner. I have a date with some steak and eggs."

"Better buckle up," Katherine warned as they sat in the Rover allowing a few seconds to let the oil circulate through the engine. Katherine put the transmission into lower drive and gunned the motor. The vehicle was instantly propelled over the terrain like a wild bucking bronco. It did not take long to get to the main road where Katherine retraced their route from the night before. It was evident that she was in much better spirits and gave Michael a history lesson as she drove headlong through the narrow twists and turns of the area known as Hudson Valley's Great Estates.

"Just north of my family's estate is Montgomery Place, arguably the centerpiece of the whole area. Of course, the families of Olana or Locust Grove might give you quite an argument, but having grown up here, I'd have to agree with the Montgomery Place camp," Katherine began. As she sped along, she pointed out many of the great homes such as Wildenstein, the home of the Stuckleys'. Michael was impressed. He just wished that he could enjoy the ride a little more instead of holding on for dear life. "Old money knows old money," Katherine continued, "or is related to old money. Most of this region goes back to the Livingstons, people who invented the term 'all in the family'. Cousins married cousins so that the great wealth and heritage of the Livingstons remained intact. The only way you could get into this family was if you were rich enough or royal enough. It may seem strange to outsiders but you have to understand that these people really loved family. The great Janet Livingston Montgomery, the widow of General Thadeous Montgomery, the first American casualty of the Revolution, made Montgomery Place the place to be for all the Livingston heirs. That tradition carried right on down to the Delafields, more relatives who made Montgomery Place a family haven until 1986 when the property became too expensive to run. They deeded it to the Historic Hudson Valley to ensure that the Livingston name would live on through this magnificent house."

They were now back on Route 9 heading south towards Hyde Park and the Every Day Diner. Michael was relieved that Katherine's driving had taken on a more civil tone.

"I guess you knew some of these people?" Michael asked. Katherine looked over at Michael and smiled. He seemed more relaxed.

"Yes, Michael, I did. You could say that I grew up on all the Livingston Estates. My family knew them all intimately. But there is more. Another Livingston married the fabulously wealthy Ogden Mills. The Mills were one of the most popular couples of Hyde Park along with the Vanderbilts, who had no children. The Vanderbilts were a generous and loving couple. Their Christmas gatherings with the children of Hyde Park are remembered to this day. But enough of the Vanderbilts, it was one of the twin daughters of the Mills who married royalty."

Katherine's voice suddenly took on an air of excitement. She looked over to Michael who already was sufficiently impressed. Katherine plowed ahead. "Beatrice Mills married the eighth Earl of Granard, who just happened to be related to the Spencers, who just happen to have a daughter named Diana, whom you might know as the wife of Prince Charles of England." Without waiting she continued, "But long before Diana, I spent a few summers with Aunty B., when she visited her nieces at Montgomery Place. Auntie B. was not really my aunt. She was one of the women in our circle who never married and sort of adopted MaryAnn and me. Oh, how they would lavish their affection and wonderful gifts on the two of us! I think I was about twelve years old the last time I saw her. She was such a love and quite a joy." Katherine made a left-hand turn into the diner parking lot and pulled to a stop. But she was not quite done.

"Of course my history with Aunty B. and the Livingstons made it easy to have access to Diana."

Now it was Michael's turn. "Are you saying that you know the princess?" He asked.

"Of course," she said matter of factly. "I've seen her many times over the years in the South of France and of course, London, and once, I believe, in New York." Before Michael could respond she said, "Remember what I said, Michael, old money knows old money."

"Come on," Michael said, "I'm starved." It was still very early and the regular morning crowd hadn't shown up yet, but their waitress was quite cheerful, considering the hour. They ordered and made small talk while Michael consumed two cups of coffee before their meals arrived. Michael jumped right into his steak and eggs while Katherine was content to watch.

"Your food is going to get cold," Michael advised her. When she did not respond he placed his utensils down and looked at her. "What's wrong?" he asked.

"Nothing at all," said Katherine. All the while she was looking at him and smiling. "I was just thinking about last night," she said. "How on earth did you know what to do? You know so much about me, but you're still a big mystery as far as I'm concerned. Maybe it's time you told me a little about yourself, Mr. DeAngelo," she said, playfully. "I mean before your life with the Chinese."

Michael sat back and looked her in the eyes. She truly was one of the most beautiful women he had ever seen. It was still hard for him to accept that they were so close. The worlds they existed in were universes apart. But she was right. Now might be just as good as any time to reveal his roots. Their relationship was really quite interesting, a sort of Cinderella in reverse. Here he was, just a guy from the neighborhood in Brooklyn, here with a princess of Hudson River royalty.

"Okay," he started, "I guess it's time for you to know a few things about me. Well, to begin with, I'm the son of a baker in Brooklyn. I come from a long line of bakers who have their roots in Rome, in the old country. Somewhere along the line, I became a Catholic priest and spent five years in missionary work." Katherine was surprised by Michael's priesthood revelation. "It was while I was stationed in South America that my life took a turn. A group of my fellow brothers and I were escorting an order of nuns across the mountains of Brazil. We ran into a storm and had to seek cover from the cold and snow. Luckily for us, the driver knew the terrain and led us to a small cave for shelter. It was he who told us to gather all the blankets we were transporting along with supplies for the poor and bring them with us to the cave. There was no dry wood for a fire so he instructed us to gather with each other just like you and I did last night. It was our only chance as it was bitter cold. That's when things got comical."

"What happened?" Katherine asked.

"Well, the two oldest priests got into a heated debate. What the

86

driver suggested would mean that all of our bodies would be pressed up against each other. As it was a mixed group, that posed quite a problem. Thank God the driver interceded, vehemently. We were starting to freeze to death. The older brother acquiesced and tried to pair us off as respectably as possible. I was the front person and the older sister was behind me just as I was with you last night. She was the oldest, but she could not have been more than in her early thirties. We covered ourselves and clung to each other for protection and warmth.

How was I to know that the sister was very well endowed? Her garments masked any evidence of that. I tried not to think about it as her body pressed up against mine. My hope was to get to sleep as quickly as possible. That was not to be. The sister quickly fell asleep, but she was a restless sleeper. Her constant moving made it impossible for me to sleep. To make matters worse I found myself being aroused as her body kept rubbing up against mine. I could not believe it. This had never happened to me. The problem was that I realized that I quite enjoyed this feeling. That was not exactly conducting myself in a priestly manner. I finally got to sleep, but the damage was done. I guess the older brothers were wiser than I had imagined.

When we got to safety, I tried to deal with these feelings by myself through prayer and meditation. It didn't work. So I got a leave to visit my old mentor at my seminary in Mount Kisco. The head father was very understanding. He allowed me to stay for a few months to try to deal with my new awareness. Finally, he told me that it might not be God's will for me to serve in the priesthood. I was devastated, but he was a very wise and kind man. He told me to take a leave and see what the outside world was like. I could come back at any time, but he stressed that there was no shame or condemnation for finding my true calling. "God loves a cheerful giver, and a happy guest," he would always say. "If I did not find joy in my labor, it probably meant that it was not what I was called to do." How right he was. Just look at me now. I still have to pinch myself at times to make sure that all this is not just a dream."

Katherine was slightly embarrassed and definitely enamored. She really liked this guy. In truth, it was she who was beginning to feel that all this was just too good to be true. "Where to, now?" she asked.

"There is someone in Brooklyn I'd like you to meet," he said. "She's like a mother to me and she'd kill me if I kept you a secret any longer." Michael's words pleased Katherine, but her clothes were posing a problem.

"I don't think I can stay in these clothes any longer. Could we go into the city first? I'd like to get something fresh to put on," said Katherine.

"Great," said Michael. " And how about a nice shower?"

"You really know the way to a girl's heart," said Katherine. They finished eating, paid the bill and headed out to the Rover.

"I promise to drive more responsibly," Katherine said

A very relieved Michael began to fasten his seat belt. Once again, Katherine grabbed hold of him and kissed him, but this time she was prevented from pulling away. She hadn't noticed that Michael had taken hold of her coat sleeves. He drew her towards him with amazing strength. For a brief second, Katherine was startled at how powerless she was to resist as Michael drew her closer to himself. As their lips touched she allowed her whole body to go limp and fall into his. Michael's passion overwhelmed her. Before she realized it, she was attempting to climb over the console onto him. The intensity of their embracing was getting quite heated.

It was Michael who realized that many of the diner patrons who had finally showed up were staring at them and were quite amused. He gently stroked her face and pointed to the admiring crowd. Katherine slowly backed into her seat, but never took her eyes from Michael. Finally she lowered her eyes and started the engine. She eased across the parking lot and accelerated onto the highway. They rode for a few miles in silence. It was Katherine who finally broke the silence. She said what she knew was true in her heart. "I'm in love with you, Michael."

# CHAPTER EIGHTEEN

As the city drew closer, Michael was starting to become more at ease with Katherine's profession of love. There was no question that Michael had feelings for her. How could he not? They had spent a lot of time together over the past few weeks and everything about her pleased him. But this was Katherine Hewett. We are talking castles on the Hudson money here. Michael's early training and deep faith would never allow him to consider one human being above another, but, all things considered, Katherine was a descendent of the Knickerbockers. He wondered what they could have in common on a permanent basis. Of course, the enormity of Manhattan could act as a melting pot for two people of such diverse backgrounds, he reasoned. He really cared for this woman and the more he thought about a life with her, the more he became convinced that it could work. At least, that's what he was telling himself.

Katherine pulled her vehicle up to the front door of Dolce and Gabbana on Fifth Avenue. She blew the horn twice. After just a few seconds the door opened and a smartly dressed woman in her early 30s came out carrying two D&G shopping bags loaded to the top.

"Michael, this is Missy," Katherine explained. The young woman and Michael exchanged nods. "You are such a love," said Katherine.

"Just put these on my bill. You're a lifesaver."

"I know, I know," was Missy's self-assured reply. "You made the morning news, you know, kiddo." Missy warned.

"Don't worry," Katherine assured her. "I'm in good hands. Call you soon, and thanks." With that, she gunned the Rover and they were off to Michael's apartment for a shower and a change of clothes before Sunday dinner at Rosa's.

From the moment Katherine and Rosa met, it was an instant click. As far as Rosa was concerned, there was nothing too good for her Michael, but madonna, this woman was simply elegant. Rosa was old school, but she knew quality. And this lady was dripping with it. Rosa had never been so close to someone who was so at ease with wealth. For three hours, they consumed Rosa's marvelous spread, went painfully over Michael's metamorphosis from the neighborhood fixture to man of the world and managed to forget, for a while, the awful events of the past day. As exhausted as she was, it was Katherine who was the most reluctant to leave. Never had she experienced three more joyous hours. This simple, loving, tiny bundle of goodness, this Rosa Santarela, had totally captivated her heart. Katherine knew that Michael could never understand how someone so innocently genuine and alive could be so attractive to one who comes from such a formal background. It didn't matter. To Katherine Hewett, Rosa Santarela was the greatest thing since wrinkle cream.

Michael, Katherine and Wee said their goodbyes and made their way to Katherine's vehicle. Without warning, three late-model Cadillac four-door sedans converged on them and came to a screeching halt, blocking the path of the Rover. Twelve large menacing men exited their vehicles and surrounded the three. 'Vinny the Chin' and a few of his boys had come to chat.

Michael took Katherine's hand to steady her. This was something totally new to her. Michael gently squeezed her hand and pulled her closer. Wee remained calm.

"You know, Mikey," barked the Chin. "It's time for you and me to talk."

You brought lot of witnesses, don't you think?" asked Michael.

Vinny laughed. "Glad to see you brought your sense of humor, Mikey."

Each time Vinny used the term Mikey, he knew that he would be provoking Michael. Michael seemed not to take notice. He knew that Vinny was just dying to get to a certain point, and he saw no need to assist him. For sure, this was Vinny's big show.

"Somebody killed my brother, Mikey, and your people were involved. He died protecting a bunch of 'chinks'. What do you know about that? No offense, pal," he said to Wee.

Michael stood motionless. He let a few seconds pass. Vinny's group seemed a little anxious to start something. Michael suddenly remembered something Walter had said a few days ago. He decided to use it here. "I am beginning to feel a little like Custer at the Little Big Horn, you know, Vinny," he said.

Vinny had a good laugh at that. "Come on, Mikey, me and my boys was just out for a little ride and then we seen you. So I think, hey, there's someone who could maybe enlighten us on some things. The boys agreed, so we thought we'd pay you and your friends here a nice visit. Besides, as far as you and me are concerned, it's just Custer and Sitting Bull here, you know?"

Michael had to smile. "So let me get this straight," he began. "If, let's say, something were to happen between you and me, hypothetically, your boys would just be, witnesses, right?"

"Witnesses," Vinny repeated. "I like that, yeah, let's say witnesses. Besides, why should I bother you, the Chinese kung fu crap legend that we hear you are?"

"Just you and me?" Michael repeated. "You don't need them, right?"

Now Vinny was starting to get a little annoyed. It appeared as though his manhood was being called into question. Vinny took a deep breath to pump himself up and took a step towards Michael. Before anyone could react, Michael slapped Vinny hard across the face. Vinny was startled. He never saw it coming. No one did, it was that fast. Then he looked over to his crew, "Nobody do nothin'," he ordered. When he turned back to Michael he was met with another slap just as hard as the first. Now he was furious. For an Italian, there was no greater act of disrespect than to slap a man. To punch him was one thing, but slapping was for sissies. Michael knew this and that Vinnie had gotten the message, twice.

In a rage, Vinny made a lunge at Michael, only to be met by the palm of Michael's right hand coming up to meet his jaw. Vinny's feet came off the ground as his body went parallel to the ground and then landed solidly and painfully on it. He was momentarily stunned. So was his crew.

Instantly one of the kids from the neighborhood ran up the street yelling "Michael DeAngelo just 'assholed' Vinny the Chin," over and over as loud as he could. In the neighborhood, 'assholeing' someone meant that you hit them and they landed on that particular part of their anatomy. Doing so to Vinny the Chin was a feat of epic proportions.

When he was twelve years old, young Vinny caught a sucker punch from one of the neighborhood kids in the schoolyard. The kid was fifteen. Not only did Vinny not go down, the contact broke the kid's hand. He ran home a crying mess. From that day forward, Vincent Cogiulo became the legendary Vinny the Chin. No one had ever assholed Vinny: till now.

"Nobody move," yelled Vinny, regaining his composure. Michael walked over to help him up. He extended his hand and Vinny took it.

"You suckered me good, Kung Fu Man," he said.

"Let's start over," Michael said.

"Cool," said Vinnie.

"Would you mind calling me Michael?" He asked.

Vinny had to laugh. "I think that would be doable, Michael."

"I'll make you a promise," Michael started. "I'm going to find out who had your brother killed, and when I do, I'm going to see that you witness his death. If at all possible, I'll make a request that you be allowed to take part in it. Fair enough?"

"Fair enough," repeated Vinny. Michael knew that this promise he just made was necessary to satisfy an Italian wiseguy. Michael wasn't sure just which family Vinny was with, but the law of the neighborhood declared that such a promise was necessary. This promise was not one that sat well with Michael, but he was a Po and as such, he knew that this is what the Pos would be required to do. Michael knew what vengeance was all about. He tried with all his might not to carry those feelings towards anyone. But the brutal slaying of Carmine cried out for Vinny's revenge. There simply was nothing that he could do about it. And, so, he honored the family way. "Now, I make you a promise. I know that somehow you are close to the Trumentas. But if you ever need me, you just call, capeesh?" said Vinnie.

"Capeesh," Michael responded. "The most important person in the world to me lives in this house," Michael said, pointing to Rosa's home.

"You got it, Michael," came Vinny's pledge.

"Be well, my new friend," said Michael.

"Benedica ,"(Italian for "God bless you") said Vinnie. He ordered his men to their cars, and then they were gone.

Michael looked over at Katherine who looked him square in the eyes, but said nothing. They got in the car and headed towards Manhattan. Michael kept looking over at Katherine who had a strange look on her face, but still said nothing. Finally he could not take it anymore. "What?" he asked.

"You goaded that man," she said. "You got him to do exactly what you wanted him to do, exactly when you wanted him to do it. That was brilliant. You have the killer instinct, Michael. My whole family would be proud of you," she said. It did not sound like a compliment.

"Do you have a problem with that?" he asked.

"Not when it's necessary, like today," she said. "But you seemed to enjoy it. There is a difference between necessity and perverse pleasure," she said. Michael knew that she was right. At no time did he ever consider them to be in danger. The whole moment was about bringing down "the Chin". This was one smart woman. He wondered if this revelation would give her second thoughts concerning their relationship. He should have known by now that Katherine Hewett was well-equipped to handle one Michael DeAngelo.

# CHAPTER NINETEEN

Katherine really liked Michael's apartment. There was, however, one glaring oversight to its design. There was no guest bedroom. It was never a consideration. So after rejecting Wee's offer to take his room, Katherine settled for the living room sofa. Michael knew that the next morning was going to be hectic. He would have to contact Walter Larkin and bring Katherine down to One Police Plaza. It would be tough on Katherine, looking at crime photos and trying to respond to a host of questions for which she had no answers. Both Michael and Katherine were convinced that the whole thing went back to that night at the Puck Building. But beyond that, they didn't have a clue.

Michael turned in early and advised his guest to do the same. He should have known better. Once Katherine and Wee were alone, they talked until around midnight. Finally, Wee tucked her in and then retired. Katherine tried to sleep but it was just no use. Thoughts of her lifelong friend, MaryAnn, who undoubtedly had died in her place, were just too much for her to bear. She sobbed into her blanket, but could not get MaryAnn out of her mind. Finally, she took the covers and quietly climbed the stairs to Michael's loft. She looked lovingly down at his serene face, a face she wanted to spend the rest of her life with. As quietly as possible she lay down near his feet and fell asleep.

About an hour later Michael was awakened by the weight of something on his legs. It was Katherine's head. He moved to see what it was and woke her up. As his eyes cleared he realized who it was.

"Katherine, is that you?" he asked.

"Yes, Michael, I'm sorry for disturbing you," she said.

"Come here," he told her. "Get under the covers." Katherine responded.

"Are you all right?" he asked.

"I'm fine now," she replied. "Michael, can I tell you something?" she asked.

"What is it?" he asked.

"Last night, when I slept in your arms, that was the safest I have ever felt in my life. I never want to be without that feeling. Only you can make me feel that way. Please let me sleep with you, that's all I ask. Just to sleep."

"As long as you wish," said Michael. Michael's thoughts drifted to the old Bible story of Ruth, who slept at Moab's feet. That union produced the mighty King David. Michael had no idea where this one was going to lead.

# CHAPTER TWENTY

The media feeding frenzy at 1 Police Plaza the next morning was everything Michael suspected it would be. The horrible murder of MaryAnn Vanooster in the apartment of Katherine Hewett was a dream come true for the television and print press. Katherine "the Lady Kate" Hewett was a society darling who was now becoming fair game for every conceivable scenario the media could conjure up. And the media was peerless when it came to heralding fiction in the absence of fact. Having fifty microphones shoved in your face by a group of screaming "asking heads" was not new to Katherine. But this was about the murderer of a childhood friend and the possibility of drugs and anything else these wonderful purveyors of the news could dream up.

Marv and the team listened patiently as Katherine related the events of Halloween evening and the subsequent threats she had received since that night. She really could not tell the police the ethnic origin of her pursuers and really, even Michael would have trouble guessing between the Chinese and the Japanese. Marv was a little surprised by Michael's willingness to help out. It was not the Po's style to be very forthcoming with the police, but even the Pos were clueless as to who or why, and right now, they had no problem accepting help from the NYPD. Han Li knew all about Marv. He respected this man who usually was his adversary. Say what you want, Marv was clean and he was good. He was also relentless, something that was not lost on Han Li.

The Pos knew that whoever came against them apparently had lost their desire to expose their dealings with Masotoma E. to the financial world. They also knew that without written confirmation no one could make a legitimate claim to their unholy nuptials. The financial details were buried in a deep hole of holding companies. Actually, it was Victor, who else, who surmised that this thing went beyond business; this had to be personal. But why? No one could figure that one out, yet. So Michael had been instructed by Han Li to cooperate fully. After all, Michael really knew very little anyway, but his friendship with Walter could prove valuable down the road. One thing was obvious through all this; as hard as it was to comprehend, the Pos and the police were on the same side. Victor had quite a laugh over that one. But it was no laughing matter to him that the problems of the Pos had a man in the middle, and that man was Michael. Make no mistake about it, Victor and Michael had become as close as King David and Jonathan, King Saul's son (1st Samuel) and Victor was not warm to the idea of his cousin being placed in a compromising position. Michael knew the risks and was eager to assist his family. Still, no one wanted to experience the revenge of Victor should something bad happen to Michael. If that were to happen, Victor would ensure that there would be plenty of mourning to go around.

Someone from the press finally put the Michael DeAngelo of Easter morning 1981 and Katherine Hewett's escort together. There would be no fifteen minutes of interest here. The more the press learned about Michael, Master Po, the more they loved him. The Pos were counting on this. Never ones to get any good press, they would now experience a tabloid honeymoon. With two high profile people in their sights, the press could drag this on forever. Marv and the team knew this and knew that the constant glare of attention would only put more pressure on them from the boys at City Hall.

"It's lonely at the top," Marv said to the team.

"The top of what?" Walter wanted to know. "If we don't start making some noise of our own, we may all find ourselves working transit."

"Gees" said Lucy, "Walter, you are the gloomiest bastard I have ever known."

"Yeah, well just don't make any large purchases, young lady. Not everybody downtown was thrilled to see this department put together. The press is going to kill them and us if we don't produce," said a very sober Walter.

"Screw them all," came Marv's shocking reply. "For every failure, we'll give them ten successes. I've been around this town longer than most of those media meatheads, and I know a little bit about manipulating those people. When I'm done with them they'll be handing us the keys to the city."

All the while Bobby had been silent. Now everyone was joining him and saying nothing. They knew when Marv was pissed and this was definitely one of those times. They also knew that Marv and Walter had made many friends over the years and most could be counted on during crunch time.

The new revelations from Michael and Katherine had filled in a few blanks for the police. After all, when you know nothing, any detail can brighten the picture. They had started many cases with less, but now they had some solid places to plant their feet. This group was great at making chicken soup out of chicken droppings.

It was a sad thing, but the death of MaryAnn Vanooster had been completely abandoned in favor of the new couple of the moment. Try as he might, it was almost impossible for Michael to completely protect Katherine. Katherine was definitely unnerved by the constant presence of the press.

"Now I know what John's life is like," she said, referring to young John Kennedy. "These people don't quit. I have newfound respect for him. His life must be hell. What the hell do these people want, anyway?"

Michael could do nothing but hold her close. There was no answer. The truth remained that someone still wanted Katherine dead and the media was killing any chance at normalizing her life. Only Michael's presence made it tolerable. She and Michael were virtually inseparable. When he wasn't close by, she could hardly breathe. For the first time in her life, she knew what it was like to be totally, completely, hopelessly in love. And she loved it.

# CHAPTER TWENTY-ONE

After a week of nonstop running from the press, Michael was summoned to the Po residence on Fifth Avenue. Katherine was left with Wee and four very tough soldiers who were Michael's top students. It would take a battalion to get through these guys. Their ultimate position was to be the last line of defense should the Po family come under attack. Michael had complete trust in their abilities and their willingness to perform them. Wee loved being left alone with Katherine, who told such juicy stories of the rich and famous. Wee just lapped it up.

Michael was surprised to see Cheun Sing answer the door. Cheun Sing was not surprised to see him.

"Please come in, my famous cousin," she beckoned. "I see that you and the society woman are quite an item."

Michael sensed that Cheun Sing's tone was not at all congenial. "Is your father here?" he asked.

"Not yet cousin, he should be along soon enough. I wonder if he is as amused as I am at your ridiculous antics; parading before the whole world with your poor little debutante. What a display you are making of yourself and of our family."

Michael was taken off guard, but did not want to get into a verbal joust with his cousin, whom he was to learn, was only warming up. "Well, what have you to say for yourself, the famous Master Po?" she mocked. Michael's refusal to answer only made her behavior turn more bold.

"Are you sleeping with your milk white beauty?" she asked. Before Michael could protest, Cheun Sing moved closer to him. "Is she good, Michael?" Cheun Sing teased. "Are you more comfortable with one of your own? How interesting. I guess we Chinese women are not good enough for you."

Michael was really starting to feel uncomfortable. He had no idea what brought this on, or what Cheun Sing would do next. He did not have long to wait. Cheun Sing grabbed at her blouse and ripped it open. She was not wearing a bra. Michael was shocked.

"Look at me, Michael," Cheun Sing yelled. Can anything your white woman have be more beautiful than these?"

"Cheun Sing," Michael exclaimed. "Please, your father will be home soon. Please stop this," he pleaded.

"You are right, Michael, he will be home soon. And when he does I'll tell him how you attempted to violate me," she proclaimed. "I wonder how my father will deal with you then," she mocked.

Instinctively, Michael backed his way to the door and retreated to the outer lobby. He was sweating heavily. A million thoughts were running through his mind, none of them good.

"Michael, my son," came the greeting of Han Li who stepped out of the elevator. "What brings you here?" Michael was nearly paralyzed. He just did not know what to do. Cheun Sing's actions would have a devastating effect on his relationship with Han Li who trusted Michael with his very life.

"Come on in," Han Li said. "Let's have a cognac. This is such a surprise."

Michael had no choice but to accept his uncle's invitation. No sooner had they entered the apartment, Cheun Sing appeared.

"Well, Father," she greeted. "I see you did not miss Michael. Did he tell you what a busy fellow he has been?" Cheun Sing was clutching her blouse. Han Li noticed, but waited for his daughter to go on.

"Come on, Michael, let my daddy hear what a naughty boy you've been," she said. Michael was speechless. Cheun Sing had orchestrated things very well. Just then, Michael and Han Li realized that the three of them were not alone. "Must I show my father what you did to me, Michael?" she taunted. Neither Michael nor Han Li responded. "What's wrong with you?" she demanded when she got no response.

Just then, Madame Po made her way across the room and placed herself squarely between her daughter and Han Li. She moved her face very close to her daughter's. "You have done the unspeakable," she hissed. "You have shamed our family beyond all reason." Cheun Sing was ready to protest.

"Do not speak," she warned Cheun Sing. "How could you compromise your cousin in such a manner? Do you not know what an exalted position he has in our family? You are beyond contempt," said Madame Po so angrily that her body was shaking. The usually composed Madame Po was furious with her daughter.

"Go to your room, now," she commanded.

Reduced to sobbing, Cheun Sing did as her mother had ordered. Han Li was totally in the dark, but that would not last very long. When his wife told him what she had witnessed Cheun Sing do to Michael, he was covered in shame. Han Li reacted as if he were going to explode right through his well-shaved head. Somehow, he composed himself. And then, he did something that Michael had never seen nor could he imagine seeing. The air seemed to go out of Han Li's body. His broad shoulders sagged measurably. Cheun Sing's actions were a humiliation beyond belief. But he was not through. He walked over to his nephew as if he were bearing the total weight of the Po Empire on his broad back and bowed lower than Michael had ever witnessed. Again, Michael was speechless.

"I, and my household, are shamed beyond imagination that you have been so horribly mistreated under our roof. That the son of my dear brother Li Xsing should be disrespected in such a manner by a member of my own family is unforgivable," was just barely audible.

Michael fought to find just the right words to comfort his uncle.

"Please Uncle," he pleaded, "do not blame yourself. I have no idea why Cheun Sing would do such a thing, but I am most grateful that our relationship has not been compromised."

Now it was Han Li's turn to be speechless. He just could not respond. Michael sensed it immediately. "Please," begged Michael. "You are my family. We will get through this."

Han Li knew Michael was right, of course, but his mind was already elsewhere. Madame Po looked to her husband; she was afraid of what he might be contemplating. Michael asked his aunt and uncle to be tolerant with Cheun Sing. He knew that he must leave so as not to prolong their shame. He made his goodbyes, left and went downtown to be with Katherine.

Han Li sat for hours in his living room. He did not go to his daughter's room; he was too distraught over her actions. Finally, he put in a call to Victor at his office in Hong Kong. Victor could not believe what his uncle was telling him.

"Are you quite sure, my Uncle?" he asked "would you not like to sleep on this?"

Han Li informed his nephew that he would not be sleeping at all that evening. They spoke for a few moments more and then bade each other farewell. Victor hit the intercom and his secretary entered the office.

"Clear all my appointments for tomorrow," he ordered. "I am meeting my cousin Cheun Sing at Kai Tak. It seems that she will be spending quite some time on the mainland." The pretty secretary raised her eyebrows at Victor's next statement. " Let's just say that hers will be an extended visit."

# CHAPTER TWENTY-TWO

The morning air was crisp and clear and Katherine was in her element; driving twenty-five miles an hour above the speed limit over the narrow winding Saw Mill River Parkway speeding towards Rhinebeck, New York. As usual, Michael was holding on for dear life while putting on a brave face.

"She'd be a killer at Gran Prix," he told himself.

The effect of speed and almost reckless abandon did serve a useful purpose, however. Michael had a very restless night recovering from his horrible encounter with Cheun Sing. He told Wee about it, but not Katherine. Wee was as perplexed as he was. Cheun Sing was a willful woman and she definitely embraced the wild life, but nothing either of them could think of could justify her bizarre behavior. Michael wrestled all night with the realization of how even the strongest of bonds could easily be put to the test. Thank God his aunt had been there. He shuddered to think what might have happened had she not.

Something else troubled him. For whatever reason, he just never looked at Cheun Sing as a woman. He had always considered her a younger cousin. Cheun Sing's latest revelation changed all that. Michael had to admit that she was stunningly beautiful. He looked over at Katherine to make sure she was somehow not reading his thoughts. He was feeling just a little guilty. But how could he not acknowledge the fact that his cousin was truly something to behold?

"How on earth can anyone so beautiful be so screwed up?" he questioned silently. He looked over at Katherine, so at peace and enjoying herself behind the wheel of her beloved Range Rover. He thanked God for his good fortune.

It was almost 11:00 a.m., when Katherine pulled into the quarter-mile driveway of Auntie Min's estate. Katherine had been going on and on for days concerning this elegant matron of Rhinebeck society who had been like a real aunt to MaryAnn and her since they were little girls.

Auntie Min had no children of her own. She had never married. But she and her family were very close to the Hewetts and many of Katherine's most joyful childhood memories included her Auntie Min.

"Her name is Millicent, but we could never pronounce it," Katherine informed a relieved Michael as the Rover was slowing to a halt. "We were four years old when we met her. To us she was always Auntie Min."

Michael got out and stretched his legs. He took in the whole expanse of the house. He concluded that it had to be one of the largest in the area. The great door opened as they approached and Auntie Min's butler Louis greeted them. He hugged Katherine and told her how lovely she looked. Louis had known her all her life.

"How is she?" Katherine asked.

"As good as can be expected," Louis replied. "MaryAnn's horrible death was quite a shock. But she is most anxious to see you."

Louis led them through the great hall to the solarium at the east wing. As they entered, they were met by an elegantly dressed, stately woman in her late 70's, standing like a queen receiving dignitaries. Michael took special note of her posture, so youthful and erect. Of course, those were things that had always interested him. He was big on body language.

Katherine hugged her Auntie Min, tightly, and then introduced her to Michael. The lady gave Michael an approving eye.

"He's more manly than the insufferable fops that run in our circle, don't you think, my dear?" she said.

Katherine flushed with embarrassment.

"Well, the truth is what it is, isn't it, sweetie. Come, let's have some tea and conversation while the staff prepares a lovely lunch for us."

Everyone took a seat and allowed the warmth of the sun passing through the glass of the atrium to set the mood. After a brief moment of silence, the grande dame spoke.

"You are all I have left, my dear. I never thought I would see the day when one of you would be gone." She paused to compose herself. "You and Mary Jane have brought me so much joy over the years. To see the pain of her parent's, grief is almost too much to bear. But I've said too much about that. Let's focus on the fact that you are still alive and well. How happy I am that you have come to see me. It's like old times. Now tell me all about your life with this handsome man of mystery here."

Katherine looked slightly surprised.

"I do watch television you know, and you must be aware that the two of you are the talk of the columns. You are even on CNN, for goodness sake. Now, come on, dearie, dish all the dirt to your Auntie."

They laughed, cried and talked for hours, through lunch and into the afternoon. Saying goodbye was not easy for either woman. Katherine was quiet for some time on the ride back.

"She's some lady," Michael said, finally breaking the silence.

"She's all I have," said Katherine through her tears. She wiped her face but looked straight ahead. She was driving the speed limit. Michael sensed she was not herself.

"I love you, Katherine Hewett," said Michael. "I love everything about you." His words were full of love and tenderness. Katherine moved her hand over to take his.

"How did you ever find me, Michael?" she asked with a tone of disbelief.

Michael could not answer. No words could properly fill that space. He gently squeezed her hand and would not let go. Nothing more needed to be said. They rode the rest of the way in silence, each lost in their own thoughts. But there was something on Katherine's mind. As they drove down Riverside Drive in the upper 90's Katherine noticed a vacant parking space and pulled her vehicle into it. She turned off the motor and slowly turned to Michael.

"May I ask you something?" she inquired.

"Shoot," said Michael, who winced noticeably as he considered his choice of words. "I never know what to expect from you," he explained, in jest.

Katherine let the mood settle back towards seriousness. Then, as if struggling to find the right words finally asked, "Do you want me as much as I want you?" She did not look away, but fixed her eyes on Michael's. She knew how serious this question was. The intent was obvious.

"Oh, yes," said Michael, quietly, but with complete conviction. "It's strange, but I cannot imagine being without you. You could say that I've been concerned about forcing the issue. I guess it's time to find out just where we stand, isn't it?" Again, there was a brief silence. But now it was Michael's turn to wrestle with the right words.

"I know that my lifestyle has placed heavy restrictions on our relationship. And you've been just great about that. But I was not sure of how much of a commitment you were willing to make. I guess what I am trying to say is that for me, marriage is the only resolution, and boy do I want to marry you. I've tried to rationalize our relationship, you know, considering our different backgrounds. I find it a little difficult to see how it could work. But I just can't imagine a life without you. So, I guess what I'm trying to say is that I'm ready to jump in with both feet if you'll have me."

Katherine spoke not a word. She unfastened her seatbelt and climbed over to Michael. She threw her arms around him and kissed him with all the passion she could muster. "Oh Michael, I'll make you so happy," she exclaimed. "As happy as you make me. New York isn't ready for the two of us. You bet I'll have you and heaven help anyone who tries to stand in the way, Mr. DeAngelo."

Then she pulled back.

"What's up?" asked Michael.

"When?" asked Katherine.

Michael was not sure how to respond.

Katherine noticed the confused look on his face. "When do you want to do it?" she asked. "It takes a few days to do the blood test and get the license. How about Sunday?" She asked

"What's on your mind, Miss Hewett?" Michael asked with mock trepidation.

"About ten of the most important people in your life at Rosa's on Sunday. That's what's on my mind. All I need is you and those closest to you. I'm starting over and I'm changing my name and my life. But there is something I just have to ask."

" There's something else? Okay, what else is on your mind?" said Michael.

"Can we renovate the apartment to accommodate a female?" she asked shyly.

Michael just shook his head in disbelief. "Whatever Madame desires," was his reply.

Katherine squealed with delight and jumped into Michael's arms. "Let's go tell Wee," she said

# CHAPTER TWENTY-THREE

The door to Victor Chen's office opened and two of his men escorted a very disconsolate Cheun Sing inside. He decided not to meet her at the airport. If there was to be a confrontation, he chose to have it happen behind closed doors. As usual, Victor guessed right. Victor could see that his cousin was quite upset that her father had actually followed through on his threat to send her to China. Cheun Sing was used to her father's threats, but they were usually just that. The spoiled younger sibling of the Pos was experiencing her first taste of the wrath of Han Li. It wasn't sitting well with her.

"Come in, cousin," bade Victor without his usual warmth. "I trust your trip was comfortable."

"I'm sure you do," was Cheun Sing's sarcastic reply. "I see you are going to be the one who will do my father's dirty work. Well, let me tell you, cousin," she said," that I'm not afraid of you. Just look at you, all regal and powerful in your high and mighty office. You don't impress me one bit."

Victor sat composed while the two bodyguards stood silently, not knowing what to expect. There was one thing they were very sure of, though, and that was that no one on earth could speak in such a manner to Victor Chen and get away with it. Victor attempted to brush her comments aside.

"Your father told me that you would not be in the best of moods when you finally got here. He knows you well."

"My father, my father, the great Han Li Po. Neither you nor my father can do this to me. How brave you both are, you two fools," came Cheun Sing's near hysterical reply.

Slowly, Victor stood up and looked his cousin in the eyes. The bodyguards shifted uneasily. "Enough," he shouted as he slammed both hands down onto his desk. "You will shut your mouth and you will do exactly as I say and you will not say another word in my presence," came Victor's cold, icy words. "If you do, you will be the sorriest person on this planet, I will personally see to that." Then he said the words that struck terror to Cheun Sing's heart, words she understood all too well.

"Your father has made a decision. You are no longer under the protection of the House of Po. You have blundered for the last time, Cousin. You are to be taken inland to Canton, where you will live the life of a Chinese peasant."

Cheun Sing collapsed in her chair in disbelief at Victor's words. She knew, all too well, how much weight they carried. His words put her in a state of shock.

"You will have plenty of time to meditate on the life you have so readily abused and taken for granted. You will learn what it means to be Chinese, really Chinese, not some undignified, characterless fool," he said. "Now take her from my sight, all the arrangements have been made."

Cheun Sing could hardly walk, so complete was her devastation. But she had no idea that this was only the beginning for her. She would soon get a thorough education concerning devastation. The princess was about to become the pauper.

The blades of the helicopter assaulted the air and vegetation as the large Sikorsky transport lowered itself down to the tiny village. Cheun Sing could hardly believe her eyes as she scanned the expanse to discover a place light years from the world she had always inhabited. There was not one building of any consequence as far as the eye could see, and from here, the eye could see quite far. A tall Chinese woman stood waiting as the singular airship touched down. Cheun Sing was led out to meet her.

The two women just stood there looking at each other. Neither spoke. It wasn't until the transport began its ascent that Cheun Sing realized that her escorts had left her and were now on their way back to Canton. There was no other way of saying it. The unthinkable had occurred; she was abandoned by her family.

"Follow me," said the woman, who briskly turned and walked back towards a lone tiny cottage approximately 100 yards away. Chuen Sing looked down and realized that she was standing in the middle of a rice field, recently drained and made ready for the harvest.

As Cheun Sing finally made her way into the hut she was struck by the meager but neatly kept interior. She realized that there was only one room and she was standing in the middle of it.

"Where is the bathroom?" she stammered.

"I am Zhoa Chu," answered the woman, "and the bathroom is out there." The woman was pointing through the window to a tiny shack about 20 paces away. "We have no running water, but there is plenty of water here to wash or to bathe yourself." She pointed to a cot and said "That is where you sleep. Whenever you need privacy, just ask. I will be happy to leave. If you are wise, you will do exactly as I say. Your survival here will depend on it. To resist my help can only lead to disaster for you. You must have made someone very angry to be sent to a place such as this. Do not be deceived by appearances; I have worked the land for thirty years and I am no one to trifle with. I will give you orders and you will obey or you will be turned away to survive on your own. We are two hundred miles from the nearest city. There is nowhere for you to go. I will be cooking dinner in a little while and tomorrow you will join the workers as we harvest the rice crop. Now get some rest."

Cheun Sing watched the woman leave, then made her way over

to the cot. She had been given a lesson in the way the natives speak: forthright, quickly and with economy. Frivolity, she would soon learn, was a word unknown to these people.

# CHAPTER TWENTY-FOUR

It was a scene of pure comedy, this gathering in Rosa's tiny living room. Victor Chen had come in from Hong Kong and stood with Han Li and Madame Po. Patty Figamo was there and so was Walter Larkin who could not suppress his appreciation for the absurd. "The Chinese, the cops and wops," played over and over in Walter's mind. He was quite pleased with himself. Lucy, he assured himself, would really have appreciated his take on all of this. Monsignor Esposito from Mount Kisco had come to perform the ceremony as a favor to Michael.

There was no one there to represent Katherine. She was true to her word. This was to be the start of a new life for her. When she walked into the living room, escorted by an ear to ear smiling Wee Fong, she was the picture of world class elegance.

Katherine wore a simple Vera Wang suit that had been made especially for her in three days time. It was made of silk to observe the ancient Chinese custom of the dress worn by royalty for such occasions. Her Dolce & Gabbana bag and shoes were masterfully understated. Everyone had to agree. The lady had beauty, class, brains and of course, great wealth. Patty summed it up best when he said, "Mike hit the lottery."

If the scene inside Rosa's house was comical, then the scene outside was purely hilarious. The sight of all the expensive cars under the protection of the combined forces of the police, standing side-by-side with the soldiers of the Italian and the Chinese was a show that the neighborhood locals would not soon forget. Somehow, the media never got wind of it. As far as Katherine was concerned, that was just perfect. She told Michael that she would allow her family to have their big day soon enough, but for now, she just wanted to be allowed to quietly marry the only man she had ever loved. No pomp, no circumstance, and certainly no old money with all its stuffiness.

By 2:00 p.m. Katherine became Mrs. Michael DeAngelo. Katherine had expressed her wish to keep the whole affair subdued, and Michael obliged. It was a gathering of their friends celebrating their nuptials. Han Li had insisted that they dine at Chin Wah, and they did. Every detail was expertly seen to. As the evening wore on Michael had a chance to speak with Victor alone. As they looked across the room where Han Li and Madame Po were seated, they both expressed their concern for the pain their uncle and aunt must be feeling at the loss of Cheun Sing.

The night wore on and it was finally time to leave. Patty saw to it that some of his people escorted Rosa home. She hugged Katherine and told her how happy she was for both of them. Katherine's affection for Rosa was unmistakable. In Rosa, she found someone so loving and warm, so unlike the stone-cold people of her youth. That is why she asked to be married in Rosa's home. She made a vow to Rosa. Now, Rosa would have two children.

The Pos saw to it that the newly married couple was secretly taken to Kennedy Airport, and placed on a charter flight headed for a private estate on Grand Cayman.

There was one last comical scene yet to be played out. At 10:00 p.m., with the police and hulking bodyguards of the Italians and the Chinese standing sentry in front of Ferrara's on Grand Street, Walter Larkin, Patty Figamo and Victor Chen shared late night cordials. Now that was really something.

# CHAPTER TWENTY-FIVE

Katherine awakened from one of the most memorable nights of her adult life. As she lay dreamily on the luxurious bedding playing over the previous evening in her mind, she welcomed the cool gentle breeze carrying the exotic fragrances of the Caribbean to her honeymoon chambers. Katherine had never experienced such passion as was lavished on her by her new husband. She stretched her arms in both directions and realized that she was quite alone. Bounding quickly from her bed, she searched the apartment for Michael. When she could not find him anywhere, she went to the back terrace overlooking a magnificent Caribbean scene spread out before her. She spotted someone standing at the edge of the water about fifty or so glistening white sandy yards from the house. It had to be Michael.

Katherine grabbed a thigh length cotton robe from the closet and made her way down to the water. She came up behind Michael and wrapped her arms around him. She brushed her face across his shoulders.

"I am very sorry, ma'am , but I'm a happily married man," he kidded.

"Very funny," Katherine said. Michael turned and kissed his wife with the same passion he had displayed the night before.

"Not tired of me yet?" It was Katherine's turn to kid.

They walked back to the house and cooked breakfast together. As they sat eating on the terrace, Katherine was startled by the presence of a large Chinese man walking across their beach. The man waved and Michael returned his wave

"That's Chow Yung," he said to a disbelieving Katherine. "Now, before you get all excited, let me explain. There is no way Victor would let me come here unprotected. Our friends are here to see that we totally enjoy our stay, and enjoy it in complete privacy and safety. Trust me, Victor would be a mess if he thought we were alone and at risk."

"Friends?" question Katherine, "and just how many friends are here to achieve this?"

"Ten, I believe," said Michael rather sheepishly. "But you will hardly notice them. They are staying in the guest house and are protecting the property from the perimeter. I have personally trained these men and they are completely loyal to me. They will not be an intrusion, I promise you," Michael assured her.

For a moment Katherine was speechless, but only for a moment.

"Why would we be in danger here? How could that be?" Katherine wanted to know.

Michael hesitated, he knew that his answer might frighten Katherine. "We have no idea who wants to harm you, back in New York. But what is also of concern for us is that we have reason to suspect one of our own. If someone among us is a traitor, then they would stop at nothing to attack us here, where they might consider us vulnerable." Michael sensed Katherine's mood changing to one of fear.

"Is our life together always going to be this way?" she asked.

"That all depends," said Michael. "Once we find out who our enemies are and put an end to them, things should be much better," he tried to assure her. "But always remember, you married a Po and the Pos are very powerful. Powerful people always seem to court a measure of danger, especially in the world we live in today. We've discussed all this before. I did not deceive you or hold anything back. This is my life, our life. It can be quite exciting, you know. I am sure that I have chosen the perfect person to share that life."

As he finished speaking, he got up, took Katherine by the hand and led her to their bed.

Grand Cayman is an exclusive island in the Caymans. It would be very difficult for anyone who didn't belong to keep a low profile. The docks and the airport could easily be monitored by the Po soldiers, actually twenty-five in number, just a few more than he told Katherine. Michael felt guilty about his white lie, but he wasn't about to frighten his bride anymore if he could help it. As for the Pos, no one was going to intrude on Michael; that was a fact written in blood. Michael had another surprise in store for his bride; he told her exactly what to wear, but not where they would be dining. It was quite a shock when the driver drove them through the gates and up to the great front steps of the governor's mansion. The DeAngelo's were to be dinner guests of the governor and his wife. Now this was the kind of surprise Katherine truly appreciated. Like dignitaries of state, Michael and Katherine dined in splendor with the governor and first lady. The women hit it off just famously. It took a grand total of twenty minutes for them to find common ground: shopping in Paris.

On the way home, Katherine placed her arm inside Michael's and leaned very closely to him. She stayed that way for the full ten minute ride, never speaking a word. As they lay in bed, having once again come together, Katherine broke the silence. She sat up, crossed her legs, and looked down at her husband.

"No man has ever made love to me like you do. How on earth do you have the stamina?" she asked. "I know you are in incredible physical shape, but," she stopped in mid-sentence.

"Is it too much, am I going too far?" asked Michael. "Do you want me to slow down?"

"Oh, no," said Katherine. "I was just wondering if you felt that you had to make a good impression, you know, given the fact that it's taken so long for us to get here. I just didn't want you to feel pressured," she explained,

"Have I made an impression?" Michael asked.

"Oh, yes, Michael you've made quite an impression. How on earth do you do it?" she questioned.

"Remember the chi," he responded, causing Katherine to look totally confused.

"Remember the chi," he said once again as he pulled her down to himself. "I'll explain it to you later, alright?"

"Oh, well, I guess it can wait," Katherine said in a resigned tone as she lowered herself once again down to her husband.

# CHAPTER TWENTY-SIX

By mid-summer much of the renovating of the apartment had been completed. Katherine had worked with the architect to convert the full 4,000 square feet into a lavish loft space with balconies and terraced living quarters. Wee was ecstatic. Katherine had made a special suite of rooms for him complete with a library. The two had grown very close. The whole apartment was an eclectic marriage of industrial Art Deco in the kitchen, grand foyer and hallway appointments to Country French dining and living areas. The dojo was moved to the floor below. Half the space became available and Michael insisted on acquiring it for the going price from his uncle. Han Li accepted, reluctantly, realizing that to Michael, it was a matter of honor. Of course, Han Li returned the money as a generous housewarming gift to the new couple.

Now Katherine was busy with plans for a reception at her father's estate in Rhinebeck, New York. It was time for the Hudson River royalty to put on their show of pomp and circumstance. The top one hundred members of the American Fortune 500 would be well represented along with many of the wealthiest barons of business from all over the world. Nicholas Thor Hewett was committed to celebrate his daughter's marriage in grand style. Katherine soon learned that her father was not going to spare any expense. The word "no" never passed his lips, no matter how high the figure Katherine or her wedding planner placed before him. He was determined not to fail her this time.

Katherine's marriage to Michael had helped ease the tension between father and daughter. The elder Hewett found, to his utter amazement, that he quite liked this formidable person who had totally captured the heart of his only child. The fact that he could actually enjoy the company of one of such meager lineage astonished him. But the truth was, he really liked this man. "How strange," he thought.

Michael escorted Katherine to the British Airways terminal for her flight to Paris. Katherine wasn't a big fan of flying so taking the Concorde was an acceptable compromise. She had been surprised when asked to be a guest of the French at their prestigious annual national charity event. All the royalty of couture would be in attendance. Versace had personally written to invite Katherine to a small lavish party he was giving to open the festivities. Katherine knew him and many of the world's great designers personally. She and Michael thought this would be good for her. She could not believe the excitement she was feeling. But when the time came to board, she suddenly became very quiet.

"Oh, Michael, I don't know," she said. "I have never been separated from you. How am I going to do this?"

Michael assured her that all would be well. It was only a matter of four days and they would be united before she knew it. Of course, he was lying all the way. The thought of being away from Katherine for more than one day made him ill. But this was a great honor and Katherine really needed to do this for herself, he reasoned. As the giant Concorde lifted off over Far Rockaway Beach and thundered upwards into the sky, Michael found he could not move.

"She'll be back safe and sound, Master," came Wee's gentle assuring words. "We must plan a party for her return," he said.

Michael liked that idea. He needed something to lift his spirits.

Besides, he was about to embark on a very strenuous two-week train-ing session with ten of the most promising recruits Victor was send-ing from China. He felt honor bound to give these young men his very best. After all, they would be expected to lay down their lives, if need be, in their pursuit of their duties to the Pos. Nothing less than his very best would be acceptable to him.

# CHAPTER TWENTY-SEVEN

The bar crowd at the Hotel Pont Royal, famous as a literary haven on Rue de Montalembert on the famous left bank, was a boisterous mixture of inter coiffure and the accompanying masses of support people of the couture elite. Once the haunts of Chagal, Miró and Buffet, the Hotel Pont Royal had become the place to be for those seeking recognition in the fashion world. It's close proximity to Musée d'Orsay, the museum of the Impressionists added credence to its reputation. Everybody who was anybody, and even the nobodies had gathered in a near hysterical environment of celebration and glad-handing. These people had come from the fashion capitals of the world to participate in one of the fashion world's three most prestigious shows, La Grande Couture de Paris.

Katherine was seated at the bar, staring into her club soda, trying to decide what to wear to Versace's private dinner party that evening. Donatella had flown in from Milan to join her brother throwing a small intimate dinner at their apartment in Rue Montmartre. Katherine loved these little gatherings of famous friends because they were rare occasions away from the glitz and theater of fashion. No pretense, no show, just the warm affection of family," Versace style.

A light tap on her shoulder brought Katherine out of her thoughts. She turned around to face a tall gaunt male in his late thirties bearing a deep tan that had long overstayed its welcome. One of the milk toast fops Auntie Min had so unflatteringly described, Roger Ortman Telker, stood inviting the expected faux kiss on each cheek that American royalty exchanged with one another as a sign of proper greeting. Katherine hesitated, momentarily, then reluctantly obliged.

"How absolutely marvelous to see you here, darling," sugared Telker.

Katherine received his greeting with mixed emotions. Roger was not part of the fashion scene and really had no reason to be there. Katherine considered him a pompous fool, with whom she once had a brief and very unsatisfactory affair. It was safe to assume that Katherine was less than thrilled to see him here. Roger could never accept the fact that their romance was halted so quickly and completely by Katherine. Most women found Roger amusing. His vast family wealth went a long way towards ensuring his popularity with the ladies. The conversation quickly became heated with Roger grabbing one of Katherine's arms amid angry mid-sentence. He released his grasp after the two exchanged even more heated words. Roger made his final statement, then turned on his heel and departed in a huff. Katherine turned back towards the bar, visibly shaken by the exchange.

A solitary observer had been sitting quietly at the other end of the room taking in the whole scene with keen interest. He got up from his chair and made his way over to where Katherine was sitting, trying to compose herself.

"Is everything all right, Katherine?" he asked.

Katherine turned to be met by the reassuring smile of Victor Chen.

"Victor," was all she could manage.

"I couldn't help noticing your little encounter with that very forward gentleman. Did you know him?" Victor inquired.

"Yes, unfortunately," Katherine slowly responded. "He's a member of my father's circle. He is not a member of mine," she strenuously declared. "Victor, this is very strange, there is no reason for him to be here. And he was talking madness. We have had no contact for at least a year or so. Yet, he shows up acting like a jealous suitor, furious over my marriage to Michael. He demanded that I leave with him or I would be sorry. If I didn't know better, I'd think this was a bad dream."

"Would you like me to have a word with him?" Victor asked.

Katherine was pretty sure where that would lead. By now, she knew all about Victor and his reputation. Wee had told her many stories of Victor's dealings with undesirables. She was sure that Telker was just a hapless fool who wouldn't harm a flea.

"I'm going to a party tonight and I'll be escorted there and back. Can I call you if I need to?" she asked.

"Of course," Victor assured her. "Just call the front desk, I'll leave instructions to put you through to me whenever and wherever."

"Please don't say anything to Michael. I'm sure this won't go any further. I just don't want him to be upset that he's not here with me. He has important work to do. It means so much to him. Besides, you are here and I feel very secure just knowing that."

Victor smiled in agreement but that was only a show to put Katherine at ease. He would make immediate inquiries as to where Telker was staying and have some of his people watch him very closely. He was content to let the evening take its course. Once his people located Telker, Katherine's safety was assured. He walked Katherine to her room and left the hotel to attend the meeting for which he had come to Paris.

When Victor arrived back at the hotel at 10:30 p.m. he and his guests were greeted by a crush of police and official vehicles. Flashing lights were everywhere. The French diplomat with whom Victor had spent the evening escorted them into the main lobby.

"Please wait here," the diplomat advised. After a few brief words with a police officer the diplomat returned.

. "There has been a double homicide in the hotel," he said. "A man and a woman, quite bloody."

"What floor?" asked Victor, coldly.

The diplomat was surprised by the question. "The tenth," he said.

"Please get me the names of the victims," said Victor.

The diplomat hesitated for a moment, then went to the concierge. He quickly returned. "A wealthy American woman, Katherine Hewett, and a Dutch businessman, Roger Telker," said the diplomat.

Victor stiffened ever so slightly. This was not good news. If it were true it would be horrible. Victor also wondered how Telker could have eluded those who were given orders to keep him away from Katherine. "May I see the bodies?" Victor asked.

Again, the diplomat hesitated, then bade Victor follow him. They took the lift to the tenth floor. As they exited they were met by a flurry of activity. The crime scene had been cordoned off. After brief introductions, Victor was escorted into the bedroom. The chief inspector was not pleased to see them, but the diplomat's presence made any objections futile. Once before Katherine Hewett had been presumed dead. Victor had to be sure that this time, it really was her. He was not happy about the task.

The scene in the bedroom was horrible. The naked bodies of Katherine and Telker were lying on satin sheets covered in blood from head to toe. Victor quickly assessed the scene. The obvious conclusion was that someone, a very angry someone, interrupted the couple's lovemaking. Victor wasn't buying into that. He immediately recognized the scenario as a ploy to cover up an assassination. Victor had employed this method himself, and he was sure that the police would come to the same conclusions. The press however, was another story, especially the French press. It would be late afternoon in New York, and Victor realized that he must call his uncle immediately, before the news broke stateside. It would be Han Li's terrible duty to be the one to tell Michael. Victor made absolutely sure that it was Katherine's body and then went to his room to make the dreaded call.

# CHAPTER TWENTY-EIGHT

Han Li stood frozen as he listened to Victor's voice filling him in on the gory details of the death scene in Paris. Victor had made arrangements to claim Katherine's body for Michael once the French finished their need for it. Victor had done his job, and now it was time for Han Li to do his. He informed a stunned Madame Po who insisted on accompanying her husband to deliver this awful news.

It was just about 3:00 p.m. when a very grave Han Li Po and Madame Po entered the dojo. Wee had no idea why they had come and bade Michael dismiss the young men two hours early, but upon seeing them, he feared the worst. There was no easy way to do it, so Han Li made Michael sit and simply told him as gently as he could. Not since the death of his own daughter and beloved brother, Li Xsing, had Han Li known such pain. He could not even try to imagine the agony his nephew was experiencing at the news. He would have given anything to change the circumstances. It just seemed all too unfair that Michael should have to once again be devastated by a lost loved one. Michael listened quietly as Han Li relayed Victor's words. Except for a lone tear, he did not react. Han Li finished speaking then took his nephew in his arms and held him as tightly as he could. Finally, he released Michael who, as though in a daze, thanked his uncle for being the one to bring him the news. He also expressed his appreciation at the un-enviable task thrust upon his dear uncle. Madame Po just stood observing at a short distance. She felt totally useless. Her heart ached for the two men she loved so much being forced by their station to remain composed, when composure was the least attractive option. Just like Marv Levy, Han Li knew that it was lonely at the top. And, now, those words were never more true.

Han Li told Michael that everything that could be done for Katherine had been taken care of. He was not sure Michael fully comprehended, so Wee was informed of everything. Wee's face was already swollen by tears of grief, but he held up beautifully to his task. He truly was Michael's right hand and now it was incumbent upon him to be even more than that.

Michael retired to his quarters; he was in no condition to carry on. Han Li broke off the training and made provision for the young men to return directly to China. No fewer than three rotating shifts of six bodyguards each were dispatched to guard Michael's residence. Michael would speak to the press when he was ready, and not a moment sooner.

At first he cried, then he raged and finally he sank to the floor sobbing, praying for this somehow to be a mistake. He summoned all his faith to be able to endure the unthinkable. Two agonizing hours passed. Then Michael realized that someone had to contact Nicholas Hewett to let him know the real facts. Sure enough, the press had broken the story with all its nasty speculation, and that is how Katherine's father learned of his daughter's death.

Michael had the elder Hewett located and then went to him. He mustered all the energy he could to meet with his father-in-law, face-to-face, to assure him that the stories in the press were not true. He knew that hearing it from Michael would be validation enough.

Michael showed up at the Hewett apartment with his full complement of bodyguards. He was ready to offer their services to protect his father-in-law's privacy if necessary or at least until Hewett could plan his own arrangements.

Nicholas Hewett looked as though he had aged twenty years when Michael first saw him. It was obvious that this whole media blitz was more than he could bear. Michael moved to shake his hand and was taken by surprise when Hewett grabbed him and embraced him. The man had been crying nonstop for hours.

"How could this happen?" he kept asking. Michael had no answers, but anger was beginning to well up into his emotions.

"The press is everywhere, sir," Michael informed him.

Hewett collapsed into his chair. Facing the press was the last thing imaginable. His doctor was summoned and was now attending to his patient. Michael instructed Wee to call for more men and when they arrived Michael and his party were free to take their leave. He dispatched six of his men to ensure Hewett's privacy. By now the elder Hewett was sedated and resting in his bed. Michael requested that the doctor stay by his side, at least for a few hours. The doctor began to protest but Michael convinced him that it would be good for the health of both him and his patient to reconsider. It was something he had learned from his cousin. The doctor acquiesced.

Michael made his way through the avalanche of media in a half stupor. It had taken all his powers of discipline to get this far. And now, he was exhausted. Han Li had him taken to the home of Woodruff Yeng, in Hyde Park. The Yengs were away and only too happy to offer their home as a retreat for Michael until he could gather himself and go to Paris to be with his beloved Katherine. After Michael spent three days there in complete solitude, the French government released Katherine's body to him. It was the loneliest three days he could ever remember. Wee was never far from his side. Not being able to reach closure as he had done with Mai Lin and Li Xsing was killing him. He hardly spoke a word, until he made final preparations to go to Paris. Victor took care of all the details and as usual, the plans and their execution were flawless.

Katherine Hewett DeAngelo was laid to rest in the family crypt at Rhinebeck, New York. Her funeral mass was attended by a who's who from every stratum of society. Had the occasion not been a solemn one, it would have made great comedic theater. Alongside the governor, the mayor and a plethora of state and local dignitaries, all friends of the Hewetts, stood the movers and shakers of the Italian and Chinese business communities and their soldiers. The collision of conflicting tailoring styles would have been hysterical under different circumstances.

Katherine had left a surprise for Michael, one she probably never expected to deliver so soon. She bequeathed her vast holdings and trusts to her husband. When the extent of her wealth was explained to Michael, he realized that her fortune rivaled his own. And now, all Katherine had possessed belonged to him.

Michael was shocked by this revelation. He sank even deeper into his pain when he realized how much Katherine had truly loved and respected him. He was reminded of how the ancient Israelites, whom he so often studied in the seminary, would throw dirt on their heads, tear their clothing and beat their chests in deep sorrow. That is exactly how he felt. More than once, the distress of his queasy stomach nearly turned to vomit. He was sick to his core. No longer able to face the apartment, he decided to gather Wee and head for the island. His departure was immediate, leaving a smut-peddling press to their own devices.

# CHAPTER TWENTY-NINE

Victor Chen stood on the bow of the Tiger Bay as she glided through the calm evening waters of the South China Sea. He was in no hurry to return home to Hong Kong. There were too many unanswered questions to suit him and his mind was working overtime to try to put some reason and order to all that had occurred since Halloween night of the past year. He instructed the captain to take a slow, steady course back. He needed some time on the open sea to sort things out and devise new plans. He was surprised by his feelings for Michael. It was at this time of tragedy, the second such tragedy he reminded himself, that he realized just how much his cousin had come to mean to him. Seeing Michael experience such misery only served to intensify his anger. Even Victor was amazed by the venom rising up in him at the thought of someone being able to inflict Michael with so much pain. Victor's jaw began to ache from the unconscious gnashing of his teeth, such was his mood. As he calmed himself down, he had to admit, grudgingly, that the Pos had more enemies than he and Han Li had imagined. The scary part was that the actions of their enemies were so brazen. Victor reasoned that their impending punishment would have to fit their crimes, at his hands of course. Arriving at that conclusion began to lighten his mood and restore his joy.

Hong Kong held more unpleasantness for Victor. He would

have to inquire how his cousin, Cheun Sing, was faring on the mainland. Han Li would be waiting to hear some news. Victor was in no hurry to find that information out. His last meeting with his cousin had not gone well. Even though the Pos wielded much power in China, there was always the possibility that his cousin might talk herself into serious trouble. Her reputation for being a loose cannon at times concerned Victor. There was no way for him to insure Cheun Sing's safety when the military was ever present. He prayed that she would be wise enough to keep silent. This was China, and here, no one cared if she was daddy's little girl. Women in China were not considered equal to men. And women who could not show a proper respect for men could find themselves staring down the barrel of serious trouble. It was a reluctant Victor Chen who would be inquiring as to the condition of his rebellious cousin, Cheun Sing.

# CHAPTER THIRTY

Michael spent a month on the island. Master Pen had Li Xsing's quarters prepared for Michael and Wee. Victor had come to spend some time, and expressed his concern for Han Li's safety during Michael's absence. Michael enjoyed his stay, but knew Victor was right. Besides, he had reached the conclusion that New York was now home. He missed Rosa and their Sundays together.

Michael chose to spend many nights sleeping in the Master's garden, under the stars. As he lay there staring up at the incredible constellations he had to admit that this was one thing the island did have over Manhattan. Here, there was no smog, no pollution to dull the heavens and mask their glory. How improbable was this life he was living. How strange the twists of fate since that fateful Easter Sunday afternoon on Bayard Street. How was it possible that he could find love twice only to lose it both times, to be left empty and alone? And what did his future hold? He would not give in to the belief that God could allow him to experience the intense love of two remarkable women only to snatch it all away as some form of punishment. With the story of Job fixed firmly in his mind, he clung to the hope of a brighter future, just as Job had experienced at the end of his tribulations. He and Wee spoke at length about testing, a calling, and the faith required to get one through. It was that faith that would have to sustain Michael, until the day when his questions would finally find answers. Yes, he must return to New York for his own good. He needed to return and get on with his life, a life that would no longer include Katherine. In such a short time, they had made Manhattan their fairyland. The parties, the openings, the theater, the galleries and the restaurants; theirs was a whirlwind relationship. And now, Katherine was gone and Manhattan would be an island filled only with bittersweet memories. There were very few places that Michael could visit where Katherine's absence would not haunt him. But go back he must, for duty was calling. He would be counting on Wee to help navigate the lonely waters. Yet again, he realized, "Thank God for Wee."

The moment Michael returned to New York he threw himself into his work with the renewed vigor. He was no longer content to sharpen his skills or even raise his own level of invincibility when challenged. Michael realized that he, like his ancestors before him, needed to search out new and innovative techniques that always seem to be emerging in the martial arts. Electronics and satellites were making the world smaller every day, and information was readily accessible to any and all who saw to it.

Young practitioners were coming along and challenging the restraints of the ancient arts. The newer forms were constantly being revised and as his training was becoming more sophisticated, so too were the endless possibilities they offered. It was at this time that Michael immersed himself in the art of grappling and in particular that of the Gracies, a Brazilian family who had taken the fighting world by storm. Ultimate fighting tournaments, once the fantasy of moviemakers, had now come to be a reality. The public could now attend a tournament where men would beat each other to a bloody pulp with few or no rules to constrain them. The public's insatiable appetite for such practices led to incredible growth and participation. The whole thing turned Michael's stomach, but he knew that this was something that he must not ignore. He withdrew even deeper from society. Only an occasional dinner with Walter or Patty could draw him out. Katherine's death signaled the end of Michael's social life. He chose to stay within the boundaries of Chinatown and except for Sundays with Rosa, never cross them.

# CHAPTER THIRTY-ONE

Sundays at Mamma Cogiulo's house in Brooklyn were becoming a place for weekly meetings with Vinnie and his brother's widow, Carla. Mamma Cogiulo had a special place in her heart for Carla. Carla had made her deceased son, Carmine, very happy as his wife. Carmine had told his mother that he never thought it possible to find love again after the loss of his first wife. Carla made him feel young again, brought a smile once more to his life and mama never forgot it. But it was Carla who maintained their relationship once Carmine was gone.

"We have each other," she told mama.

When Mamma C. protested, telling Carla that she should meet someone else and get on with her life, Carla simply asked her, "Who could take the place of someone like Carmine?"

Carmine was respected, a made man. His allegiance to his crime family was legendary. Now his brother had taken his place, but times were changing. The days of the shoot em' up wise guys were coming to an end. The Jamaicans, Colombians and Asians had established their territories. It was getting more difficult not to step on someone's toes.

The Italians were more interested in investing their time and money into gaming and more legitimate enterprises. Of course, they still maintained their stronghold on the unions, the building trades, and let us not forget, the granddaddy of them all, sanitation.

All the other factions were warring over drugs, protection and black market enterprises. While the Italians seemed to be distancing themselves from such endeavors, it was still possible that they could be counted on to float a few loans or lend financial backing when invited. No one seemed to know what the truth was, but conventional wisdom and their lengthy track record were usually sufficient to provide answers to  questions concerning their involvement.

Vinny the Chin was now the man to see when problems arose on the Brooklyn docks, a most lucrative and strategic piece of his family's pie. When a rival family recruited Jamaicans to try to wrestle the docks from their control, it was Vinny who was chosen to see that their plans failed, and painfully.

Vinny proved to be more than just the possessor of a steel jaw. His encounter with Michael led him to the Trumentas and in particular, Patty. Vinny told Patty about the decking he had experienced at Michael's hands. Patty had a good laugh at that one. Vinny's overtures to the Trumentas were a stroke of luck for both sides. The Trumentas were always accorded a certain respect by those who controlled the docks, but if the Jamaicans were involved, that could become troublesome. Getting into bed with Vinny's family to keep control of the docks would greatly ensure future dealings for them. Patty knew Vinny and more importantly, Carmine. Like Carmine, he had a reputation of unshakable loyalty. As he was now the head of his family, he was in a perfect position to ensure their future. Vinny's real stroke of genius was realizing that any dealing with the Trumantas included the Pos.

Han Li was only too happy to give his blessings and a hundred soldiers to go along with them. Once Vinny was able to identify all the parties in the rival camp, he passed that information on. It took a mere seven days and nights for the combined forces of the Trumentas and Pos to rid Brooklyn and Queens of anyone who had any ideas about acquiring the rights to the Brooklyn docks. No fewer than seventy people of Italian or Jamaican descent died at the hands of the Trumentas and their very able partners. That number never reached print. The combined media was content to report only that many had died in related gang war activities. A full disclosure of the circumstances and the true number of the deceased would have sent shock waves through the city.

Vinny was now the new fair-haired boy of Brooklyn. To everyone, Vinny was now "the man". The Trumentas were honor bound to cover their new allies. Everybody was happy. But there was still one situation requiring Vinny's attention: Carla.

Vinny could not deny that he thought Carla was one of the hottest females he had ever known. She was Carmine's widow and he respected that. His love for his brother would never allow him to covet his brother's wife. Even after Carmine's death, he just never gave much thought to Carla's availability. Being a big man around the borough, Vinny had little trouble attracting the ladies. He had quite a reputation where they were concerned. But he always admired Carla's class. She never dressed trashy or exposed too much of herself like the other Italian girlfriends or wives. Carla always stood out in the crowd, the picture of the understated. It would have taken a tent to hide her physical attributes, and that is what Vinny most admired about her. Her respect for her man was always on display while the other woman of their circles stumbled and bumbled along their way in a vulgar attempt at sexiness that was pure 'Donna a' putona'.

It was your typical hot August night. Breathing was labored as the air blowing in off the ocean seemed to lack oxygen. Vinny was really sweating as he escorted Carla to the door of her house.

"Would you like to come in for a cold drink and some air conditioning?" Carla asked.

Totally surprised by her question, Vinny wasn't sure how to respond. Carla had to laugh.

"What's so funny?" Vinny asked.

"Nothing, it just reminded me of something that happened a

long time ago," she said. Carmine had given her the same response to her directness. "Are you in a hurry to go someplace or is it that you just don't want to come in?"

Vinny looked down at her. He was not quite sure what would come out of his mouth, but he knew he had to say something or face the possibility that Carla would think he was some 'mook' off the streets.

"Sure, sure I could go for something cold," he said.

"Good," said Carla as she turned and walked through the door.

Vinny followed her to the kitchen. As he walked through the house, he noticed how tastefully decorated it was. Vinny was more cultured than he allowed people to know. Guys in Brooklyn would have had a problem respecting a tough guy who was cultured. Vinny was well read and a fan of art and design. But that was not something he chose to advertise. He was tough alright, ask anyone who challenged him, but he also went to the opera. Truth be told, he had a number of inspirational CDs including one by the Brooklyn Tabernacle; in his line of work Vinny reasoned that a little help from above could not hurt.

Carla bade him sit as she poured iced tea. "I don't drink," she said.

"Good for you," Vinny responded. "It's a lousy habit."

"Glad you approve. So let's cut to the chase, okay?" said Carla.

"What's on your mind?" Vinnie asked.

"You… and me," she answered. Now Carla was looking him straight in the eyes. "You and me," she repeated. "And don't say what about you and me. I see the way you look at me when you don't think I'm looking."

"But, you are…"

"Carmine's widow?" She cut him off. "Don't you find me attractive?"

"Ain't no man on the planet that would not find you attractive. I'm just not sure if it would be alright, you know, carrying on with my brother's widow."

"What would you do if I had never known Carmine?" she wanted to know.

"I think you can guess the answer to that," he responded.

"Did you know that in some ancient cultures, it was a brother's duty to marry his brother's widow?"

Vinny thought for a moment. Then he said, "You know, I actually do know that. But I want to show proper respect for my brother. Our old man died when he was fourteen and I was four. All my life he looked out for me. He was always my big brother. He never let me down, he was always there for me. I would never do anything to show him disrespect."

Suddenly the room was quiet. Carla moved closer to him and took his hand in hers. "I loved your brother. I was a good wife to him; not for any other reason but that I wanted to be. He was my man. He was the only man who ever looked out for me, protected me. Carmine made me feel safe, for the first and only time in my life. I would've done anything for him. But ours was not a high school, first love kind of thing. It was a love of two people who grew to know and love each other. We respected each other. Let me tell you this, your brother was no father figure for me or any of that bull. He was my partner, my confidant. Some bad people took that away from me. That's something I'll have to live with. But you..."

"What about me?" Vinny asked.

Carla stopped to think for a minute. Then she lowered the pitch of her voice and continued. "You, I want you to hold me, to take me in your arms and kiss me with all the passion you've got. I want you to gather me up in your arms, just like they write about in those paperback romance novels. I want you to want me and then, I want you to do something about it. Let's face it, Vinny. We need each other. I just need to know if we want each other."

Vinny felt the passion growing up inside him. He stood up and grabbed Carla by the arms. Then he lifted her up and kissed her full on the lips. Carla wrapped her arms around his neck and smashed her mouth into his. Then he moved his arms down to hold her at the waist. He held her up, her feet dangling above the ground as they clung passionately to each other. Slowly, Vinny lowered her as each tried to catch their breath.

"Don't leave me tonight," she said. "I don't want to be alone. I don't want you to go. I want you to stay with me," said Carla.

Again, Vinny was speechless, unsure of what to say or think.

Carla quickly set him straight and cleared up any ideas he may have had. "Don't worry, Vincent, there is only one way you can have me. That should give you something to think about."

Vinny stayed the night and Carla was true to her word. Three days later they flew to Las Vegas and were married at Caesar's Palace. On the night of that occasion, Carla showed Vinny why his brother always had a smile on his face. Two months later they stood before the parish priest and renewed their vows. This made Mamma Cogiulo very happy.

# CHAPTER THIRTY-TWO

Six months had passed and Michael had formed a dialogue with the famous grappling Gracie family from Brazil. Their patriarch, Poppa Gracie, was a man in his early sixties and was the possessor of a legendary reputation. Michael had met one of his sons at a tournament in New York. The Gracies invited him to their headquarters in Brazil and Michael was only too happy to accept. For the first time in years, Michael found himself in the role of a student. He was thrilled. It also marked the first time since Katherine's death that he began to feel alive. This new knowledge and his friendship with the Gracies seemed to energize him. He would soon discover the value in all this in response to a vague comment Victor had made concerning a possible special journey that he might be required to take.

Michael slowly replaced the phone to its cradle and stared blankly at the wall. Victor was coming over and he was bringing a mystery guest. Michael knew Victor well enough to know that whoever his cousin was bringing was sure to be high profile with a strong desire to go unnoticed. Victor did not disappoint.

Aaron Schiller was a man in his mid-sixties who appeared to be a good 15 years younger. He stood a very fit 5'10" tall and was a member of Israel's defense ministry, here to meet secretly with American

Intelligence. The State Department was professing a stance towards Palestinian concessions on the left bank, but Schiller's presence begged to tell a different story. It was commonly accepted, in the intelligence community, that Yassar Arafat, the Palestinian head, was not a man to be taken at his word. It was widely believed that the Palestinian chief spoke out of more sides of his mouth than could be counted. Arafat was a fact of life, one that caused much trouble for both sides. Aaron Schiller's reason for visiting with Michael was strictly business; Israel defense business.

In a conversation Victor and Michael had recently, which at the time seemed to have no significance for Michael, Victor had informed him of a long-standing friendship between the Pos and the Mossad, the fierce secret police organization of the Israelis. It was now that Michael would learn just how much that conversation would relate to what he was about to hear.

"I knew your father, Li Xsing," said Schiller, after all sides had exchanged pleasantries. "He was very helpful to Dyan when the state of Israel was in its infancy. We knew that the land given us would always be contested. Not for one moment did we delude ourselves with any notion of a lasting peace. That is not our history."

Michael nodded acknowledgment, then bade his guest continue.

"The great Master Po stressed the importance of hand-to-hand combat skills to our military leaders who were very receptive to his theories. It was decided that every member of our military and law enforcement agencies would be trained in these methods. No one was exempt. Your father understood our part of the world all too well and he knew how treacherous our opponents would be. The Mossad went one step further and sent our people to your island to confer with Master Po. He was very gracious and only too happy to lend assistance. Much of what we learned on that island is found in Krav Maga, our ultimate fighting system. It has served us well over the years. I am sure that you are also aware of Haganah, a more street fighting system that has evolved over the years. Victor tells me that you have been focusing on a Brazilian judo-like fighting system called grappling. Your cousin felt that we should speak concerning this grappling. He feels that it might be something we would want to investigate with the possibility of incorporating it into our own training. What do you think of Victor's idea?"

All the time Schiller was speaking, Michael could not escape the feeling that Victor was now moving his favorite cousin into a new and more exalted realm. It was true that Michael was a master to the Pos, but Li Xsing was a master everywhere, and Victor was probably sending a message to Michael that the time had come for him to fully assume his father's position of eminence. Michael also understood the gravity of the question and the answer he was required to give. He did not hesitate.

"The Brazilians are winning many of the freestyle fighting competitions. They are combining very close quarter jiu jitsu techniques to subdue their opponents who find it very difficult to fight with an opponent who is hanging and crawling all over them. You can imagine their frustration. The Brazilians have proven that the older practitioners of their discipline can easily subdue and defeat much younger opponents. This flies in the face of most martial arts and boxing systems employed today. I have seen it done, and believe me it is very frustrating and embarrassing to those on the losing end."

"I can then assume that your belief is that such a system would be of significant benefit to us by incorporating it into what we are already doing," said Schiller.

"Yes, but it would take careful planning and intense training to ensure that focusing on this new element would not disturb or detract from the old tried and true. That could prove disastrous. Great care would be needed to integrate it successfully," Michael warned.

Aaron Schiller liked what he was hearing. "Are you familiar with our country?" he asked.

"There was a time when I was required to study your history at great length. I have always been fascinated by Jewish history and I've always had a desire to visit the Holy Land."

Schiller looked over to Victor and smiled. "You may soon get your wish," he said, turning his attention back to Michael. "It would be my very great pleasure to invite you to my country at your earliest convenience. What would you think of that?"

Christmas was rapidly approaching, and Michael was not looking forward to being in New York during the holiday season. It would be too painful. He would miss Rosa terribly, but she would understand. She always did. And besides, she had formed a great friendship with Wee. Gossip and soap operas had become a Wee specialty. He and Rosa would spend hours in deep conversation. This pleased Michael. He would feel very comfortable leaving Wee to be at Rosa's disposal. And really, how long could this take?

"Allow me to confer with Victor and my uncle, Han Li. If they have no objection, Christmas time in the Holy Land would be very inviting to me. Give me a few days. I'll let you know before you leave for home. Is that agreeable?"

Schiller was most pleased.

# CHAPTER THIRTY-THREE

The El Al airbus touched down so flawlessly that it took a few seconds for the passengers to realize that they were safely on the tarmac. Michael was exhausted from the trip, choosing to fly into Rome and then directly to Tel Aviv with no layover. Victor was still in New York, his business with Han Li not yet completed. Both he and his uncle were convinced that this trip would be good for Michael on many levels. You might say that this was Michael's first assignment as an ambassador for the Pos. This was the first time in years that Michael and Wee were separated. It would only be for a week or so, but Israel was no day at the beach. The danger was too great and the landscape too hostile. He certainly did not want Wee exposed to that. Michael reasoned that he could never achieve what he was brought to do with Wee's safety constantly on his mind. Wee was not thrilled by the decision, but as always, he honored the directives of his master.

Trained to be observant, Michael took note of the flight attendants on Israel's airline. The two females, in service in first-class, displayed formidably well-developed figures, evidenced through non-revealing uniforms. Maybe he was just too tired to focus elsewhere or maybe he was beginning to allow himself to take in beauty, wherever it might appear. Nevertheless, his interest in Israeli females had been piqued. Were these two fine specimens of female pulchritude an honest representation of the local female population? He concluded that this would bear some investigation. On the other hand, he was here on important business. He was also a guest of the Israeli government. Diplomacy and discretion would have to rule the day. But what about the nights?

Michael collected his luggage and made his way to the customs area. He marveled at how clean everything was. He decided to visit the public toilet. That would be a true test. To his amazement, it was spotless. No less than three attendants were in full service. Or just maybe it was the Israeli Army officers standing by with automatic weapons that was suggesting order. Michael finished his business and made his way to the gate where a driver would be waiting for him.

Michael noticed a man in uniform holding a sign calling for Mr. Michael. Once again, Victor was making his wishes known. Michael assured the man that he was the passenger the man was there to escort. The escort identified himself as Sam Levi and guided Michael expertly through the terminal to a waiting Mercedes sedan. In less than thirty minutes, Michael stood in the offices of the Defense Ministry.

"Ah, Michael, how good to see you," came the warm greeting from Aaron Schiller. Schiller took Michael into his office and made a call to a subordinate. "Sergeant Nathan will be at your service during your stay. We have taken the liberty to book you at the Tel Aviv Hilton. I'm sure you will find it to your liking. It has a world-class spa and a very attentive staff. Sgt. Nathan will be responsible to insure that your stay with us is most pleasant."

Michael was too tired to be in a critical mode. A clean room with a good mattress was all that was on his mind right now. Michael was seated with his back to the door so he did not see his guide enter the room.

"Ariel," announced Schiller. "Please come in and meet Mr. DeAngelo."

Michael rose to his feet and turned to greet Sgt. Ariel Nathan of the Mossad. Sergeant Nathan was five feet six inches of one of the most exotic women Michael had ever seen. Her jet black hair was pulled tightly back, but it was her body, hardly able to be contained by her uniform, that really got Michael's attention.

"For me?" he silently mused. Quickly snapping out of his reverie, Michael took the sergeant's hand in greeting and after a few more moments of pleasant conversation, followed Sergeant Nathan out.

"Please wait here, sir," she said. "I have to sign some papers. I'll only be a moment."

Michael did not respond. He just stood there like a dumb school boy, observing his first real babe.

"She's really something, wouldn't you agree?" asked Sam Levi whom Michael hadn't noticed standing there. Michael turned but made no response.

"That's okay, my friend. Ariel has that effect on most men. You should see her in a bikini. We were at a conference last year at Naama Bay and spent an afternoon at the seashore. A great many tongues were left hanging out at the sight of our fair sergeant. When she came out of the water, well, maybe you saw Ursula Andrews in Dr. No? Trust me, Honey Ryder had nothing on our sergeant here."

"We are all set, sir. I will take you to your hotel. Dinner is at 8:00 p.m.. You'll have enough time to get some rest and freshen up. There are a lot of people who are most anxious to meet the son of the legendary Li Xsing."

Michael followed Sergeant Nathan out. During the journey, he concluded that the rear view was every bit as enjoyable as the frontal.

The telephone next to his bed began to ring, bringing Michael out of his two hour slumber. Schiller had understated Michael's accommodations. The suite at the Tel Aviv Hilton was world-class, stocked with everything and anything Michael would require. The marble shower with its eight headed water system brought Michael out of his stupor while, curiously, relaxing him. The four-ply towels thoroughly soaked up the water from his body while gently wrapping him in the embrace of luxurious cotton. Michael returned to sit on the edge of the bed to contemplate the evening's festivities. There would be a diverse group of military leaders and statesman, who, along with their wives, would be dining with Schiller's guest. Sergeant Nathan had informed Michael that some of the military were not at all thrilled with the thought of an outsider being brought in to improve upon the fighting capabilities of their proud fighting forces. Michael had been especially warned concerning a Major Zim, head of security for the Mossad. Zim was in a tug-of-war with the State Department and especially Schiller. It appears that Schiller's motives went beyond the self-defense ruse Michael was led to believe.

The military and the State Department always seemed to be at odds between statesmanship and diplomacy in direct conflict with the military's position of using sheer force of arms. The pols had to answer to their constituency in matters of national security and of course their very existence in the white-hot Middle East. They also have to walk a fine diplomatic line with their American allies. The military shared no such burden of philosophy. No one voted them in or out of office. The sooner they could exterminate their foes, the better. What was the sense of constricting their military supremacy? They were smaller in number in the region, but make no mistake about it, they could really kick ass if necessary. Like the Po warriors, theirs was a service to the death. And when dealing with the religious fanatics, a good old-fashioned sit down just wouldn't cut it. Total annihilation was their only acceptable course of action.

As Michael greeted each dignitary he quickly assessed who was for him and who was not. A handshake told a lot about one's personality. Major Zim's was stronger and more determined than the others. Michael had no allusions of the major coming over to his side during dinner. His best plan was to be respectful to the major while being as gracious a guest as possible to the others. Schiller ran interference and helped move the evening smoothly along.

It was just after the dinner plates had been cleared away and the group was waiting for their after dinner cordials that Michael chose to share the story of his life in the seminary and of his intense interest and study of Jewish history. More than one member of the group was silently embarrassed by Michael's superior knowledge of Abraham's seed and of the new State of Israel. To put it mildly, Michael wowed them with his knowledge and the eloquence with which he conveyed it. Sergeant Nathan was beginning to get an uneasy feeling that she felt herself being drawn to this intriguing stranger. Michael had been presented as a man of war. No one expected him to be a person of letters. Major Zim had to admit that there was more to this person than he had anticipated. But Zim was a warrior and he was not about to relax his guard at some pretty words.

On the way back to the hotel Sergeant Nathan informed Michael that the major would probably challenge Michael before ever allowing him to proceed with any instruction. Michael expressed concern, as he had no desire to embarrass anyone. The sergeant informed him that Major Zim could not allow any subordinate to challenge Michael. Such a move would cause him to lose face. Michael would have to defeat him with dignity. This would be no easy feat as the major was very proud and quite an accomplished fighter.

Schiller would be paying close attention to their meeting. A lot was at stake here politically and Michael knew it. He wondered how Victor would react when he learned of Schiller's deception to bring him here. Then he smiled a knowing smile. Of course, this would be right up Victor's alley. All Victor would be concerned with was how well Michael conducted himself. As Michael prepared for bed, he pondered his circumstances. He concluded that the Pos had sent him on a mission of self-awareness. As he dozed off, he had firmly grasped the reality that this was his baptism of fire. Nothing short of complete success, on every level, would be acceptable. The Pos, along with Schiller, would be watching and waiting.

# CHAPTER THIRTY-FOUR

Sergeant Nathan joined Michael for breakfast in the hotel restaurant. Michael then returned to his room to wash up and prepare for this morning's session at the headquarters of Mossad in Tel Aviv. The Mossad had many installations in Israel, and all locations were kept secret. This morning, Michael would be meeting the best of the best. Major Zim would be sure to put Michael to the complete test. Michael would be addressing Israel's elite. There would be no room for error.

Michael addressed the group wearing a short-sleeved cotton shirt and cotton slacks, which drew quite a buzz from the ranks. When Major Zim questioned his choice of dress, Michael informed him that there was no appropriate dress to subdue and possibly kill someone. That response quieted the ranks and caused the major some embarrassment. Michael chose a direct businesslike approach with no attempt to exchange pleasantries. He quickly set a mood suited to his liking. Everyone would soon get the message.

"Do you have a knife?" he asked the major.

The major assured him that he did. Michael instructed him to take it out and use it. "Attack me any way you wish, but be very determined to do me harm because I have every intention of harming you," he stated in a sober tone.

Everybody was taken aback by Michael's bold approach. If anyone was unsure of what to expect, Michael immediately cleared that up. Sergeant Nathan held her breath; she knew that the major would not allow himself to be made sport of.

"Why are you hesitating?" Michael inquired, rather smugly. "I don't take part in mock exercises, Major. You are an Arab sent to kill me, a Jew. Kill me if you can," he goaded.

Slowly, deliberately, the major inched his way towards Michael. He made a few false lunges to see what Michael's body reactions would be. Michael hardly reacted at all, he simply gave sufficient ground to keep the distance equal. He then allowed the major to close ground. Then the major exploded towards him with no attempt to lessen his blow. He actually got closer to his target than he could ever have imagined such a move being defended. At the last possible second his arm was intercepted by Michael's left hand which slapped the major's wrist as it went by, causing the major to be turned slightly to his left. As he tried to recover, Michael had already thrown himself onto the major's body. Michael grabbed the knife hand with his right hand and wrapped his left arm around the major's throat. He then placed his right leg between the major's legs and wrapped around the major's right leg from the inside out. He placed his left leg behind the major's and using his full body weight forced the major to the ground. The combination of Michael's weight and the choking off of air to the major's lungs made the move fairly effortless. Michael rolled the major over onto his right side using their combined body weight to render the knife hand useless as he drew his own right hand up and further locked down on the major's throat. Just as the major was about to lose consciousness, Michael relaxed his grip. He reached over and took the knife that had fallen from the major's limp grip and proceeded to mock stab the major many times. Those who witnessed the conflict were stricken speechless. Their invincible major had been rendered helpless in a matter of a few seconds.

Michael motioned for one of the group to assist the major. After a few moments, the major stood up and faced Michael. He gathered himself and then with some effort spoke.

"It is an honor to have you here, Master Po," he said as he extended his hand, which Michael quickly accepted. "It appears that you have something to teach us. It is our good fortune that you are here to instruct us." Obviously, the major needed no more proof.

With that, all the members applauded. Michael led a three-hour session and then they broke for lunch. The major and Michael shared an animated discussion of war tactics and the challenges of fighting the type of conflict going on in the Middle East. Sergeant Nathan sat at their table, but confined her contributions to ensuring that the two men were not disturbed. Michael chose to concentrate his instruction on the mastery of two moves, which would be the basis for repelling an attack and gaining a position of contact with your opponent. The session went on for five hours with a few breaks. Each fighter had to work with each member in the room. It was an exhausting workout, but the Israeli soldiers never showed any signs of fatigue. With each passing hour, Michael gained more respect for them. After five days of two a day sessions, which covered nine basic and fundamental moves, Michael was convinced of the superior reserve of these men he had come to instruct. For their part, the Israeli soldiers formed a very real bond with their visiting mentor. Michael had earned high scores on all sides. The military had gained invaluable fighting knowledge and the diplomatic corps was breathing a sigh of relief. Schiller's plan had worked beyond even his own expectations. This was one decision made by the State Department that the military had to concede was prudent and valuable. Michael gained a new friend in Israel. He and Major Zim spent every free moment in deep discussion of politics and war. And then, of course, there was Sergeant Nathan.

# CHAPTER THIRTY-FIVE

It was Saturday, the Sabbath, and Sergeant Nathan had prepared to take Michael on a two-day tour of places he most wanted to see before he had to leave and head home. That list included Bethlehem, the Wailing Wall, the Mount of Olives and Gethsemane, the Sea of Galilee, Masada, the Negev, the Golan Heights and Israel's amazing irrigation system beginning at Mount Herman. Sergeant Nathan knew the territory well and had mapped out a route that would satisfy Michael's desires while allowing sufficient time to leisurely explore each site. The trip would require two one-day excursions beginning very early in the morning in Tel Aviv and would reach its conclusion back in Tel Aviv late into the evening of day two. The sergeant brought bottled water and protein bars along to satisfy any cravings along the way. Water was essential as most of the trip was in open country. It is winter in this part of the world and winter usually includes some degree of rainfall. However, the forecast was for clear skies for at least the next two days, so that Sergeant Nathan's itinerary brought them to Jerusalem where Michael was able to experience things he had studied, researched, and even preached. The tour began at the Mount of Olives and Gethsemane, where Jesus came face to face with the sin he was destined to take on and the fate he was about to endure on a cross at Golgotha, the place called the "skull." They even stopped at the place where legend claims Jesus was buried. Michael was visibly moved. Few words passed between him and his guide. He could not explain all that was going on in his head. Somehow, he reasoned, coming here was linked to that fateful day on Bayard Street and the death of Li Xsing and his two wives. Being a man of the cloth, Michael knew well that priests believe in acceptance of what is and the expectation and hope of the future. But right at this moment, he was moved to more than he had ever been in his entire life. There were no words sufficient to explain it, nor was there energy enough to try. Michael chose to take it all in and just let it work its way towards making some sense or reason. Sergeant Nathan allowed him plenty of space. When Michael made a request, she obliged. Beyond that, she remained a silent, respectful companion.

When he was ready, Sergeant Nathan directed Michael to the remains of Solomon's Temple and the famous Wailing Wall. Again, Michael was speechless. All his studies, and the knowledge of the centuries past, were not sufficient to prepare him for the sheer reverence on display before him. He was well aware that those standing before him would spend hours in prayer before the great ancient wall. It seemed amusing to him as he recalled having dealt with the parishioners of his Brooklyn church, complaining that a forty-five minute Sunday service was too long. He wished those disgruntled faithful could experience what was on display before him. Maybe they would get it. And, then again, maybe not. Patience and perseverance were two words traveling towards extinction in America. "No wonder the world doesn't trust us," he mused. "To them we don't seem to stand for anything. We have no reverence for our past, our history. For places such as this, our conduct seems incomprehensible."

"Are you all right?" the sergeant inquired.

"Yes, I'm fine. I was just thinking about back home," he informed her.

"Do you miss it?" she asked.

"Right now, my thoughts are of a different nature," was Michael's reply; one that surprised the sergeant. She decided not to inquire further but suggested they begin their trip to Bethlehem and then the Negev.

By the time they reached the Dead Sea, the sun was in deep descent in the sky. Michael could not believe the way his body floated effortlessly in the great salt body of water. For the first time that day, he and the sergeant shared laughter. The drive back to Tel Aviv was much more animated than hours earlier. The sergeant was relieved, as it was not her intent to take Michael on a journey of gloom and despair. Michael could not help looking at this beautiful Israeli woman who seemed to know just what to do and just when to do it. He had to forgive himself for observing how beautiful she was. It seems her inside was proving to be as attractive as the outside. And as far as her outside was concerned, well, Michael was fighting mightily not to go there. But he was losing.

Michael had dinner sent to the room, opting to shower and turned in early. Tomorrow's trip would be a little more taxing as he and the sergeant would be heading across country to Masada and then north to the Sea of Galilee, strangely, the place Michael most wanted to see.

The warm sun and the desert air were pleasing and most temperate for this time of year. In a matter of hours Michael found himself at the base of the plateau called Masada. Here, centuries ago, the Romans were shocked to find the whole city of Jewish zealots, men, women and children who chose death rather than bow to the superior heathen Roman legions. After enduring a siege of more than two years and a period of starvation, the entire population of Masada committed suicide. The eerie quiet of the city strewn with lifeless bodies greeted the legionnaires as they finally gained entry into the city. The officers and most of the tough fighting soldiers had experienced much in their years of Roman conquest and wars. Nothing could have prepared them for Masada. Writings by the historian Flavius Josephus found years later confirmed that few of the more than

10,000 ever got over it.

"Masada shall not fall again," a phrase sworn at induction by Israeli soldiers, just seemed to come out of Michael's consciousness and into his spoken words.

"You are quite knowledgeable, Master Po," said Sergeant Nathan. After Michael made quick work of his encounter with Major Zim, the major issued a directive that everyone under his command was to address Michael as such. "Do you know what it means?" she asked.

"Just what it says," was Michael's response. "Masada, Israel for that matter, will not fall, not now, not ever."

Sergeant Nathan gave a satisfied smile in response, acknowledging she and Michael were on the same page. Recognizing that Michael had substituted the word will instead of shall assured the sergeant that Michael possessed a complete grasp of where Israel and its people stood. After more than three hours of inspecting the fortifications, cisterns, the hot baths and countless points of interest including the remains of what many believe to be the oldest synagogue in the world, Michael and Sergeant Nathan entered the cable car to begin their descent to the bottom of the mountain.

"That's quite an amazing place," said Michael as the sergeant gunned the motor and shifted gears heading out onto the highway.

"You were impressed, I assume?" she responded.

"Let's just say that even though I have read so much about Masada, and studied its history, I am nevertheless quite taken by its magnitude. I believe that fact gets lost somewhere in the process. I had no idea how large a place it was. But then again, for over 1000 people to live there, it had to be big. I just never thought of it in those terms," Michael said.

"That seems to be a common observation, you are not alone. They are often surprised at how big things are here. It's really quite amusing."

Michael broke off the conversation concerning Masada as they passed an abandoned excavation site.

"What's going on there?" he asked.

"Oh, they are always finding new places to dig up. There is still so much in our country to be discovered. That particular site will be abandoned for just a few days until some rather sophisticated machinery can be delivered," said the sergeant.

Michael eased himself into a relaxed position, closed his eyes and allowed the warm desert air to caress his face as the sergeant sped the vehicle along the road that would lead to the Sea of Galilee, Michael's most anticipated point of interest. Michael had insisted that their visit should be as evening approached. This caused Sergeant Nathan some concern as the trip back to Tel Aviv would be conducted in darkness, introducing the possibility of danger as Golan bordered Syria, Lebanon and Jordan where rebel extremists might be lurking. She chose to keep her thoughts to herself and concentrated on their trip up Mount Hermann and the Golan Heights.

Michael's breath was taken away by the vistas in view from the Golan Heights. Only the view of China's Gobi Desert could compare in magnitude. "This is what Jesus saw," he silently marveled. "This is where He walked and lived. How extraordinary," were his innermost thoughts.

"It's time we moved on ," said the sergeant in a tone that suggested some concern. Michael followed her lead, but did not choose to address what he suspected was a hint of tension in the sergeant's voice. Now it was time to visit Capernaum and the shores of the Sea of Galilee.

The sergeant directed their vehicle to a deserted area at the far end of a small fishing village. Considering how important this part of the journey was to Michael, a fact he had stressed on more than one occasion, the sergeant decided to provide him as much privacy as she possibly could. Michael took his time exiting the vehicle and slowly made his way towards the water. When he reached the point where the water was only a few feet away, he stopped to take off his shoes and socks. He placed his hands on his hips, paused for a long moment to look out over the storied body of water. For some reason, the thought "This is why I am here," kept repeating over and over in his mind. Finally, he lowered his hands and walked a few feet out into the water. The warmth around his ankles caused a soothing sensation to come over him. For some unexplained reason he began to feel a sense of sadness. Without warning, he dropped to his knees and lowered himself into the gentle surf. Now his mind was racing. Tears began to stream down his face.

"What do you want from me?" was all he kept asking while raising his eyes towards the heavens. Then he seemed to gain a sense of peace and sat very still in the water. Sergeant Nathan observed all this from a distance. She didn't quite know what to do, but surmised that if Michael required any assistance, he would let her know. That not done, she proceeded to give him all the space he needed. After ten or so minutes, Michael got to his feet, bowed his head ever so slightly and returned to the shore to gather up his shoes and socks.

He and the sergeant returned to the vehicle and after putting his shoes back on he leaned back in his seat and closed his eyes. Sergeant Nathan again chose to wait for instructions.

"I have a friend," Michael began, after a brief period of silence. "A Jewish friend as a matter of fact, who, by the way, has absolutely no faith or belief in anything but the business he is in and the cares of his own life. He once told me about a trip he made with his father, a most devout Jew, to the Holy Land and that on Christmas Eve, he found himself here at the shore of the Sea of Galilee. He told me that there were no words to describe what he experienced. And this is a man of no faith. I believe I understand what he meant. For you, this place is probably old hat, but for me, well, it's true, I can't possibly tell you what went on out there. But whatever it was, it was amazingly powerful."

Sergeant Nathan responded by starting the engine and slowly maneuvering her way out of the ancient village onto Highway 90 towards the far end of the sea and then back to Tel Aviv. She wasn't sure what to make of what she had just witnessed or heard. Her thoughts were focused more on the possible danger of driving near the Golan Heights late into the evening. She did not want to think about having to face her superiors should Michael be placed in harm's way or, heaven forbid, injured in any way.

Now it was Michael's turn to give his companion space. He could feel the tension in her demeanor as they streaked towards the cut-off that would take them through Jerusalem and finally Tel Aviv. The sergeant drove at a steady pace for a while when Michael sensed a sudden increase of speed. He looked over at the sergeant who kept looking into her rear view mirror with great interest.

"Two vehicles just came out of nowhere and are gaining on us. There are no roads connected to the highway along the stretch. If I am correct, they will be Hezballa out of Lebanon with mounted gun stations on their vehicles," said the sergeant.

"Can we outrun them?" Michael asked.

"They are probably driving modified Mercedes vehicles and if they are, our all terrain Toyota will not be able to avoid them for very long," the sergeant said. "We will be no match for their firepower."

"How far to those ruins?" Michael inquired.

The sergeant looked over at him and flashed a broad smile. "Very good, Master Po, very good," she said. "You read my mind. The ruins are just up ahead. We can hold them off there until help arrives."

The sergeant drove off the highway and up onto an elevated section of the excavation site. "I was just here a week ago. I know where we can place our vehicle so that whoever is after us will have a difficult time rushing us. I should have enough ammunition to keep them at bay," she said with an air of confidence. Michael had little trouble believing.

The sergeant drove up a slight incline to where two walls intersected and placed her vehicle on an angle covering both sides. The only way their pursuers could reach them was up the incline that was right in front of them. It would not be easy to launch a frontal attack. Such an action would surely lead to a few lost lives. The sergeant radioed headquarters and was informed that an Israeli gunship would be there in forty minutes. Sergeant Nathan would have to keep her pursuers busy for at least that long. She was not the least bit concerned. Her training had prepared her for this. The high command expected her to act valiantly and confidently. The sergeant was prepared to do whatever it would take.

It wasn't long before their pursuers arrived and started firing their automatic weapons up at their position. They gave every indication that theirs was going to be a very aggressive siege. Sergeant Nathan returned fire judiciously. She moved back and forth behind their vehicle and fired from both positions. Her intent was to convince their attackers that there were two people up at this position with guns.

Michael was not at all pleased to be content ducking bullets until help finally arrived. Sergeant Nathan was too busy to notice that he left the safety of their position and made his way along the rocks under the cover of darkness. He and the sergeant had agreed that there were at least six attackers. Michael made up his mind to even those odds. He made his way to an opening in the cliff, halfway down to the attackers' positions. He noticed a deep shadow that made this position twice as dark as any other. It wasn't long before the sergeant realized that he was gone. She checked to see what progress the Israeli military had made. She was informed that they had left and were on their way. The dispatcher could not specify exactly when they would arrive. This was not good news.

Michael realized that his position was in a perfect line to intercept anyone who was bold enough to attempt a roundabout pursuit of the sergeant's position. Of course, the attackers had to assume that she had called for help and that help was sure to be on its way. If the gunship arrived before the attackers could achieve their purpose and then slip away, they would be totally vulnerable and completely defenseless against the awesome firepower of the American-made Sikorsky gunship employed by the Israelis to combat their enemies. The performance of these marvelous machines was without equal. It was during Desert Storm and their use by the Americans, that they rose to nearly legendary status. And, with any luck, one would soon be putting in a convincing appearance to obliterate some would-be assassins.

Michael was not entertaining any such ideas. From the moment of his first training under his deceased father, he had been preparing for a time such as this. A shocking sense of anticipation came over him as he prepared to meet his attackers on his terms. For the first time in his life, Michael was in completely uncharted territory. Never before had he been required to fight for his life in a place completely foreign to him. He could hardly believe the excitement he was experiencing.

"Well, Father," he said silently to the great Li Xsing, "let's see if I really grasped all that you tried to teach me." His silent dialogue was cut short by a sound coming from his left side. It was hardly audible but it was there. Michael slowed his breathing down to where it almost disappeared, almost. He was in a perfect position to see the terrain clearly. He intentionally positioned himself at the darkest part of the digs. While Sergeant Nathan traded fire with the group below, Michael stood motionless, anticipating the arrival of the man moving very deliberately in his direction. At the precise moment the intruder unknowingly reached Michael's position, Michael reached out and yanked him into the darkness. With lightning quickness, Michael struck the man in the throat with his fist as his victim bounced like a rag doll off of the wall Michael had unceremoniously flung him into. As he slid down, barely conscious, Michael shot his right foot up to meet the defenseless man's jaw, crushing it while driving it halfway up into his skull, leaving him dead where he came to rest. Without hesitation, Michael turned to assess the terrain before him and consider his next move.

The two all terrain vehicles of the attackers were positioned about 100 feet apart opening the way for Michael to deal with one with little possibility of resistance or aid coming from the other. Sergeant Nathan and the attackers were still exchanging fire while the two men positioned nearest to Michael appeared to have no intention of leaving their relatively safe position. Michael hugged the rocks for safety as he steadily made his way towards his prey. He was mindful of the danger of Sergeant Nathan's firing in his direction. He moved with the grace of a cat, stalking his intended victims. It appeared that one of the men had become concerned by the amount of time having passed since his comrade had left. He and the other man shouted back and forth and Michael surmised that one had decided to break off to investigate the whereabouts of the third man.

Michael began to retrace his steps back up the wall until he reached the place where he would have cover. Before long the second man was approaching his position. Before the man could react Michael used his right arm to act as a hook as he attacked the second man with such force that his legs went out from under him causing him to come crashing to the ground with the full impact of his own body weight. Before he could react, Michael took part of the scarf the man was wearing and began shoving it down the man's throat. Michael saw the terror and disbelief in the eyes of his victim. He banged the man's head into the rocks, then lifted the man to his knees and in one motion extracted the man's knife from its sheath and plunged it into his chest. Within a few seconds, the man's body convulsed and then gave up its life. For a brief moment, Michael was exposed, having no idea where the next man was. And then that puzzle was solved. Michael had backed a few steps away from his second victim when the third party came upon the scene. The man appeared horrified at the sight of his companion's dead body. That brief second was all Michael needed to reach the man and secure a grip on the wrist of his gun-carrying arm which he had lowered from the shock of seeing his comrade's dead body. Michael forced the man's arm to his body then applied pressure to his hand forcing him to discharge his weapon. A horrific scream of pain shattered the night air as two bullets struck his right foot. In one continuous motion, Michael bent the man's arm and guided the hand carrying the gun up into the man's midsection. Once again the force of Michael's grip compelled the gun to fire again and this time discharged three shots into his stomach. A look of total disbelief came over the third victim and then he was no more.

More shouts from the direction of the other vehicle quickly drew Michael's attention. Not realizing what had happened to their comrades, they chose to split up and rush Sergeant Nathan's position. Michael would have to act fast.

A deafening roar of blades brought the action to a full stop. The bright lights of the Israeli gunship totally illuminated the area while temporarily blinding everyone on the ground. A huge explosion was heard as both the attackers' vehicles were destroyed in a blaze of massive firepower.

Two of the attackers foolishly attempted to trade fire with the giant machine. It was a bloody, costly decision. Both men went down in a hail of bullets. The third was not so lucky. He had the unfortunate fate of trying to escape in Michael's direction. Michael placed himself squarely in the man's path. The man drew his knife and ran screaming towards Michael. Michael allowed his attacker to get very close, almost colliding with him before he dropped to the ground and wrapped his legs around the man's legs, bringing him to the ground with amazing quickness Michael never stopped moving, a product of his Brazilian friends' instruction to be all over his opponent. Michael wrapped one arm around the man's throat while grabbing his knife hand to control it and guide it out of the way. Slowly, he rolled him over so that his victim was lying on top of him but with little chance of survival, let alone any ability to do any damage. The man's body went limp as Michael choked the life out of him. Once the knife fell to the ground and his opponent lost consciousness, Michael released his grip. He released his victim, pushed the man off of himself and slowly stood to his feet.

The gunship was lowering to the ground. Michael took a few moments to look around trying to locate Sergeant Nathan. He was surprised by two gunshots that came from behind him. When he turned, he saw Sergeant Nathan standing about 10 feet away, smoke coming out of the barrel of her weapon.

"Never trust these people," she said to Michael. She walked over to the man's body and kicked a hand gun away from the body. "He had another weapon," she said.

"Lucky for me you were in the neighborhood," said Michael. He proceeded to inform the sergeant of the location of the others he had disposed of. Sergeant Nathan inspected the remains of all three men and then came back to Michael and the soldiers who had come to mop up.

"I will be sure to relay the particulars of this incident to Major Zim. I am quite sure he will be pleased to know that you are most capable of practicing what you preach, Master Po. It is obvious that you are a force to be reckoned with. Nicely done, sir," said Sergeant Nathan.

In the battle, Michael had killed three Hezbollah and participated in the death of a fourth. He did not know it but he was sure to be awarded the Golden Star of Zion, Israel's highest award to a civilian, for his heroics. Sergeant Nathan looked at him with new respect. It was one thing to disarm and subdue an adversary, but this tall stranger from America had shown almost ruthless disregard for those who attacked him. The sergeant wasn't sure what to believe about this man who talked and acted with such gentleness yet killed with deadly precision, showing no signs of hesitation when taking a life. In this case, three lives. The sergeant had never encountered someone so paradoxical.

Michael sensed the shift in her attitude, but knew he was powerless to give an explanation. Basically, even he was confused by his actions.

"Your training served you well," said the sergeant. Before Michael could respond the sergeant broke away and began to engage in a deep discussion with the officer in charge of the attack group. The officer then walked over towards Michael and extended his hand.

"It is a pleasure to meet you, sir," he said. "My men and I have been stationed in Gaza for some time. I had heard about your visit with us but didn't think I would actually get the opportunity to meet you. I guess I can thank these poor bastards for affording me the pleasure."

Michael shook his hand and thanked him for his quick response and of course, the kind words. Then Sergeant Nathan invited Michael to join her in her vehicle and continue their return to Tel Aviv. It was 11:00 p.m. when they reached the entrance to the hotel. The sergeant shook his hand and thanked him for a job well done. Michael disappeared through the front entrance and went straight to his room. He showered and called room service for coffee.

# CHAPTER THIRTY-SIX

Back in Brooklyn, Michael would face the prospect of many lonely nights with a good strong cup or two of Brooklyn Joe. Before long there was a knock at the door and room service made its delivery. Michael poured, added some cream, then sat on the couch and savored the rich aroma. Before he could drink it, there was a knock at the door. Michael went to the door and looked through the small peephole. He could hardly believe his eyes. He opened the door and bade Sergeant Nathan enter. The sergeant was out of uniform and her gorgeous mane of thick dark hair was down, dancing over her shoulders. Michael was speechless, and just managed to have enough presence of mind to close the door.

"Ariel," Michael stammered, saying the sergeant's first name for the very first time since he arrived. "Why are you here?"

"I know how lonely you are and the pain you are living with. A man such as you should never be alone," she said. With that she began opening the buttons to the white silk blouse she was wearing.

At first, Michael stood watching as the sergeant continued to expose her beautiful sun bleached body. Instinct made him grab her hands to stop her.

"Please," he said. "You don't understand. We can't, we just can't," he repeated, almost pleadingly.

167

"You don't want me?" the sergeant asked.

"Oh, Ariel, you have no idea how much I want you."

"Then what is stopping you?" she wanted to know.

Michael was at a loss for words. Finally, he found them.

"I have never been more sure of anything in my life; if we made love tonight it would be one of the most memorable nights of my life. You know that I have not been able to take my eyes off you the whole time I've been here. I know you realize this, I'm sure of it. You must be quite used to men looking at you as I have. But I am a priest. I have taken a solemn vow never to be with a woman who is not my wife. And in the life I lead now, I hold a position that must stand for something. I could never compromise myself and until now, I never thought it possible that I would even consider it. You must believe me," he said as his grip on the sergeant's arms tightened. "It is taking all the reserve I have not to give into my feelings. I don't know what else to say but I'm sorry. I am so sorry. And to thank you, that you would come here for me. I will never forget your kindness."

Ariel was greatly confused. "I have been with this man for over a week and all that time he has been nothing but open and honest. No man could have made such an impact on all of these tough, seasoned soldiers, unless he were completely honest," she reasoned. It would take a giant leap of faith, but she chose to trust him. She allowed herself to fall into Michael's arms. She did not speak.

"I have a favor to ask of you," said Michael after a long silence.

The sergeant pulled slightly back and looked up into his eyes, and waited.

"Will you please stay with me tonight?" he asked. "I don't want to be alone, and this may sound crazy but I really don't want you to leave. I'll understand if you do not wish to stay."

Without hesitation she answered, "I will stay with you, Michael," saying his name for the first time.

Michael sat down on the sofa and pulled Ariel to him. He took her in his arms and savored the sweet smell of her body next to his. They soon fell asleep. Michael's last recollection of the evening was to wonder what possible reason there could be for this happening. He would soon be leaving for home and Sergeant Nathan would be staying, period. She made it very clear that her life was in Israel and that would always be. Once again, Michael was left to ponder his fate. "Job, where are you when I need you?" he wondered as he dozed off.

When Michael awoke, he found himself alone. There was a knock at the door. He slowly crawled from his abrupt awakening and made his way to the door with some difficulty. A groggy look through the peephole showed a smiling young man in the hotel service uniform holding a large tray. Michael opened the door and bade him enter. The tray held a large pot of coffee with a note that read, "I hope this will atone for the coffee my visit caused you to miss last night." It was signed "Ariel." Michael smiled, tipped the attendant and then sat down to enjoy his breakfast brew. Before long the phone rang. It was Ariel, calling to tell Michael he had one hour to prepare to meet a gathering at the Ministry of Interior building. They made small talk while Michael consumed his coffee and then broke off as Michael went to shower and collect his things and check out of the hotel.

Once he convinced the hotel manager that he had thoroughly enjoyed his accommodations, Michael exited the hotel to meet up with Ariel, who had a car ready. There was a strange tension in the air. Ariel chose to drive in silence. Strangely, neither wanted to speak first.

"There will be many high-ranking officials at this meeting. Both the military and the State Department bigwigs will want to meet the man who helped train our troops and then help defend the life of one of their soldiers." Ariel said, finally.

"Don't they know I was fighting for my own life?" Michael asked.

"Of course, but that's of little consequence here. Relax, Master Po, they are dying to make you a hero, and of course get in on the act. That is a way of life here."

"I liked it better when you called me Michael," he said.

Sergeant Nathan eased the car over to the side of the road to avoid the ongoing traffic. She stopped the vehicle and turned around to address Michael who was sitting in the back seat. "I too am honor bound, just as you are, Michael. I will always consider you my good friend, my very special friend, Michael. But here, and in my official capacity, I must follow my orders, even when no one is present to know the difference. I have been ordered to address you as Master Po, and so I will. Besides, attention to honor and duty are very valuable allies in such a dangerous part of the world. I trust you understand."

"Yes, I understand," said Michael. Both parties knew what must be done and both would place honor before desire. Not in his wildest dreams could Michael have envisioned meeting someone like Sergeant Ariel Nathan in his visit to the Holy Land. He half joked that God owed him a special blessing for the sacrifices he had made where the sergeant was concerned. On further inspection, he wasn't so sure that it was a joke.

Major Zim pinned the Silver Shield of Zion on Michael's lapel. The Shield was the highest award possible for a civilian to achieve. Very few had ever been granted to a non-citizen of Israel. A tumultuous applause broke out from the crowd who had come to get a closer look at this mysterious stranger who had won over so many in such a brief time here. They also came for the food and, of course, the chance that their picture might just get in the local press. Occasions such as this one did not occur on a regular basis, so it would be safe to say that there were as many agendas present as people.

# CHAPTER THIRTY-SEVEN

Michael adjusted his seat to a slight incline. He had just politely declined a beverage from the flight attendant. It was time to lean back and close his eyes and reflect on his last few hours in Israel. He had been in the air about thirty minutes and the expectation was little or no turbulence all the way back to Hong Kong and a waiting cousin Victor. Schiller's embrace of Michael at the official reception spoke volumes of the gratitude he was experiencing over Michael's visit; the success of his instruction to the troops and his magnificent display of heroism in combat left Schiller almost speechless; almost. He managed to spew a few thousand words of praise and acknowledgment in Michael's direction. It didn't hurt that Michael's visit served to explode Schiller's stock in the State Department. And, he gained a new ally in the military who had to admit that their lot had been made better by his intervention. This was as much Schiller's day as Michael's. But he was gracious to a fault. After all, he was first and foremost a statesman who knew all too well that Michael would soon be gone and all the accolades of his deeds would come to rest at Schiller's modest feet.

Saying goodbye to Major Zim and the troops was emotional. All sides had gained more than they bargained for. As anxious as Michael was to leave, he could not escape feelings of reluctance. He had learned so much in these brief few days. The Holy Land was a place he would never forget, a place that exposed him to a danger and evil not possible to be experienced on CNN or Fox news. Michael would remember well that there was a place on this earth where one moment you would experience all that was good and spiritual and the next you could be fighting for your very existence. He understood how his new friends lived, every day. Unlike him, they could not just fly away. He was touched with a sense of sadness, but also a love and respect for good people whose way of life was a constant and increasing vigilance towards a maniacal people hell-bent on their destruction. And then, there was Sergeant Nathan.

The hardest part of leaving was saying goodbye to a young woman who had etched an indelible impression. Sergeant Nathan extended her hand at the security checkpoint. Michael took it and pulled her to him. Their embrace caused a few raised eyebrows. A few of the soldiers on guard knew her and her reputation. By now, all the local military personnel recognized Michael as he walked down the long corridor to board his plane. Michael's mind was racing from the crush of so many emotions. With any luck, the flight back to Hong Kong would provide some time to sort things out.

# CHAPTER THIRTY-EIGHT

No sooner had Michael grabbed his luggage and headed into the terminal was he met by the jubilant face of Victor Chen.

"This is a surprise," Michael said.

"Oh, Michael, how proud we all are of you. Uncle Han Li is bursting. But he will have to wait. Now I have you. How are you?" Victor asked.

"I'm so glad you are here. I am really tired. Seeing you here is just what I needed," Michael said.

"Schiller must've called five times from Israel to regale your exploits. And that battle; I always knew you had it in you," said Victor in his proudest voice.

"You knew more than I did, Cousin," was Michael's reply.

"Come, let me take you to your hotel so that you can get some rest. We'll meet later for a quiet dinner and you can tell me all about your exploits. How proud we are of you," he gushed as he grabbed Michael's luggage and personally carried it to the car. Very close by was Victor's contingent of bodyguards. It hardly seemed possible, but Michael's own stock had just taken a big bump. Victor's Rolls-Royce and the two accompanying Mercedes-Benz sedans sped off to the Central District.

The two cousins enjoyed a very quiet and relaxed dinner in the hotel restaurant. Victor insisted that Michael share the details of every moment spent in the Holy Land, a place where Victor longed to go, but sadly, never had.

After a much needed good night's sleep, Michael joined Victor for breakfast and then made the ride to Kai Tak.

"I am sorry to see you go so soon, but I will be joining you in New York next week," Victor said. "Han Li is anxious for your return. Your presence is very reassuring to him and our aunt. He holds you in the same regard as Li Xsing did, if that is possible. To him, you are more than a son," said Victor to a very surprised Michael.

Before Michael could respond Victor spoke. "It is time for you to leave. I trust this parting will be less emotional than yours and Sergeant Nathan's."

Michael just stood there and looked at his cousin. "Is there nothing that escapes you?" He inquired half mockingly and yet half amazed. He just shook his head, smiled and grabbed Victor's waiting hand. Then he turned and headed towards the giant airbus and the journey home.

# CHAPTER THIRTY-NINE

A subdued Christmas came and went. Rosa's home became a home away from home for Michael and Wee. Michael loved Christmas time more than any other time of the year. And even though the events of the past few years were constantly on his mind, Michael managed to keep his spirits up for Rosa and Wee, who were just grateful to have him home. Han Li and Madame Po tried their best to make the season festive for all, but their concerns for Cheun Sing were never far from their thoughts.

As summer arrived events took a startling turn.

"Master, Master," Wee yelled. "Cheun Sing has returned home."

Michael looked at his friend with inquiring eyes.

"There was some trouble in Canton and Victor had to intercede. There were some tense moments, but you know Victor. He always finds a way. And your uncle and aunt are meeting her and Victor at Kennedy, as we speak."

"Victor is here too?" Michael inquired.

"Yes, yes," said Wee. "He has come to insure safe passage back to her parents. Han Li and Madame Po are overjoyed.

Just then the phone rang. Wee answered it and called to Michael. "Victor is on the phone and wishes to speak to you."

Michael was pleased to hear the sounds of Victor's voice. "Han

Li and our aunt are going to take Cheun Sing to the apartment," said Victor, after greetings and salutations. "Why don't you meet me at the Four Seasons, say in one hour?"

Michael was only too willing to oblige.

"What on earth happened?" Michael wanted to know as he eased into his chair at Victor's table.

"It's wonderful to see you too, my favorite cousin," Victor joked.

Now, Michael was embarrassed. "I am overjoyed to see you. This is a great time of year to be in New York," Michael said. "We have much to catch up on. I didn't expect to see you until the Fall. This is excellent."

Victor was appeased. "Uncle Han Li wishes to have a big celebration in a few days time. But he and Cheun Sing have much to discuss before that happens. However, now that I am here, there is some business that we can conduct, but not before dinner. I am famished. The events of the past few days have greatly altered my eating schedule. Tonight it is prime rib and Dom Perignon. And, as I stated before, my favorite cousin will be with me to share it. What could be better than that?" Victor exclaimed.

Michael and Victor shared a most enjoyable evening. The management of the Four Seasons made sure that security was heightened when someone of Victor's stature was their guest. Over the years, they extended a courtesy to Victor's bodyguards, a concession shared only by the United States Secret Service.

Victor spent fortunes in the hotel on an annual basis and the management was damn well determined to ensure his privacy, to say nothing of his safety and continued good health, while in their charge.

During their time together, Victor informed Michael that Cheun Sing had requested that she be the one to explain the events leading up to her return. It was a request Victor found intriguing, but, nevertheless, one he would honor. Cheun Sing promised that the time of revelation would be soon. Now Michael was intrigued, and a bit surprised.

# CHAPTER FORTY

The mood at Chin Wah was most festive. The owners had outdone themselves, dressing their restaurant up in style. Michael and Wee entered and were greeted by Michael's own security force. Michael had spent most of the day going over security measures. He supervised them himself, even employing bomb sniffing canine, courtesy of Walter Larkin and the NYPD. Snipers took up places on strategic rooftops. The alleyways in the immediate vicinity of the restaurant were patrolled by no less than four roving squads carrying automatic weapons. Victor's assessment was this was a slight case of overkill, and he loved it.

"Your security measures are admirable, Cousin," were the first words Michael heard upon entering.

"I'm so glad you approve," Michael said. "I can assure you, no one is going to spoil our uncle's evening. I can see how happy he is. I have not seen him like this for some time." Victor had to agree.

"Observe our cousin," said Victor, directing Michael's attention to the far side of the room. Cheun Sing sat next to her mother as a princess next to the queen. She sat receiving all the invitees who waited patiently in line to offer their greetings and of course, their gifts.

Michael waited for a while, observing his cousin's placid demeanor. Something was different, he reasoned. Cheun Sing seemed almost embarrassed by the attention. For a woman who had strutted the catwalks of Paris and Milan, wearing the creations of some of the world's greatest designers, this seemed a bit confusing to him. Finally, the line ended and Michael took Wee in tow and headed cautiously across to where she and Madame Po sat. As they approached Michael noticed a broad smile on his aunt's face. To his surprise Cheun Sing rose to greet him, something she had not done for any of the other guests, not even family.

"It is so good to see you," said Michael, extending his hand.

Cheun Sing gently took his hand but did not raise her eyes to meet his. "My cousin does me a great honor coming this evening. You have made my parents most pleased by your presence and by all your preparations." Finally, she looked up slowly with a look of gratitude. "Thank you, Michael," she said, in a voice barely above a whisper.

Madame Po greeted Wee and directed his attention to her daughter.

"I believe you know the joy you have given your parents. Your safe return has brought happiness once more to the house of Po. It is so very good to see you again, Mistress Po," came Wee's eloquent words.

Michael stood by, impressed at Wee's words. He stood for an awkward moment wondering, "Why on earth couldn't I say something like that?"

Wee noticed that more guests had arrived and were waiting patiently to greet Cheun Sing. He and Michael excused themselves and went over to where Han Li was holding court. After a brief exchange with his uncle, Michael and Wee made their way over to the sumptuous sprawling buffet for some of Chin Wah's finest. Soon, Michael would be making the rounds outside to check on his people.

Michael felt a slight tap on his shoulder and looked around to see his old friend, Lewis Fong, standing there. Michael quickly rose and exchanged greetings with one of his favorite Po soldiers.

"Mistress Cheun Sing would like to see you if you would not mind," said Fong.

Michael looked over to where Cheun Sing had been seated and noticed that she was not there.

"The Mistress is out back, Master Po" Fong informed him. "It is very pleasant outside and she wished a private audience with you. Do not be concerned, she is well guarded. Your men have seen to that," Fong assured him. Michael let Fong lead the way and before long he and Cheun Sing were standing face to face.

"Cousin, there is something I wish to say to you," said Cheun Sing.

"Only if you address me as Michael."

Cheun Sing smiled, bowed her head in agreement, then continued. "Oh, Michael, I am so sorry for the way I have treated you over the years," she began.

Michael attempted to stop her but Cheun Sing forcefully, but respectfully, intercepted his efforts.

"Please, Cousin, you must allow me to say all the words that I have in my heart to speak," she pleaded. Michael stepped back and allowed her to continue. "I have had much time to ponder these things and I am beyond embarrassed by my disgraceful actions towards you. All you have ever done is to bring joy to our family while I have gone out of my way to make your life miserable. Uncle Li Xsing considered you a blessing to his life after he lost his family. Your companionship and, then, your rise to master, under his charge, brought joy beyond his greatest expectations. He was the most brilliant among the Pos and your years with him meant more to him than all the vast holdings he possessed. And, as for my dear sister, you filled her life when she was resigned to have no life. You helped erase the disgrace of her youthful transgressions. Every report of her to my family bore the unmistakable joy you gave both her and Uncle Li Xsing, who loved her as his own. Until you came along, nothing seemed to ease her sadness for her terrible mistake and separation from our family. And now, you'd lay down your life for my parents while I do nothing to show you the honor, respect and gratitude you so rightly deserve. Can you ever forgive me?" she pleaded, as she began to weep softly.

Slowly, Michael took her in his arms and held her gently.

"Cheun Sing," he said, "your return is such a healing for your family. Your father has been so upset with himself, blaming himself for failing you. Every one of us wishes we could possess the power to go back in time and to redo all the things we feel that we failed at. I have not seen such joy on your father's face in years. What you are doing is good. I do not have it in my heart to hold onto the mistakes of the past. I'm only interested in what lies ahead. Being a Po is dangerous enough. We do not need to be at odds with each other. I am sure you will do the right thing. As for me, consider me your friend as well as your cousin. Whatever you need, you have only to ask."

With that, Cheun Sing hesitated for a moment, content to be in Michael's arms. Then she stepped slowly back. She looked up into Michael's eyes, but did not speak.

"What is it?" asked Michael.

"Well, there is one little thing you could do for me," she said shyly. "I was going to wait, but since you have offered, I do have one request."

"And, that would be?" Michael asked.

"I would very much like for you to train me. I cannot trust anyone else. I know that you will not make it easy for me just because of who I am. My father and Victor hold you in the highest regard and I know that after time, you will get the best out of me. After what I have seen, I can accept nothing less from myself. I know who I am, Michael, for the first time in my life, I truly know who I am and what is expected of me. I will not ever forget who I am and who I represent. My parents will never again suffer even one moment's embarrassment because of me. I am appalled by my actions and I vow to spend the rest of my life acting like a Po. Will you help me, Cousin Michael?" she asked.

Michael just looked at Cheun Sing for a moment, allowing her words to sink in. "Whatever my cousin needs, she has only to ask." Then Michael took Cheun Sing's hand and escorted her back into an awaiting party. Madame Po leaned gently into her husband as they entered, pleased by what she observed.

# CHAPTER FORTY-ONE

"Uptown, Michael," announced Victor. "We're going uptown to a whole different world."

Michael enjoyed the few times when Victor was in a jovial mood. Victor was obviously relishing the thought of taking Michael to a place in Michael's own city where Michael had never been nor had he any knowledge of. That place was Harlem. Their destination was 125th Street, the storied thoroughfare of Small's Paradise and the Apollo Theater. The former, a legendary jazz club where the giants of jazz had played over the years, and the latter, the hallowed Temple, the very home of black soul. Everyone from Billy Eckstein to James Brown had graced its stage and rocked its audiences.

The large Mercedes sedan exited the Harlem River Drive and headed west down 125th Street. Before long, they came to a halt in front of Little Ed's, a nightclub famous for chicken, ribs, jazz and soul. Michael had to suppress a laugh observing the glitzy flashing neon sign bearing Little Ed's name. It was 4:30 in the afternoon and the sun was still blazing in the sky.

"Your eyes will need some adjusting," Victor warned as they entered the club. Inside, it was pitch black except for tiny blue laser-like lights placed like stars in the ceiling. Victor and his two soldiers led Michael past the long bar area to the restaurant section. Just as Michael's eyes began to get accustomed to the darkness, he caught the site of the smiling behemoth coming in their direction.

"Some bodyguard," Michael surmised, as a six foot seven inch, four hundred pound mass of humanity lumbered to meet them.

"Little Ed, meet my cousin, Michael DeAngelo," said Victor with much pleasure. The look of disbelief on Michael's face brought a giant laugh from their host. Michael was still staring with surprise as Little Ed's mammoth right hand took hold of his in greeting.

"It's a long story," said Little Ed with a reassuring smile. "Come on, gentlemen, let's have a seat. Our other guests should be here any minute."

Michael and Victor joined their host at a table for four. While Michael wondered who the fourth party would be, he had become sufficiently acclimated to his surroundings to notice two rather hefty young men who joined with Victor's to make sure the area remained secure.

By the time Patty Figamo and his two soldiers arrived, Michael had learned that Little Ed got his name during an undersized youth. His father, Big Ed Thompson, was a local high school three sports star, who stood 6 feet 1½ inches tall and weighed two hundred sixty-five pounds in his playing days. In Big Ed's day, that was National Football League big. Everyone was shocked when Little Ed grew from five feet eight inches tall as a fifteen-year-old to his present six feet seven inches tall by his 20th birthday. Of course, his weight was a product of twenty more years of a dedicated love affair with food: soul food.

Once Patty settled in and everyone had their drinks, Michael's being seltzer with lemon, Victor began the meeting.

"We have a very special problem, Michael, requiring your attention. Our associates in India are in need of protection. Obviously, we cannot spare you, nor would we be comfortable with your going to India, so we have decided the next best thing would be to have their people come here for training with you. Your job will be twofold. First, you will be training a group of people sent here to be able to protect our associates, and while you are doing that, you would be training a group of our men that I have selected for this operation. Our men will go to India to support their people and also to train more until our presence is no longer needed. This is a most urgent situation, Michael. Speed is of the utmost importance. But we must make sure that these men are capable. Their foes are very dangerous and very committed."

"I can get started as soon as you like, my Cousin," said Michael. "But, India?

That got a laugh out of everyone.

"Ever hear of the Order of the Yellow Scarf, Michael?" Patty asked.

"I read about them somewhere a long time ago. Why don't you fill me in?" said Michael.

"For over one thousand years, an organization known as the Thuggies terrorized travelers in India. They believe they are descended from a group commissioned by an ancient goddess to slay a many-headed creature she was fighting. Legend has it that Kali, the goddess I mentioned, was able to slay the creature, but the blood of her victim served to revive it and bring it back to life. Kali devised a scheme to strangle the creature by means of a yellow scarf. Then there was no bloodshed and the creature was slain.

For about 800 years these Thuggies, the order of the Yellow Scarf, killed unsuspecting travelers by the tens of thousands along the traveling routes of India. These fellows were very crafty. Often, they would join travelers along their destination. They were very friendly and very adept at putting people at ease. At some point, at night, they would attack, strangle and kill the unsuspecting travelers and steal their possessions and bury them along the way. There is a burial site that was discovered a few years ago that held five hundred corpses, all strangled.

Around the 1800's a British soldier aided the Indian nobility in eradicating them. Almost one hundred thousand of them were captured and killed. The people of India believed that they were gone for good. They were wrong.

In the late 1940s, India became independent, and almost immediately, there was a conflict between the Hindus who had ruled forever and the Muslims. When the Hindus started killing the Muslims,
a man named Garwood Ibraham, a rich building developer took his
revenge and began the slaughtering of Hindus. A war broke out in
the Bombay underworld. Here is how we become embroiled in their
problems.

India's movie industry has exploded. Bollywood, as it is known
worldwide, has become one of the largest industries in all of India.
Their movie stars are held in even higher regard than our own, in the
States. To these people they are gods and these gods represent a fortune in revenues annually.

Little Ed has large interests in foreign movie imports and those
of India are growing every day. Ed enlisted the aid of the Trumentas,
who supplied him with all the capital necessary to fund the network
to facilitate this very lucrative industry. We are now offering to let
our good friends the Pos share in this windfall. And that is where you
come in, Michael."

Before Michael could ask, Patty continued. "Some people in the
Bombay underworld have decided to revive the Thuggies and the
Order of the Yellow Scarf to try to take control of Bollywood and
extort great sums of money with their fear tactics. They have already
proven how committed they are as several of the biggest moviemakers have either been hurt or killed. They need our help, Mike, and are
willing to pay for it. Believe me, money is no object to these people.
But, we need to move quickly. What do you think, Mike?"

"I think we should start tomorrow."

Everyone liked his response. Another round of drinks was ordered and the group began to relax and enjoy. Michael's attention
had shifted to the far side of the club where a young couple appeared
to be attempting a sexual encounter while dancing fully clothed. The
wailing of a saxophone coming from the club's sound system seemed
to be driving them into a frenzy. The more the music honked and
growled, the harder the couple slammed their bodies into each other.

Slowly, Michael began to become aware of Little Ed's laughter, which started deep in his throat and grew to a roaring staccato, coming in short bursts.

"'Bump and grind', my man," said Little Ed, "'bump and grind'. Big stuff in the 50s."

"It would seem to be experiencing a resurgence," said Michael.

"King of the 'bump and grind': Sam the Man," he said. "Sam the Man Taylor could really work them up with his Harlem Nocturne, probably the greatest 'bump and grind' record of all time."

Victor was not in total agreement. "I believe you would have to agree with me that Sade's 'Pearls' by David Sanborn is a worthy challenger to that crown," said Victor, catching the group by surprise. Little Ed, Michael and Patty listened intently as Victor dissected Sanborn's virtuoso performance.

"The song starts out mysteriously, then, builds slowly on its theme, all the while keeping a steady tension. Then the artist begins to ascend and build even more tension until he climaxes with what sounds almost like an animal's cry. It is a marvelous piece of work," he concluded. 'Come Rain or Come Shine,' on the same CD has many of the same qualities, but it never matches the intensity of 'Pearls'."

Michael stared at his cousin in disbelief. Patty just smiled a knowing smile and nodded in agreement. Over time, he had become very familiar with Victor Chen; nothing Victor said or did surprised him.

Victor looked over at his cousin. "Michael," he said, " you seem shocked that I would possess such knowledge. Did you not accompany your father on his trips to Shanghai?" he asked. "And what did the great Li Xsing indulge in on those trips?"

"Ballroom dancing," said Michael.

"Exactly," said Victor. "So, why do you find it so surprising that another Po has knowledge of the arts? Is it because I have a somewhat dangerous," Victor paused and raised his eyebrows, "reputation?"

Michael and the group all had a good laugh at that one.

"A point well taken, Cousin," Michael conceded. "Once again, I am impressed by my esteemed cousin." With that he raised his glass " A salute, my cousin," he gestured. Patty and Little Ed raised their drinks and joined him.

The following day, Victor brought two young men to Michael's residence. The two men had traveled from India with a group of ten to begin training. Michael was impressed by how intelligent and articulate they were, but he was even more moved by their tales of murder and extortion being carried out against their employers. It was agreed that their training should begin immediately.

Michael spent two weeks in the dojo with the group from India and Victor's men. It was one of the most exhausting periods of time he could recall. The men trained tirelessly; they had little choice. The group from India was keenly aware of what they would be facing upon their return home. They focused on every word and technique thrown at them. Michael came to be very attached to them. Victor's men knew exactly what to expect from Michael.

Michael reminded them all that Kung Fu is believed to have gotten its origin from Indian monks who came to China. Although the group from India was aware of this, they were even more impressed and gratified by Michael's candor. It was hard to see them leave. Unlike the Po soldiers who knew they could face much danger in their service to the Pos, these men faced almost certain death upon their return. Michael could only hope that his training would be sufficient to prepare them to protect themselves. Victor was again proud of his cousin's work. Michael spent almost every day and night in this project. The Pos held up their end of the bargain.

Over the next eight months, Michael visited the island for several two-week periods to train more of the young men from India. It was good to see Master Pen. As always, the people of the island considered Michael's visits a time of celebration. The island was an astounding success. The spa was considered a peerless adventure. Those who paid a small fortune to go there were always satisfied.

Many were repeat visitors. Only the wealthiest could afford to be its guests. Michael's training sessions and visits never interfered with the daily routines. Master Pen had turned the island into a well oiled machine. Li Xsing would have been proud of his old friend.

# CHAPTER FORTY-TWO

The sweet smell of an oncoming spring filled the air with the promise of fresh clean relief from a long, messy winter. It was Friday night and Cheun Sing was looking forward to another tough workout with Michael. Michael's intense training methods always provided a welcome relief from the stress of her weekly grind at Po headquarters. She had become a valuable aid to Han Li, and as time passed, she gained access to much Po business. She sensed her days of walking across town would soon be coming to an end. She had become too valuable and knew far too much to go unprotected. Han Li had shared as much with his reclaimed daughter and declared that he was not about to lose her again. The wheels have been set in motion, but for today, Cheun Sing was free to enjoy her stroll, which helped serve as a warm-up for her sessions with Michael. She was totally unaware of the soldiers strategically placed along the route to protect her. Such were her father's wishes and Michael's execution of his uncle's orders. Wee buzzed her in and met Cheun Sing at the elevator. The look on Wee's face startled Cheun Sing.

"Wee, what is wrong?" she asked.

"My master is sick. Please come in. Master Hong has asked his nephew to examine Michael," Wee said.

"What has happened to Michael?" she demanded.

"Master Hong suspects either food poisoning or a viral infection. As the Master and I have eaten the same food prepared by my own hands, I might add, it appears to be a viral infection. Master Hong's nephew is head of internal medicine at University Hospital. He is with Michael now," said Wee.

Just as Wee concluded his comments to Cheun Sing, the door to Michael's bedroom opened and Master Hong and a slight man in his early forties appeared. They spoke in their native tongue.

"I am pretty sure your assessment is correct, Uncle" said the doctor. "Keep a close watch over him this evening. Call me first thing in the morning if you feel my assistance is necessary. But I am confident that you can deal with this," he assured his uncle.

Master Hong thanked his nephew and bade Wee show him out. Wee complied, then hurried back to speak with Master Hong.

"I am concerned that the Master is shivering. That is a sure sign of fever. We must do all we can for him," said Master Hong. Master Hong spoke no English. He and Wee carried out a short animated conversation in Chinese, which, of course, Cheun Sing understood. "Too bad there are no young virgins available to sleep with the master," said Master Hong, to a surprised Wee and Cheun Sing. "Forgive my boldness," said the older gentleman, but I am reminded of the biblical story when old King David could no longer stay warm at night. A young virgin was chosen to sleep with him and to keep the old king warm. No sex was involved," he added. "Such a person would come in handy right now to give aid and comfort to Master Michael. Well, now I must take my leave. Wee, please call me later. I am at your disposal."

Wee escorted Master Hong down to the lobby and then returned to the apartment. When he entered, he observed Cheun Sing ending a phone conversation.

"I have made a decision," she informed Wee. "Come," she ordered.

Cheun Sing opened the door to Michael's room and walked over to his bed where Michael lay heavily bundled in covers and

190

shaking uncontrollably. "I'm not leaving," she declared. "I can't take care of the virgin part, but I am very capable of doing the rest."

With that, Cheun Sing began to unbutton her blouse. Wee ran for the door.

"Just call if you need me," he yelled as he quickly exited the room, without looking back.

Cheun Sing looked down at Michael, removed her clothes with the exception of her underpants and climbed into bed. She wrapped her arms around Michael and pressed her body against his. In a few moments the warmth of her body started to take effect and Michael's shaking began to lessen and become more controlled. Before long both were sound asleep.

At approximately 4:00 a.m., Michael got out of bed, went to the bathroom and vomited. For a short period of time, he lay on the bathroom floor. He tried to gather himself and slowly rose. He groped for some mouthwash in the medicine cabinet. With great effort he took some, swished it around, spit it out and then lumbered back to bed; his legs felt like heavy lead objects. He got under the covers and rolled up into a ball. Once again, Cheun Sing's body was on his. This time he was aware of it, but believed he was dreaming. He was still slightly delirious.

At eight o'clock that morning Cheun Sing opened the door and exited the room, being very careful not to make any noise while closing the door. She was fully clothed. Wee was on the sofa. He quickly jumped up to meet her.

"Michael is resting comfortably," she told him. "The fever has left him and he is sound asleep. I suspect he'll be out of it for a few days. Why don't you go and look in on him?" she said. "I'll let myself out.

"How can I ever thank you, Mistress Po?" he asked. Cheun Sing just smiled.

"Go ahead, Wee, and see for yourself. I'm sure with a few days rest, Michael will be as good as new," she assured him.

Wee went into the bedroom to check on Michael as Cheun Sing made her exit. To her surprise, Louis Fong was waiting outside to take her home. She was very grateful for her father's thoughtfulness. She was prepared to hail a cab on Houston Street, but Han Li's Mercedes was much better by far. Now she would go home to her expectantly waiting parents and tell them all was well with Michael. Of course, she would omit the part she had played. She didn't think they would understand.

# CHAPTER FORTY-THREE

Cheun Sing was in the best of moods. She spent the day anticipating dinner with Michael, who insisted they forego their usual Friday evening sessions. Michael had expressed a desire to repay his cousin for her gracious help during his brief illness. Cheun Sing was only too happy to oblige. She tried not to read too much into it, but was well aware that Michael rarely, if ever, found an excuse to miss training. She made sure to wear one of her best Hugo Boss man-tailored business suits. Cheun Sing theorized that this particular outfit, drop dead sexy and gorgeous, worn with only a sheer lacy Vera Wang camisole, could not hurt. Neither would the fact that her Jimmy Choo stiletto heels made her powerful legs appear to be a mile long, extending down from the skirt's playful slit.

It was not unusual for Cheun Sing to be the last to leave the office on Friday evenings. It was the end of the business week and one of her many responsibilities was to make sure that all business was properly completed in the office, made ready to go, come Monday morning. Over time, she had gained great knowledge as to the ways Po business was conducted. And, now, her father had entrusted this most sensitive obligation, the locking down and securing all of Po headquarters to his very capable and loyal daughter. Michael's coming to meet her eliminated the need for the usual presence of her bodyguards.

Michael emerged from the main foyer at exactly 6:00 p.m., right on time, as usual. Before he could offer Cheun Sing a proper greeting he was dumbstruck by her appearance. Cheun Sing feigned not noticing Michael's reaction, but inwardly she was filled with delight. As usual, Michael was dressed in understated elegance. His simple slacks, shirt and loafers outfit, while completely devoid of pretentiousness, came with a combined price tag of about $1500. Cousin Victor's influence was obvious. Secretly, very secretly, Cheun Sing was most pleased by what she was seeing.

"I am just about ready," said Cheun Sing. "Your timing is perfect, Cousin."

Michael smiled and reached to take her by the arm to lead her to the elevators. As the elevator door began to open, Cheun sing let out a gasp. "Oh no," she exclaimed, "I almost forgot Han Li's papers."

With that, she turned and raced back to the huge wooden doors. "I'll just be a moment," she called back and disappeared.

Within a few seconds, Cheun Sing was soon exiting the office and activating three large locks that secured the massive doors. She was struggling to maintain control of the leather-strapped portfolio precariously secured under her arm and the papers she was juggling in her hands. Michael moved swiftly forward to lend assistance as some of the papers appeared to be falling out. As he got close, Cheun Sing made an awkward attempt to gain control of them, but managed only to slam into an oncoming Michael head first. Bodies and documents were sent in every direction. There was nothing either one could do but to sit on the plush carpet and laugh hysterically.

"Now, I'm going to move towards you to help you up and hopefully retrieve your papers," Michael informed her. He said this with his hands held in a mock defense pose bringing even more hysterical laughter from Cheun Sing. As promised, Michael got to his feet and reached down to assist Cheun Sing. His powerful grasp raised her quickly to her feet. They stood there for a long moment, Michael still maintaining his hold on her. Cheun Sing could do little but wait to see what he would do next. She didn't have long to wait. Michael drew her to himself and kissed her in one unbroken movement. Cheun Sing responded by gently raising her arms, wrapping them around Michael's neck, while pressing her body to his. Neither made any attempt to break off their embrace. It was a sign that each had contemplated such an occurrence. Both knew that a frivolous dalliance between them was utterly out of the question. Should they go any further, there would be no turning back.

They entered the elevator still wrapped in each other's arms while somehow, Cheun Sing managed to not release her hold on him and successfully secure the strapped portfolio over her shoulder. After hitting the ground level button, Michael drew Cheun Sing forcefully to himself. They crashed against the back wall of the elevator, never relinquishing their hold or embrace. This was new territory for Michael. Not even as a teenager had he experienced such raw passion in the arms of a female. Holding onto each other, they made their way to the street and hailed a taxi.

Michael had made reservations at Tribeca Grill, the famous eatery in the tony new hot Manhattan neighborhood called Soho where celebrities of every avenue converge to experience excellent food and relative peace from paparazzi and other menacing newshounds. The taxi ride did not take very long. Still, Cheun Sing and Michael never came up for air. This truly was new territory for Michael. Never in his life had he experienced such an intense desire. Two spectacularly beautiful and amazingly sexy women had inhabited his life, but never had the touch and the smell of a woman giving birth to such passion welled up within him. As the taxi pulled over to their destination, Michael took Cheun Sing's face in his hands, but did not speak.

"What is it?" Cheun Sing asked.

"I cannot believe how beautiful you are," he responded with an air of total disbelief. It was said with complete honesty. It was almost as if Michael could not believe that she was really here, and all this was happening. But it was.

As they were led to the farthest end of the restaurant to the secluded table Michael had requested, Michael was flattered by how many people acknowledged him. He never expected that, but Michael never truly realized how famous he had become on the New York scene. The whole affair with Katherine and the Hewetts, his fame as the legendary martial arts master and member of the infamous Pos and of course, his unlikely friendship with a certain police detective, not to mention his relationship with the mayor, made it practically impossible for him to blend into the woodwork.

Michael and Cheun Sing settled into their booth and ordered dinner. It wasn't long before they found themselves locked in each other's arms. They hardly touched their food. Actually, they never realized that it came. At some point, they ordered coffee, and it was while they were enjoying their rich brew that Michael leaned back and enjoyed a revelation with himself.

Over the years, Michael had, on occasion, observed couples who were not exactly young, kissing and "making out" as they used to say in public; making a public display of themselves. Michael recalled how foolish they appeared to him, how absolutely ridiculous were their actions. And now, here he was, Mr. New York sophistication, clawing and groping Cheun Sing in an overcrowded restaurant like some teenager in heat. He let out a laugh and then attempted to explain it to a confused Cheun Sing. Eventually, they both shared a hearty laugh over it. They agreed their actions really were sophomoric. It was Cheun Sing who broke the mood when she looked into Michael's eyes and said, "Do not be afraid to love me, Michael."

Her words caught Michael completely by surprise. This was the first time they had ever been alone for such an occasion. Truly, they had been together for only a few short hours, but somehow, Michael did not feel Cheun Sing's words were inappropriate. Quite the contrary, Michael was finding it difficult to explain what was happening between them, and, strange as it may seem, the word "love" seemed to have its place.

Michael looked into her jet black eyes. His look spoke a thousand words. He and Cheun Sing had spent many hours together over the past year. There always seemed to be a combustible chemistry being held under control by both. They knew their place in an impossible world: the family, danger and wealth. It was obvious that both had spent much time thinking about the other. And those thoughts were not platonic. Somehow, in the back of Michael's mind was a vague recollection of the night with Cheun Sing's fabulous body wrapped around his. That definitely was not platonic.

They made their way to the street and decided to walk back down towards Chinatown. Neither could believe that the whole evening felt so natural. It was obvious that what they needed in their lives was each other. Michael seemed to be trying to piece it all together. Cheun Sing allowed him his thoughts while guiding them expertly through the streets to lower Manhattan. It was on the corner of Canal and Mulberry streets that Cheun Sing brought them to a stop and, once again, looked deeply into Michael's eyes.

"Michael," she cooed, "I would love dessert."

"Oh, yes," was Michael's wholehearted response. "And what does my Lady desire?" he asked.

"Cheesecake and cappuccino at La Bella Ferrara and lots of it" she proclaimed.

"Excellent choice," said Michael. Within minutes they were gulping down their delicacies and ordering more cappuccino.

We hardly ate dinner," Cheun Sing offered in their defense.

"Dinner? What dinner?" Michael wanted to know.

Michael gave the taxi driver Cheun Sing's Fifth Avenue address and instructed him to take them through Central Park. It wasn't until they realized that they had reached their destination that they would have to become untangled and say goodnight.

The look on the doorman's face caused Cheun Sing to look into the large mirror in the lobby. The two swollen faces looking back at her and Michael alerted her that it might be better if Michael didn't escort her upstairs. After all, the Po soldiers in the hallway might find their appearance awkward. Michael agreed, reluctantly.

"Meet me for breakfast," Michael said.

"I love Balthazaar on Spring," was Cheun Sing's response.

"True French roast coffee," Michael acknowledged.

"Nine o'clock?" Cheun Sing inquired.

"Nine o'clock it is," Michael responded.

"I have a story I want to tell you; one that I want you to know. It will tell you much about me; much that you should know."

"I can't wait," said Michael.

They kissed and then Cheun Sing disappeared into the elevator that would take her to the Po penthouse.

It was over two years since Katherine's untimely death. The only two women Michael had ever loved had been ruthlessly taken from him. The pain of that was something he carried with him every day of his life. Obviously, that was in the back of his mind as he contemplated a relationship with Cheun Sing. He honestly questioned whether it was possible for him to have a lasting relationship, one that would not end in tragedy and pain. He decided he had to take a chance. He did not want to spend the rest of his life alone. Only love could convince him to try again. For some strange reason, he had complete confidence that Cheun Sing's love could make that happen. Michael grabbed the taxi and went home to a very inquisitive Wee, whom he reasoned would be coming out of his skin waiting for Michael to divulge even the smallest of juicy tidbits concerning his evening with Cheun Sing. The chances of that happening were next to none.

# CHAPTER FORTY-FOUR

Morning finally came to put an end to a night of little sleep. The smell of fresh brewed Puerto Rican coffee prepared by his trusty Wee momentarily took Michael back to those wonderful Sunday mornings, so long ago, when Rosa would cook her amazing breakfasts for him. So much had changed. And now, Michael had the very real feeling that once more his life was about to take a drastic turn.

Cheun Sing had accomplished what Michael believed could happen only in romance novels. She had completely intoxicated him. Michael had never experienced anything like the events of the evening past. He and Cheun Sing had made a public display of their mutual longing and now, Michael would be heading over to Spring Street and Balthazar for French breakfast and who knows what?

The forecast was good: clear skies and warm temperatures. Once again Michael relied on Wee to choose suitable clothing for today's adventures. It would be cotton shirt and slacks and a most comfortable pair of walking loafers by Kenneth Cole. Michael acknowledged that Wee had chosen well.

The site of Cheun Sing exiting the taxi proved an early morning feast for Michael's eyes. Her v-neck Dolce & Gabbana cotton T-shirt revealed just enough without succumbing to the vulgar breast baring frocks that had become so fashionable. Her slightly clinging knee length skirt would be comfortable and practical while keeping

Michael's attention solely on her. Her strapped Ferragamo sandals were the perfect finishing touch, appropriate for whatever transpired during the day.

They kissed and entered Balthazar. The wood and glass eatery, so reminiscent of French bistros, was alive with locals. They ordered authentic French roast and croissants to start. After a few sips and pleasantries having been exchanged, Cheun Sing took the lead. Her first words startled Michael, but that was only the beginning.

"Last night was the best night of my life, Michael."

She paused to let her words take hold. "Now, I would like to reveal to you what only my parents and cousin Victor know."

Michael leaned back in his chair and gestured that she go on, and she did.

"When the helicopter that took me to the mainland rose to leave me in Canton, I was devastated beyond belief. For the first time in my life, I experienced fear and total abandonment, a helplessness that can never be described. I quickly realized that I was at the mercy of the people there and that my father had finally made the decision to disinherit me. I truly believed that I would never see him or my mother ever again. I was beyond devastated.

For the first month there, I lived in a small cabin that possessed neither plumbing nor an indoor bathroom. I slept on a cot and did all my business outside. I was laid bare. The woman in charge treated me sternly but fairly. Soon, I was working in the rice fields with the rest of the laborers and strangely enough, I began to sense a peace I had never known. At night I would look up at the stars and think thoughts I had never considered. In retrospect, I realize that I had been so spoiled, so sheltered all of my life that I never gave consideration to anything outside my own self-indulgent nature. I started to wonder how I could miss my home so much and yet fall in love with my heritage, for China was beginning to consume me.

I soon realized that my lodging was only temporary. It was pre-arranged that when I adjusted to my new life, I would be transported to a local village where everyone I knew lived. It was a few scant miles away, but I was led to believe that the workers traveled a great distance each day. Once I moved into the village and into the home of my guardian, Zhoa Chu, I began to embrace my new life and made friends. What surprised me most was how easily I adjusted to that way of life, which I might add, was vastly different from the one we enjoy here in America. Oh, but of course, the village had plumbing and the bathrooms were, mercifully, indoors. I was also amazed at how well I was able to perform my duties and how self-sufficient I had become.

Even in the most remote regions of China, it is becoming apparent that China has experienced great and historic change. The Central Committee, to its credit, is doing all it can to adjust without feeling that it is relinquishing too much authority or holding too tightly to centuries of tradition and control. To add to their concerns, there are two very strong ideological movements taking place today. A great Christian movement is happening in all parts of China and that is of much concern to the Central Committee. The Christian movement is of a quiet, peaceful nature which, while strong and growing, is non-confrontational. The other movement I refer to is the Fow Lun Gong. This movement has a more foundational focus which causes the government considerable concern. The Fow Lun Gong will conduct peaceful but public demonstrations to protest which, by its very nature, is a threat to the Committee's authority. It would appear that, for the moment, the government is more threatened by the Fow Lun Gong, at least for now, anyway.

I tell you this because the village where I was staying was a Christian community. As I became more interested in their makeshift services and gatherings, (I was allowed to attend worship) I had to pass a test before gaining their confidence and being granted permission to join them. At first, I was chosen to be a lookout, to make sure that the village was not caught unawares by patrolling bands of government soldiers. After a few months I was given a position of attendant to Zhoa Chu, my guardian who, I discovered, was the main organizer of all the religious activity in the area.

The Fow Lun Gong were thought to be operating nearby, but we had seen no evidence of them. Suddenly, one day, a group of government soldiers surrounded our village and accused us of being Fow Lun Gong. Zhoa Chu confronted the officer in charge and vehemently argued with him. Without warning, the man drew his weapon and murdered her. I screamed and fell to the ground, taking her in my arms.

"How could you do such a thing?" I screamed.

The officer walked over to me and grabbed me by the hair, lifted my head and was about to shoot me also. One of the soldiers noticed the cross I was wearing and yelled to his superior. All of a sudden, the man seemed frozen, unsure of what to do.

"Are you a Christian?" he asked.

"We are all Christians," I yelled, hysterically. "Just look at what you have done. We have no knowledge of the Fow Lun Gong. They have no place with us," I said through my tears.

The officer released his hold on me. Without a word being spoken, he holstered his weapon, turned abruptly, and left our camp. Not another word was spoken. As I held Zhoa Chu in my arms I cried uncontrollably. Her death was like my very own. She had taken me in and loved me, mentored me, and helped me to find myself: the real me, the one I am most proud of. And now she was gone. I was inconsolable.

The villagers were fearful for my safety. They were afraid that the officer might have second thoughts and decide to return to get me. They showed no regard for their own safety. Later that evening, under the cover of darkness, two men from the village took me downriver in a small boat to a place where Victor could be reached by satellite communication. As usual, Victor acted swiftly and decisively. Within hours I was in Hong Kong and under the safe protection of Victor and my family. I am most concerned for those I left behind. Victor assures me that all is well with them. I pray constantly for their welfare.

Michael reached across the table and took Cheun Sing's hands.

"Let's take a walk," he said.

They left Balthazar and secured a taxi. Michael gave instructions to drive to the upper 70s and Madison Avenue. During the ride Michael gently put his arm around Cheun Sing but said very little.

"Let's just walk," he said after exiting the cab and paying the driver. They began to walk slowly down Madison Avenue. Michael tenderly took Cheun Sing's hand in his as they walked in silence.

"That was some story," said Michael, finally breaking the silence.

They made small talk until they reached Sephora, the famous cosmetics oasis. Cheun Sing pleaded to go in. They exited about 15 minutes later, but they were not empty-handed. By the time they reached Bloomingdale's, the conversation had become more animated. Once again, Cheun Sing insisted they stop and go in and see what was happening at the famous Bloomingdale makeup area. Some new additions were made and more bags left with the couple.

"If you keep this up," Michael began, before being assured by Cheun Sing that she was finished shopping and pledged to devote all her attention to their little journey. This seemed to please Michael. On the corner of 61st Street and Madison Avenue, Cheun Sing brazenly confronted Michael, who was carrying all the packages, wrapped her arms around his neck and kissed him passionately.

"You're just full of surprises aren't you?" said Michael.

"Michael, I have looked death in the face and I am determined not to waste any more time in my life. I have years to make up for and I am willing to accept the consequences of my actions."

As they walked over by Central Park, Michael announced, "I'm hungry. How about lunch?"

"That sounds great," said Cheun Sing. "Where would you suggest?"

"How about over there?" said Michael, pointing to a vendor selling pretzels.

"Outstanding," said Cheun Sing with a laugh.

They purchased two giant pretzels, then located a vacant bench nearby. They ate, talked and kissed until the pretzels were consumed.

Then they entered the park and walked back uptown towards Tavern on the Green, the world-famous eatery that has seen itself majestically displayed on the silver screen in countless movies. They stopped at John Lennon's famous Strawberry Fields and kissed unashamedly. What they were not aware of was that a lone paparazzo, on his way to do a simple errand, had spotted them and immediately recognized Michael and was now taking photos of them at a safe distance.

By mid-afternoon they found themselves laughing and pouring down espresso at Viande on Broadway. It was here that Michael turned serious. "You know that we have crossed the line here," he said. "There will be no way to dismiss our behavior to Han Li. I have to be very sure of your intentions so that I will not bring an offense to the House of Po."

Cheun Sing looked into his eyes; she did not turn her gaze from his. Cheun Sing knew well that it was not possible for her and Michael to carry on a frivolous romance. Her response more than proved her awareness of family honor and her determination to act with old dignity.

"When I was in China, I thought of you constantly. I tried to make sense, gain some understanding of why I treated you so poorly. When I got my answer and I realized the truth I was embarrassed and confused." Without hesitation she looked directly at Michael and said, "I find I have always been in love with you. Even before I met you, when I would hear the reports sent over from uncle Li Xsing I envied my sister so. When I finally saw you, I could not get you out of my mind. My shameful conduct when you were with your Katherine was an act of insanity. All I can offer as an excuse is that at that time I was drowning. I had no focus or purpose. My life was one big mass of confusion. My father was right to act as he did. As I lay at night, looking up at the stars, my thoughts were constantly of you. Since I have been back, I have tried mightily not to influence you or to inflict myself upon you. When I lay with you that night, I dreamed of what it would be like to be with you always. Leaving that morning was very difficult. As I have said, I have looked death in the face and

I am convinced that all that has happened to us in the past was meant to lead us to this. I said it before and I say again, Michael. Do not be afraid to love me."

Michael's response was immediate. "I don't wish to be alone anymore," he said. "I need to have someone in my life to share it and my work. To some, being a Po may be scary, but for me it is the best of lives. My life has meaning and I love the work that I do. It is an honor to be a Po and to be the son of Li Xsing. If I were to have you," he said, "my life would be complete."

Cheun Sing was so moved she found she was not able to offer a response.

"Cartier is not far. If you could find a way to reignite that shopping spirit of yours, we could go over and check out their engagement rings. That is, if that is something you would be interested in doing," he said, with a touch of sarcasm.

"Oh, Michael," Cheun Sing replied, "I don't know what to say."

"Yes would be good," he replied. "Then I won't continue to sit here feeling like some foolish twenty-year-old."

"Yes, yes, oh yes," Cheun Sing exclaimed, her voice growing louder with each response.

Patrons nearby quickly realized what was happening. An impeccably dressed elderly woman motioned to Michael if he had just proposed and Michael gave an affirmative head response. The look on Cheun Sing's face was all anyone needed for confirmation as a huge round of applause rose up from the patrons nearby. One of the waiters came over to the table; he obviously recognized Michael.

"Congratulations, Master Po," he said. "Viande is honored that such a wonderful thing has happened here," he offered in classic Bronx accent. "Our congratulations to both of youse," he blurted out, with a smile. "This one's on us, folks. Please accept it as your first gift, from Viande," he beamed.

Totally embarrassed, the joyful couple got up, thanked the waiter with a large tip, hugged half of the people in the place and ran out into the street, laughing all the way.

"Come on," said Michael. "Let's grab a taxi. My legs are too numb to attempt to walk across town." No sooner had Michael given directions to the driver, Cheun Sing leaped into his arms.

"Oh, Michael, I am so happy. Are you sure? Are you really sure?" she asked.

"Completely," was his immediate response. "I spent a great deal of time last night thinking, and came to the conclusion that this was the only answer for us. You are right when you say everything that happened to us before was meant to lead us to this. I now believe that this is our destiny. The House of Po needs this. We need this. I too have done everything in my power to resist encouraging a relationship between us. But since you have been back, I have been able to think of little else but you. This is all too perfect. I know in my soul that we are meant to be together. I have no reservations."

Michael paid the driver and took Cheun Sing's hand to head towards the front entrance of Cartier. Cheun Sing tugged at his arm and brought him to a halt.

"What is it?" e asked. "Is something wrong?"

"I have one very important question to ask you, Michael, one that concerns me," she said.

"What is it? What do you wish to know?" he said.

Cheun Sing hesitated momentarily as though gathering herself to ask the next question. "After we are married, will I be able to feel totally secure should you be required to travel to some distant place: Israel, for instance?" She asked.

Now it was Michael's turn to be momentarily speechless. "Victor," he blurted out. "What did Victor tell you?"

"Oh, Michael, do not be concerned. Actually, my father and cousin Victor were greatly impressed by your show of self-restraint. From what I hear, your Sargeant Nathan was very beautiful. Victor made her seem so desirable that if I were a man, I believe I would have pursued her. But you didn't and that says much for you. I have only one question for you: are you over Sergeant Nathan?"

"My place and my heart are with no one else but you. I doubt very much that she or anyone else but you could complete my life. I will always have fond memories of my time in Israel and they are not confined solely to a female officer of the Mossad. You are my life now. Now, are you ready to go in and choose a symbol of our future?" Michael asked.

Cheun Sing's answer was direct; she grabbed onto Michael's hand and pulled him through the doors.

# CHAPTER FORTY-FIVE

Michael and Wee entered the Po residence and were led directly out to the terrace with its magnificent views of the Park by Louise, the Po's longtime housekeeper. Everything was in order. The coffee was waiting and ready along with croissants, bagels, fresh baked blueberry muffins. They were greeted by Han Li, Madame Po and Cheun Sing, who were seated and waiting. Customary greetings were exchanged, then all took their seats allowing Louise to take their breakfast orders. Sunday breakfast with the Pos usually meant scrambled eggs, sausage, bacon, new potatoes and whatever else anyone desired. For instance, waffles with fresh blueberries with whipped cream, French toast or pancakes were always available thanks to the very capable Louise.

Wee took his place next to Michael, between Michael and Cheun Sing. Madame Po sat directly across from Michael who could not help noticing the society section of the New York Times resting in front of her. Madame Po had a strange expression on her face.

Without delay, she said, "Michael, it seems that you are becoming quite a celebrity in our city. There is an article about you here in the society section of the Times."

Michael was taken aback. For the moment, he had no idea what his aunt could be referring to. That moment would quickly pass. Before anyone could respond, Madame Po continued.

"It seems that you and a very attractive mystery woman were observed making quite a display of your mutual affections for one another and in more than one location yesterday."

Han Li, who showed no interest when the conversation began, was now sitting upright and was all ears.

"Michael DeAngelo, more famously known as Master Po of the powerful Po crime family, here in New York, was seen romancing a gorgeous Asian female all over Manhattan. It was obvious that Master Po had eyes and every other part of his anatomy only for the statuesque stunner," read Madame Po from the Times article.

"Well, Michael," she paused with a wry smile, "who is this statuesque stunner they are referring to? It appears that you have been concealing someone from us."

Madame Po was having great fun playfully teasing Michael. But it was she who was about to be caught completely off guard.

"Now don't be shy, Nephew," she said. "I believe it is time that you reveal your little secret to your family. I am sure we all wait with great anticipation to know who this lucky young woman is. And, Asian, now that really is intriguing."

Wee squirmed uncomfortably in his seat while Cheun Sing merely lowered her eyes so as not to look in Michael's direction. Michael knew he had no choice but to respond.

"I am saddened, dear Aunt, that you had to find out about this in such a shabby manner," Michael said. "It was my intention to tell you myself, but all this came about so quickly, I just didn't have the time. In fact, I was going to tell you this morning, but I had no idea that I was being observed. Not that I was being discreet, by any means. I guess I just did not consider myself as being newsworthy. I am sure the article is vividly contradictory."

"Michael," said a now very interested Han Li, "enough of the apologies, for heaven's sake, who is this person?"

Michael hesitated for a moment and then looked at Wee whose expression left little doubt that he had no desire to contribute.

"The beautiful, gorgeous, statuesque Asian stunner they perfectly described is seated right here, next to my aunt, Madame Po," said Michael.

At first there was silence. Then, Madame Po shot a glance in Cheun Sing's direction.

" You?" was all she could muster.

"Yes, Mother, it is I," Cheun Sing answered.

Amazingly, the group fell silent. Finally, Cheun Sing said, "May I continue, Michael?"

"Of course," Michael responded, gratefully relinquishing the floor.

Cheun Sing's deferring to Michael, such a simple and seemingly harmless act, bore testimony that she was already assuming a position of subordination, which she fully understood and fully intended to honor. She had witnessed this many times in her life as a child of the Pos. This did not go unnoticed by her father.

"Michael and I are very much in love and have already pledged to marry as soon as possible. We ordered our rings yesterday at Cartier. We hope this news gives you both great joy," said Cheun Sing.

After a few seconds of stunned silence while everyone had a chance to gather themselves, Han Li exclaimed, "It has been years since joy of this magnitude has been shared in the home of Han Li Po." Again he paused. "Now, I fully understand the happiness my brother Li Xsing experienced, Michael. You have made our joy complete. The House of Po takes a giant step forward with this union. Never could I have imagined such a wonderful thing happening. All that we have is at your disposal, my son. It is an honor beyond description that our daughter and the son of Li Xsing would be united," said Han Li, hardly able to contain himself.

Madame Po just sat in silence. She had been completely upstaged, but realized she had been given a gift of immense importance. A union between the Houses of Li Xsing and Han Li, at this place and time, was of monumental significance to the Po Empire.

"By the way, Uncle," said Michael, "you should expect a call from Victor in about fifteen minutes. Of course, he already knows. I could not go to sleep last night without informing my cousin. He's probably bursting, waiting to make his call to you."

Cheun Sing rose from her chair to stand beside Michael, who was now standing and placed herself in his arms. Not in her wildest dreams could Madame Po imagine that what she was seeing was possible. "Finally," she thought to herself, "peace among the Pos."

Michael and Cheun Sing had decided to spend their wedding night in a penthouse suite at the Four Seasons where the wedding would be taking place. Victor had other ideas. One week before the wedding, Victor, Han Li and Madame Po took the couple to lunch at the Montauk Yacht Club in the tony Hamptons, on Long Island. After an enjoyable meal and good family conversation overlooking the harbor, Victor led the group over to the private yacht basin. Neither Michael nor Cheun Sing suspected anything. The guard greeted them and let them enter as if they were longtime members. When they reached the far end of the pier Michael took notice of a very large vessel about 500 feet out into the water. It was the largest boat in the harbor. At first, Michael did not allow himself to believe what he was seeing. "After all," he thought, "how could it be possible?"

"Victor," he said, "is that the Tiger Bay?"

"Why yes, I believe it is the Tiger Bay," Victor said, rather coyly.

"How is that possible?" Michael asked. But before Victor could answer, Michael realized that just about nothing was impossible for his favorite cousin. "But, why?" he wondered.

"It is my wedding gift to you both," said Victor. "The Tiger Bay has been one of my most prized possessions. It is only fitting that I give her to you. I know that you have many cherished memories of your times spent on her in China. Wee has told me how much you love her. Well, now she is yours. But do not fret, dear cousins. I have my eye on one that I am guessing will come on the market just as I will be arriving back home. I trust the owner will realize that he wants to sell."

Just then, a launch pulled up to the pier and the party went aboard. Cheun Sing had never seen the Tiger Bay. She was about to be given the grand tour of her new sea home.

# CHAPTER FORTY-SIX

If the wedding of Michael and Katherine Hewett seemed like something out of a romantic comedy, the scene at the Four Seasons for his wedding to Cheun Sing was nothing less than hysterical. Security was everywhere. Even the security was under scrutiny. This wedding, ballyhooed by the media for three long weeks, would be the perfect place for treachery to be carried out by anyone who wished to do harm to the Pos. Neither Han Li nor Victor would ever allow himself to believe that those who came against them at the parking garage massacre were finished with the Pos. They were confident that those parties were not done with their business. Even the long passage of time would not diminish the possibility for danger. In fact, it might lead to a false sense of security. As long as Victor was alive, the Pos would never suffer a false sense of security.

Three Po family heads from Shanghai, London and Malaysia arrived with full entourage and security two days before the event. There were many rounds of festivities and family gatherings, and of course, conspicuous displays of security. The mayor, although invited, could not possibly attend. Through Marv Levy and Walter Larkin, he authorized a heavy police presence to guard the perimeter. The Trumentas would do their part on the day of the wedding, but until then, they would be noticeably absent.

Valentino was flown in from Milan, at a very hefty price, to supervise the final fitting of a gown he personally created for the event. Having no desire to don a ballooning, overly ornate frock, Cheun Sing chose an elegant, formfitting, strapless creation of Chinese silk and cotton blend. The dress and Cheun Sing were breathtaking.

To ease his jitters, Michael chose to take complete control over all security for the event: no small task. The grand ballroom had been transformed into a lavish replica of ancient Chinese gardens, a landscape complete with large stone statues, hanging lanterns by the hundreds, mountains of flowers of every description, huge potted trees and a remarkable decorative stone replica of the Great Wall of China. Walter had enlisted the aid of the local theater scenery establishment, who, after viewing hundreds of photos and drawings, sat back and allowed New York's famous union theater professionals, hired for the event, to work their magic. And magic it was.

Most of the invited guests had seen just about everything imaginable where weddings were concerned. Still, few had ever witnessed anything like what Han Li had prepared for the guests of his only child's nuptials. Lucas and Spielberg would have been impressed. The society wags would be rehashing this little party for weeks to come.

First, Michael had to make sure that the safety of his visiting family was fully insured. Next, was the daunting task of orchestrating the intricate deployment of the police, Chinese and the Italians to be foolproof , yet not in any way intrusive  to the atmosphere of the Four Seasons and its guests. That got a little tricky, but Walter, Patty Figamo and Victor worked selflessly to achieve harmony and cooperation. As usual, Walter was able to make light of any tense moments and get all the parties to see the big picture. Patty and Victor marveled at Walter's complete disregard for the fact that he and they were supposed to be on opposite sides. Thank God for Walter Larkin.

To ensure Cheun Sing, Han Li and Madame Po's safety,  Michael assigned his favorite and most trusted soldiers. Of all his many security details, this group was the one he had the most confidence in. One final issue had to be attended to, and there was only one person on the planet Michael could turn to with complete assurance. That person was Wee, and the issue was food. The chefs at the Four Seasons were top notch. Michael knew that everything they prepared would be perfect. But would it be safe? That was his main concern. Wee brought in the chefs from Chin Wah to assist him in monitoring all the food prepared. Every box, case and foodstuff would be totally scrutinized, and every morsel would be tasted at random by the chefs preparing them. Extensive background checks were done on all the chefs as well as setup people, wait staff and delivery services, compliments of Marv Levy who reached out to old friends at the F.B.I. for assistance. Not even the president of the United States enjoyed a more complete and exhaustive preparation.

The ceremony was held in the grand ballroom. The vows were exchanged under a large rose covered arbor that was then quickly pulled to the side to make room for the huge head table which magically appeared. Rosa took her place with Han Li and Madame Po where she and Madame Po held a ceremony-long contest to see whose smile could be the widest. Victor served as best man and his toast nearly brought tears to the eyes of many in attendance. Few could ever recall a time when Victor displayed such eloquence and pure emotion. Such was his love for his adopted cousin and his respect for Cheun Sing.

Patty acted as head usher of a bridal party of twenty. Cheun Sing chose as her attendants only the women she worked closely with at Po headquarters. It was a great honor for them and a genuine display of affection by Cheun Sing who valued their friendship and work ethic. She was determined that this affair would be about family and love. No headliners would be needed. There were enough barons and kings of crime to satisfy anyone's need for glitterati.

Valentino begged off attending the reception. As soon as the "I dos" were exchanged, Michael had him spirited away to Kennedy to catch a plane back to Milan. He was very satisfied at the way his wonderful creation had been displayed. A large, and very real gasp arose from the crowd as the bride made her royal appearance. Michael seemed transfixed at the sight of her, that is until Han Li gently took his hand to meet Cheun Sing's. For Michael, this was the third time he had pledged love and devotion to someone whom he loved deeply. This time, he felt a confidence and peace he had never experienced before.

The reception seemed a blur as course after course was served, temporarily interrupting the music provided by Harry Coniff and a twenty-two piece orchestra. Guests ate and danced long into the evening. The event went flawlessly.

There was only one minor incident. Michael had hired a photographer friend of Cheun Sing to record the occasion, but also agreed to permit local press photographers to gain access to the wedding at a specified time and in one designated place. Foolishly, a lone paparazzo, the one from Central Park, tried to crash the party. The poor man spent the night at the local hospital having his broken arm and many bruises attended to. One week later, a Po soldier delivered a large check to his apartment: payment for the replacement of his cameras, which were accidentally destroyed and of course, for any inconvenience caused him. Reluctantly, the photographer opened his door to take the check from a very large Chinese man whose eyes bore a hole through his. The poor man quickly closed the door to his apartment and then remembered to breathe. Surprisingly, his little stay at the hospital never made it into the local media.

# CHAPTER FORTY-SEVEN

The majestic Tiger Bay rocked gently with the tide. A full moon beamed down magical illumination, silhouetting her beauty for all in the harbor to take notice. Normally, there would be a full crew of four plus chef and captain. And, in keeping with Po tradition, three bodyguards in attendance. But for tonight, Victor had seen to it that three smaller launches with four soldiers each carrying automatic weapons had taken a position nearby to ensure privacy for the newlyweds. Only Wee and the captain were aboard. They did their best to keep out of sight while providing any service needed.

Michael lay in bed, waiting for Cheun Sing to emerge from their marble appointed master bath. The room was dark, but the moonlight sweeping through the portholes was all that was required to set the mood. As Cheun Sing drew near, Michael noticed her holding something in her hand.

"What is that you have in your hand?" Michael asked.

"This was Victor's idea," Cheun Sing responded. "He said you would understand."

Mysterious music began to fill the room from the Bose music system. Cheun Sing released her robe and laid her naked body alongside her husband.

"It is a David Sanborn, I believe," she said, responding to Michael's inquiring eyes.

Michael just smiled, "That Victor is truly something else," he

216

said as he drew Cheun Sing close and began to kiss her passionately. Their bodies immediately began to respond to the driving pulsation of Sanborn's searing saxophone work. Victor had instructed Cheun Sing on how to place the music system on repeat play and by the second time the music reached its soaring climax, both Michael and Cheun Sing were totally versed in the primal scream Victor had so masterfully described. As they lay breathing heavily in each other's arms, Michael instructed Cheun Sing to turn the music system off.

"I don't think we'll need any more outside inspiration," Michael whispered in her ear.

# CHAPTER FORTY-EIGHT

Detective Lucy Ferrigno welcomed the warmth of the sun wafting over her as she locked the door behind her and walked down the few steps to the street. Her journey up Spring Street always included a visit to her favorite coffee shop before continuing her daily walk to work at number One Police Plaza in lower Manhattan. As Lucy exited the shop with coffee in hand, she noticed a large black Cadillac with heavily tinted windows parked out front. Before she could respond, she realized that she was surrounded by three young Chinese men, all dressed in business suits.

"Please do not be alarmed, Detective," spoke the tallest of the three. "We mean you no harm, but we must insist that you come with us," he said as he motioned to the waiting Cadillac. "Do not even consider reaching for your gun or we will have no choice but to shoot you right here with all these pedestrians passing by."

Lucy realized she had no choice, so she allowed the speaker to come close and remove her service revolver as inconspicuously as possible .Then, she entered the back door of the Cadillac. It didn't take her long to recognize the young Chinese woman sitting next to her. It was the very same girl she had arrested over a year ago in Little Italy. Before Lucy could say anything, the girl hit her with her fist across the face.

"Quickly, place a bag over her head," the girl ordered her associate. "Now tie her hands," she barked.

Lucy strained to remain conscious.

"Let's go," she ordered the driver who immediately hit the accelerator and sped the auto away towards the East River.

Lucy could not tell what the two in the backseat were saying, they were speaking in Chinese, but they were obviously having a heated disagreement.

"I have decided to ask for more money to do this job," she informed her associate who was taken totally by surprise. "I have decided to take our guest to my uncle's warehouse so that I can make a better deal."

"You are not acting wisely," the tall man said. "Your uncle left explicit instructions that we were to synchronize our actions with his. He would be most upset."

"Screw the old fool," said the girl with obvious contempt. "I do not wish to follow the path he is on. He is willing to die to gain revenge on his enemies. I am not. We will need a lot of money to make our getaway. The Pos have people everywhere. But I know a place where even they cannot harm us. Now keep silent and help me."

Just then, Lucy felt the car ascending and making a wide turn. She realized they were going over the 59th Street bridge and heading to Queens. The sound of the tires against the steel grate roadbed convinced her she was right.

At about the same time, Madame Po was settling into her seat alongside Lee Hong, who was charged with taking Sung Lee up to Bridgeport, Connecticut to spend a few days visiting with her cousin. The driver navigated over to Second Avenue and then headed uptown to catch the FDR drive north to the Bronx and the New England Thruway to Connecticut. She thought it strange when the driver did not take the 72nd Street access. The driver made a right turn on 92nd Street and headed east. The car slowed and entered a building on the right making a descent to the lower parking garage.

"Lee Hong, what are you doing?" she asked. "What does this

mean?"

"I am very sorry, Madame Po, but you will not be going to Connecticut today. I have chosen another destination for you. Please do as you're told as I would not want any harm to come to you."

"Are you insane? You know very well what Han Li will do when he finds out what you have done," Madame Po declared.

"I know exactly what to expect from Han Li, and Victor, for that matter. However, it no longer matters to me. I no longer fear your family, my dear Madame. My only desire now is to inflict as much pain on them as has been suffered by me. I am confident that I will die at their hands. And you, Madame Po, are going to die at mine," said a very resolute Lee Hong.

The driver pulled the Mercedes sedan into a parking spot next to a Toyota Land Cruiser. A Chinese man got out of the Land Cruiser and opened the side door to escort Madame Po out. He took her gently, but securely around and placed her into the Land Cruiser. Lee Hong got in to join her. Sung Lee looked over just in time to see the man in the front seat of the Mercedes shoot the driver and ease his lifeless body back into the seat. The Land Cruiser quickly pulled out and ascended the ramp to 92nd Street and entered the FDR at 96th Street heading north towards Hyde Park and Rhinebeck.

# CHAPTER FORTY-NINE

Lucy found herself tied up in a chair with a hood still over her head. She found her captor to be very talkative so she decided to try to provoke her. "Are you sure you have the stomach for this?" she said. The girl stopped what she was doing and turned towards Lucy.

"What do you mean by that?" she asked.

" Well, here we are, me all tied up with a hood over my head so I can't see or even move. It takes a real brave person to pull that one off. I'm kind of defenseless here, or didn't you notice?" Lucy chided.

The girl paused for a moment, then walked over and yanked the hood off of Lucy's head. "You think you're something special, don't you, just because you are a cop," the girl said.

"No, I'm not so special, but at least I don't go into a confrontation making sure the other party is defenseless," she challenged. "I guess you haven't forgotten our last meeting," she taunted.

Again, the girl was silent. She walked over to where Lucy was and stood right in front of her. Then, after some thought, she smiled, walked around back and began to untie Lucy's restraints. When she completed her task she walked around to once again face Lucy.

" I see you have a gun. Are you going to allow me to get mine so we can shoot it out, Wild West style?" Lucy asked. "How about we draw on each other, Clint Eastwood style?" she mocked.

Again, the girl simply smiled then walked across to the far side of the room. "You have a real big mouth," said the girl as she placed her gun on the floor. "I think it is time to settle things between you and me."

With that, both women slowly approached each other. Lucy took up a defensive posture, seeking to let her opponent attack so that she could deflect and counterattack. After a few fake assaults, the girl launched a full attack seeking to land a roundhouse with her right leg. Lucy countered by moving very close and both women began struggling and fighting for superiority. The girl quickly realized that Lucy was stronger and proceeded to break off her hold and landed two quick fists to Lucy's face. Lucy countered with a strike of her own, causing the girl to stagger backwards. Sensing an opening she charged in only to be met with a foot to the midsection. Lucy bent over in pain. Now the girl sensed an advantage. She cautiously advanced and easily deflected Lucy's attempt to strike with her fist. Next she took hold of Lucy's arm and twisted in one direction and then another aikido style, flipping her painfully to the floor. As Lucy struggled to get to her feet, she was met by a solid fist to her jaw. Her instincts took over and she countered with a right of her own to the jaw. The girl was surprised. She landed another right but Lucy, surprisingly, again returned fire. Both women just stood there for a moment. Lucy made the first move; it was a mistake. The girl deflected her punch, then grabbed her arm and twisted it behind her back. Lucy cried out in pain. Next, the girl spun her around and landed a hard right hand to her jaw. Lucy was staggered by the blow. She never saw the powerful right leg crescent kick that landed squarely on her jaw and sent her to the floor, unconscious. The girl walked over to lift up Lucy's head to satisfy herself that the fight was over. She grabbed her mobile phone and left the room to make a call.

"That's right," she informed the person on the other end. "You tell that decrepit old witch that I'm through killing people for her. I want one million dollars or I'll let the cop go and turn myself in. I will make a deal with the D.A. and you, my uncle, and that old maid can all burn in hell for all I care. You have one hour or I'm calling this whole thing off. Now get a move on. I'm not going to wait one minute longer."

The girl closed her phone and headed back into the room where she had left Lucy.

"Got to get this one up and see if these fools respond," she said to herself.

She entered the room and was met by a right fist that collapsed her nose. Momentarily stunned, the girl reached up to feel the blood gushing from her face. Her eyes were watery, impairing her vision, but she recognized the voice she heard.

"Remember me?" said Lucy.

"Witch," the girl yelled. She managed to strike out and land a punch. But it did not have much effect. Lucy returned the favor, knocking the girl backwards. Then she landed a right and left, half turning the girl around. She slammed the girl face first into the wall. Grabbing her hair with her left hand to secure her she then landed three powerful fists to the girl's kidneys, causing her to scream in pain. The girl managed to turn around, barely holding herself up against the wall and tried to raise her hands to protect herself. Lucy landed a powerful right hand to the girl's midsection. Then, she landed a right cross that sent her staggering a few feet backwards, before collapsing to the floor. Lucy went over to the chair where her belongings had been placed and grabbed her handcuffs. She walked back over to the girl who was lying face down on the floor. With her left knee, she came down full force onto the back of the girl who cried out in extreme pain. Lucy mirandized her as she handcuffed her hands behind her back. The girl had passed out.

Lucy got her mobile phone and dialed the home of Michael DeAngelo. When the answering machine responded, Michael being away on his honeymoon, Lucy left the following message. "Master Po, I believe the time has come for me to take you up on your offer of training, if you are still interested. I'll explain when you return my call. Thank you, Inspector Lucy Ferrigno."

Next, she dialed Marv. "Where are you?" he barked.

"I believe I'm in Long Island City, in a warehouse of some sort. I'm looking out the window and I see this billboard for Wonder Bread. Can you trace my signal?"

"Hold on a minute," said Marv who made a call downstairs. About thirty seconds later, he was back on the line. "Yeah, we can trace it. Hold tight, Walter knows that area. He and Bobby are on the way. They'll be there in less than twenty minutes. You going to be all right?" said Marv.

"Yeah, I am okay. Just tell my husband to hurry up and come and get me."

# CHAPTER FIFTY

Wee came running down to Michael's cabin and knocked on the door.

"Master, Master," he yelled. Victor is calling. It is urgent." Michael opened the door to let Wee in. At Wee's instruction, he went over to pick up the ship's phone.

"There is a plane on the way to pick you up on Block Island. I am very sorry to disturb you at this time, Cousin, but an emergency makes it necessary. Our aunt is missing and I fear the worst," said Victor.

"How could this happen?" Michael wanted to know.

"Lee Hong was escorting her to her cousin's home in Connecticut, but they never arrived. There was a bulletin on the news that a body of a man of Chinese ancestry was found in a parking garage on 92nd Street. The man was Lee Hong's driver. Uncle Han is beside himself. I don't have to tell you what this would mean if our aunt has been harmed. A car is waiting for you at Kennedy. I would come myself but I do not dare leave our uncle right now."

"I understand, Victor. I will tell Cheun Sing and we will be back as soon as possible. Tell our uncle not to worry. We will get to the bottom of this," said Michael.

As Victor replaced the receiver, something about Michael's tone caught his attention. There was not a moment of hesitation in Michael's voice. In fact, it was full of conviction. Victor rather liked that. Within two hours, Michael was back and deeply involved in strategy with Victor. Quan Yee had become a valuable member of the family and he asked to be there. Speculation was running rampant as to whether Lee Hong was a victim or somehow responsible for this mess.

"I have my suspicions concerning Lee Hong," said Quan Yee. "I mentioned this to Han Li months ago, but he waved me off. He and Lee Hong go back many years and he counts Hong amongst his most trusted allies. That is dangerous as far as I am concerned. Hong has a niece who is always in trouble and he is always bailing her out of jams. She hangs with a radical crowd so it is very difficult to get a fix on her. But she is a whack job. She even assaulted a female police officer about a year and a half ago. Some big time, uptown lawyer bailed her out. No one knows who he represented, but his firm only handles mega-wealth. I don't know if this means anything, but I would not be surprised to find she is mixed up in this somehow. And if she is…"

"Lee Hong is," said Victor, finishing his sentence. Victor really liked Quan Yee and had learned to trust him. "See what you can find out," Victor ordered. "And do not worry about bruised feelings. Turn our organization upside down if you must, but get me something fast. I fear for every moment my aunt is not with us." Quan Yee made a hasty exit as Louise entered the room holding a telephone.

"It is for Michael," she announced.

Michael took the phone and recognized Walter Larkin's voice on the other end. "Walter, what can I do for you?"

"Maybe we can help each other, friend. Can you meet me at Ferrara's on Grand Street.? I believe we are joined at the hip in some nasty business, my friend, and the boss has asked me to speak to you, personally. Michael, I know what is going on. Meet me now and I'll lay it all out for you," said a determined Walter Larkin.

Michael explained the conversation to Victor who immediately called for a car to take Michael to lower Manhattan.

Michael and Walter ordered their espresso. Walter wasted little time and charged right in. "Lucy Ferrigno was abducted today by a group of young Chinese thugs," he began. "She's okay but that's not the case for Madame Po is it?" Michael nodded in agreement and gestured for Walter to continue.

"This crazy Chinese chick and a few of her buddies abducted Lucy on her way to work and took her to a warehouse in Long Island City. Guess who owns the warehouse?"

"Lee Hong," said Michael.

"Right you are, my friend. Now, guess whose niece Mary Chen, the young Chinese girl is?"

"Lee Hong's," Michael answered once more.

"You're really good at this," said Walter. "Michael, this Mary Chen is some piece of work. When she got to the station, she immediately tried to cut a deal. We called the D.A. in and boy, what a tale this young lass did weave. It seems her uncle is really pissed off at the Pos for working a deal with Masotoma of Japan. Ever hear of the massacre of Nanjing, during the Second World War?" Walter asked.

"Sure," said Michael. "I was at a meeting up in Hyde Park where Masotoma told our people all about it. He told us all about Nanjing. It was horrible," said Michael.

"Well, you can just imagine how old Lee Hong felt when he heard about the deal. It seems most of his family was wiped out in that little fiasco. The only survivors were he and his sister. They happened to be away at the time. His only sister had a child and later on she had a child, one Mary Chen. It seems the kid grew up with nothing but hate, specifically, hate for all things Japanese.

That was the girl we saw down in Little Italy that Lucy arrested. The lawyer who bailed her out represents Millicent Carlyle of the Rhinebeck moneyed Carlyles. The grand dame hates Lucy for cracking the Carlyle porn case. When she saw in the news that Mary Chen was arrested, she got her lawyer to go down and bail her out. It wasn't long before the Carlyle woman and Lee Hong hooked up and that's where you come in, my friend."

"How can I possibly figure into all this?" Michael wanted to know.

"I'm sorry to have to be the one who tells you this Michael, but the Chen girl killed MaryAnn Vanooster. The old lady was crushed when she learned of the mistake. She orchestrated Katherine's trip to Paris and then sent the girl to kill her. She blamed Katherine for the Vanooster girl's death in her place.

Now, we believe Lee Hong has Madame Po up at the Carlyle estate. She's not going to be alive for long. But, we are not one hundred percent sure she is there. Only one person can tell us that, and if we go through normal channels, I'm afraid your aunt is not going to make it. Michael, somehow, you have got to get to her lawyer. He knows what is going on, but he won't be in any mood to tell us. He'll be trying to cover his own butt. Maybe Katherine's father can put you two together. But you better act fast. And Michael, keep me in the loop. You'll need me to make all this work."

Michael digested all that Walter had said. Considering his revelation concerning Millicent Carlyle's involvement in Katherine's death, it was a lot. He realized that Walter was right. Only Walter could orchestrate keeping his family out of trouble while doing what they had to do. His only hope was to get to Nicholas Hewett. He did not waste any time.

"Michael, so good to see you, son. And I guess congratulations are in order. So glad to see you are happy, son. Now, what can I do for you?" asked Hewett.

"I've waited a long time to tell you what I'm about to reveal, sir. Please, sit down," said Michael. Michael waited for Hewett to take his seat before continuing. "I know the name of the person who killed Katherine ," he began. Her name is Mary Chen, and she is in jail. She has admitted her guilt, so there is no doubt."

"But, why?" Hewett asked. "What reason could this person have for doing such a terrible thing to my Katherine?"

"Money and adventure," said Michael. "She is a sick young lady, but she was hired by one who is more sick than she. And that person is Millicent Carlyle."

"What ?" Hewett exclaimed. "Impossible. I've known Millicent all my life. She could not possibly do such a thing. What you suggest is utterly preposterous."

Michael began to explain. "When the police exposed her brother, she harbored a vendetta against the female member of the team who discovered Dr. Carlyle's sordid past. MaryAnn Vanooster died in Katherine's apartment. The killers believed she was Katherine. Millicent Carlyle loved Mary Ann as if she was her very own. By now, she was deeply involved with members of my family who harbored bad feelings towards us and who started all of the killings back in Halloween at the Puck Building. Many people died and one of our own caused this: his niece, Mary Chen. Mary Chen killed Katherine to please Millicent Carlyle and now, Millicent Carlyle is in the middle of an abduction of my aunt. I fear for my aunt's safety. Only one person can help us and I need you to help me get to that person."

"Who is this person?" Hewett asked.

"Your lawyer, Thomas Lake," Michael said.

Hewett sat back in his huge leather chair and took some very deep breaths. Slowly, the muscles in his face began to relax. He picked up his phone and dialed the speed number.

"Thomas," he said. "Fine, fine, but I'm afraid I need a favor, old chum. My son-in-law needs to see you. How soon can you see him? It is urgent or I would not bother you." He waited for his lawyer's response.

"Thanks so much, Tom, let's do lunch soon. I owe you. You too, goodbye."

"He is in court all morning tomorrow. He will skip lunch and meet you at 12:15 in his office," said Hewett. Then he turned very serious. "You will always be my son-in-law, Michael. You are the only man my Katherine ever loved. And you loved her back. No parent can ask for more. I am very grateful that you have deeded much of her estate back to us. You are a very honorable and caring man, Michael, and the Hewetts owe you a great debt of gratitude."

"I am the one who owes you, sir. For a short while, I was able to move in a circle someone like me could only dream of. And to do that with Katherine, well, that was special. To have Katherine, that was beyond special. I might need further help if my aunt is being held on the Carlyle estate. And I make you a promise. If she is, I'll make sure you are there when we bring Millicent Carlyle down. Katherine deserves that. And that would give me much satisfaction."

Michael returned to the Po residence to meet with Han Li, Victor and Quan Yee. No matter what, tomorrow had to be the day to act. There could be no more delays. It was agreed that Victor would accompany Michael to visit the lawyer.

At 12:15 p.m. Michael and Victor were ushered into the offices of Hanover, Seeley and Lake. Thomas Lake was surprised to see Victor, since he was not informed that Michael would not be alone.

"How may I help you, gentlemen?" he asked

"We need to know if Millicent Carlyle is involved with the abduction of our aunt. We need to know if our aunt is being held at the Carlyle estate," said Michael, boldly.

"I'm afraid you gentlemen are mistaken. Millicent Carlyle is a client and as such, she is privileged. I could not possibly discuss anything concerning her with you. I'm afraid you've wasted your time," said Lake.

Before Michael could advance any objections, Victor asked him to please wait outside so that he and the attorney could have a private moment. Reluctantly, Michael obliged.

Victor waited until Michael closed the door behind him, then he and Attorney Lake were alone. "I know you don't know me, Mr. Lake, and until last evening I did not know of your existence. But things have a way of changing rapidly in times when needs arise," Victor started. He then reached into his suit pocket, took out a group of photos and gave them to Lake. As Lake looked at the photos his face turned ashen. They were pictures of his home, his wife and his children. There were also pictures of his brother and his family who lived on the upper East Side.

"What is the meaning of this?" Lake demanded to know.

"Someone in my family is about to be harmed. How would you react if your family were placed in the very same position?" Victor returned.

Lake thought for a moment. "Look, I'm on shaky ground here. Against my wishes and my advice, my client has gone off the deep end. I honestly don't know what to do."

Victor reached into his side pocket, pulled out a card and handed it to Lake. "Call this number, now. They'll take your call," Victor instructed. Lake did as he was instructed. The voice on the other end was one that he was very familiar with. He listened intently to that voice who informed him just who Victor was and what he could do for him should he find himself in dire straits. Lake hung up the phone and looked at Victor through new eyes.

"These people are going to drown me," he said. "This firm has been here for over one hundred years. We have always prided ourselves on our integrity. And, now, one of our most prestigious and influential clients has gone crazy. I fear that she will bring us all down with her," said a very deflated Thomas Lake.

"I can help you. I will help you," said Victor. "Tell me what I need to know, nothing more, and I will place my whole family in your debt. Friends of the Pos fear no one. Never has a Po asked a lawyer to compromise himself. We hold honesty and integrity above all else. True, we can be ruthless at times, but only in retaliation. We never start a fight. The strange thing is that no one has yet to figure out that we win because we are smart, smarter than anyone else. We always position ourselves for success. We do not take up with goons. Sooner or later, thuggery leads to disaster. We have no desire nor any interest in such practices. We'd rather beat you in a game of chess. Now, is she there? Yes or no?"

"Yes," Lake answered.

"We are in your debt. You will not be sorry. Now, call this man,"

Victor instructed as he handed Lake another card. "He is a detective with the NYPD. He will tell you what to do. Be honest with him and he will see that you and your firm come out of this smelling like a rose. In the meantime, as a gesture of our goodwill, whatever business you lose over the Carlyles, the Pos will match and better. I think you will be amazed at how much cleaner our hands are than those of your former client."

Victor made his goodbyes. He and Michael went to meet with Nicholas Hewett. Now that it was confirmed that Madame Po was being held at the Carlyle estate, plans had to be made to orchestrate a safe but effective assault. And, just as Michael had promised, Vincent Cogiulo was invited to take part along with members of the Trumenta family. The plan called for Nicholas Hewett to take Michael up the Hudson River to the back end of the Carlyle estate. Then Hewett would go to a designated spot to be picked up by Walter Larkin. He would also contact the local police to instruct them to go for an extended break for coffee and doughnuts between the designated hours of the operation.

It was decided that the best time to strike would be just before dawn. Michael would come up the back end of the property to try to gain access to the house. The Pos and Trumentas would take up flanking positions near the main gate so no one could escape. A NYPD S.W.A.T. team would handle the main assault. Theirs was the job of taking down the enemy. Michael's job was to locate and secure Madame Po by whatever means necessary. Everything was ready.

# CHAPTER FIFTY-ONE

## Revenge Is A Dish Best Served Cold

At 4:00 a.m. Michael's driver pulled into the yacht basin at Tarrytown-on-Hudson, just north of the Tappan Zee bridge to meet up with Hewett. Hewett was waiting for him and led Michael down the long wooden walkway to a gorgeous twenty-three foot wooden beauty. Michael released the lines and Hewett expertly directed the vessel out of its slip through the maze of yachts to a waiting Hudson River. Once clear, they accelerated to and maintained a speed of twenty knots all the way up to Rhinebeck. Michael wondered how they would find the exact spot. He need not have worried. Hewett knew the territory well. He steered the vessel easily through the overgrowth to an old dock which was in sad shape due to years of neglect.

Hewett had instructed Michael to bring a change of clothes as he would have to climb a waterfall at the back end of the property. It was the only access that would not be guarded. Hewett produced a waterproof duffel to carry his dry clothes in.

"Take these," Hewett instructed. They are night goggles. They will help you to avoid being surprised. When you get to the service road you will be about two hundred yards from the house. Stick close to the tall brush. It will hide you all the way up to the house. When you get near the house, be aware of the large trees just to the right.

They probably will be used for lookouts. You can also gain access to the second floor of the house by them. Get past the guards and you will have easy access."

They shook hands and Hewett wished Michael well. Michael got onto the dry land and made his way towards the waterfall. It was larger than he anticipated.

"Stay far to the right," Hewett had instructed. "No matter what happens, just stay as far as you can to the right. If you don't you could really get yourself hurt." Michael kept repeating these words over and over in his mind as he made his ascent. The night was warm but the water was surprisingly cold and slippery. The rubber soles of Michael's boat shoes aided in the climbing, giving a sense of stability to his feet as they pressed against the rocks. His climb was slow and deliberate. When he reached the top, he was soaking wet, just as Hewett had predicted. He opened the duffel and took out the night goggles to locate a place where he would feel safe to change. Once he located a suitable area, he quickly changed into dry clothes and sneakers. With the goggles in place, he began his journey towards the house.

Sunrise was at 6:03 a.m.. The guards would probably check in every half hour. Michael timed it so he would have a good half hour to dispose of any guards before he could be detected. Then there would be little time for those in the house to react. At daybreak, the assault team would begin its operation. Those in the house would be divided. It was a good plan.

Michael made his way along the dirt road to a spot approximately one hundred yards out where he spotted a lone guard leaning against a tree pouring coffee from a thermos into a plastic cup. Michael made his way to the other side of the road and settled down into the brush. He checked the terrain in all directions. Satisfied that he and the lookout were alone, he took off his night goggles to allow his eyes to adjust. Finally, he made his way towards the guard. The man was Chinese, but Michael did not know him.

"Nice night for a walk," he said to the startled lookout. The man dropped his coffee while nearly jumping out of his skin. Michael landed a spear blow with his fingers to the man's Adam's apple. The man grabbed at his throat as he began choking. Michael grabbed the back of his collar and slammed his head into the tree until his lifeless body fell to the ground. He put his night goggles back on and resumed his trek. He went another twenty-five or thirty yards and observed another guard positioned low in the brush. He made his way ever so slowly over towards him. He had to move painfully slowly, as there was no noise in the area to divert the man's attention. It was dead calm. Again, he removed his goggles. Almost out of instinct, Michael spoke Chinese to the guard.

"Seen anything out here?" he said. The startled guard tried to reach for his gun but Michael was instantly on him and threw the man to the ground face down. Michael quickly scaled his back and took the man's chin with both hands and snapped his head back violently, breaking his neck. As Michael reached for his night goggles he was surprised by a voice only a few feet away. Another guard was moving towards his position, complaining in Chinese about having to be out so late.

"It's about to be over soon," said Michael to the unsuspecting guard. When the man realized that it was Michael and not one of his crew, he quickly drew his knife and lunged at Michael. With his right hand, Michael deflected and grabbed the man's knife hand while simultaneously coming across to land the blade-like strike across the man's face and eyes. As the man relaxed his right hand to respond to the pain in his face, Michael directed the knife hand back up to strike him in his neck. As the man sank slowly to his knees he muttered "no man can be this fast," in total disbelief. He fell dead at Michael's feet.

Michael looked down at his two victims. Their deaths did not please him. He knew, of course, that they surely would have killed him. And, who knows, they might have taken great pleasure in doing it. But that was them and not he. Long ago, Michael had reconciled himself to the fact that people would die at his hands. He accepted the fate dealt him. He accepted it with much sadness. As Michael drew nearer to the house he noticed one lone guard standing on the porch on the second floor. Two giant elm trees stood nearby and offered access to that porch position. Night was ebbing quickly. In a few short moments light would be coming up and he would be totally exposed. Quickly, he mounted the tree furthest from the house. If he were noticed, he would have some protection. He climbed effortlessly to a branch parallel to the porch. Surprisingly, the guard was nowhere in sight. Michael scaled the limbs to reach the porch smoothly without making a sound. He noticed an open door, about ten feet from him on a diagonal to the limb on which he was standing

The flickering light of a cigarette appeared in the darkness as a guard came through the door and placed his weapon down. He picked up a pair of night goggles to scan the property. He heard a noise behind him and when he turned to see what it was, his face was met with the soul of Michael's shoe which struck with great force. The man's head shot backwards striking the wall behind him. As he began to collapse to the ground Michael grabbed him and lifted him back upright. He pivoted and landed a brutal side kick to the man's midsection nearly causing him to bring up last night's meal. Hardly conscious, he could do nothing to stave off Michael's final blow, another foot strike to his jaw which sent him over the banister and down to the ground below. His life ended with a thud.

Michael gained access to the house and made his way down the servants' back stairwell, which led to the kitchen. Hewett had described the home perfectly for him. As Michael made his way through the kitchen to the entrance to the dining room, he witnessed a great mass of confusion from the men in the house. The sun had come up and now the police presence was very noticeable. It wasn't long before both sides began exchanging fire. Michael knew we had to react quickly. He located the staircase to the second floor and made his way up.

He heard voices coming from what Hewett had described as the master suite. A man and a woman were yelling at each other. Michael slowly opened the door and could see Madame Po seated in a chair near one of the windows in what was the sitting nook. A great noise was coming from below. Voices screaming and the sounds of many guns exchanging fire were everywhere. The sound of bullets ripping through the structure of the home and of the shattering of windows was almost deafening.

Madame Po noticed Michael and motioned with her eyes that Lee Hong and the Carlyle woman were in the next room. Michael entered the room and formed a pistol with his hands, asking Madame Po if Lee Hong had a gun. Slowly, she made a negative response. Michael closed and locked the door behind him. Then he took a chair and wedged it under the handle to deny entry from the other side. He loosened Madame Po's bonds then made his way across the room to where Lee Hong and the Carlyle woman were still embroiled in a heated conversation. Michael came around the wall and entered the room.

"Michael," gasped Lee Hong, not believing his eyes.

"Time to die, Hong," said Michael.

Hong stood for a moment not sure what to do. Michael's showing up was something he had not considered. Hong's plan was to use Madame Po as a shield and once she had been killed by the bullets of those coming to rescue her, he would then charge them and die in a blaze of gunfire. Such was not to be his fate. Believing that Michael would kill him quickly by launching an assault, Hong charged Michael, who simply sidestepped him and grabbed him by the collar, and lifted him off the ground, dangling the poor man hopelessly in the air. Michael brought him down and applied a pressure point to the place where his neck and shoulder met, putting him to sleep.

"It's not going to be that easy for you, old man," said Michael, as he slowly lowered Hong's body to the expensively carpeted floor.

Just then, a gunshot rang out from behind Michael. The Carlyle woman had taken a pistol from her nightstand and pointed it straight at Michael's back. Lucky for Michael, Sung Mae intercepted her and knocked her to the floor, thus redirecting the bullet's flight. Michael walked over to retrieve the pistol, picked Millicent Carlyle up and placed her in a chair. All her fight was gone. She slumped back into the chair and began to cry.

"What have I done, what have I done?" she sobbed. She was the last of the Carlyles and, because of her, her family name would live on in infamy, and she knew it. She wished she could die right there. Madame Po would have been most willing to oblige her.

The shooting outside had stopped and now there were loud voices just outside the room.

"Police," barked an officer. "Open the door."

"I'm opening the door," Michael responded, loudly. "We are unarmed."

The officers had instructions to keep their weapons ready until it was confirmed that Michael and Madame Po were safe. Michael opened the door and saw Walter Larkin's face behind two large police officers dressed in full combat gear.

"Wait here," Larkin instructed the officers. "Make sure the house and grounds are completely secured," he ordered.

"We had an agreement, Walter, one that I expect you to honor," said Michael.

Michael knew he had to turn Lee Hong over to his family so they could take their revenge. But, he also knew that Walter's honor and trust were at stake here. Walter's value would be worthless if the Pos and Trumentas could not trust him at his word.

"I assume this is the Carlyle woman," said Walter, pointing to Millicent Carlyle who was sitting lifelessly in the chair.

"Yes," Michael responded.

"Are you all right, Madame Po?" Walter asked as he moved his attention to her.

"It is very kind of you to ask, Detective," Sung Mae responded. "My nephew has seen to my safety."

"Your uncle has a car around back. Take your man down the back stairwell. Be gone in less than ten minutes, Michael. The local cops will be coming soon," said Walter. " Coffee break is over."

Michael quickly picked Lee Hong up and flung him over his shoulder, then led Madame Po down to the back exit. Han Li could hardly contain himself at the sight of his wife all safe and sound. He and Sung Mae shared a long embrace.

"Quickly, Uncle," warned Michael. "You must leave now."

"Throw this dung in the trunk," Han Li ordered. "Victor and the Trumentas have organized quite a reception for him in Brooklyn."

Michael responded and then watched as Han Li's cars sped off towards the main gate. Nicholas Hewett stood on the front steps waiting to see Millicent Carlyle coming of the house out in police custody.

"I read her Miranda," the head SWAT officer informed Walter.

"Good, now take her to the city and book her," Walter instructed. 'Just a minute," he said, as he stopped the officer's progress. He motioned for Hewett to come over to where they were standing. Hewett walked over and stood in front of Millicent Carlyle whose head was bowed.

"Got anything to say to this woman?" Walter asked.

Slowly, Millicent Carlyle lifted her eyes to meet those of Hewett. The look of sheer contempt and disgust in his eyes made words unnecessary. The look in his eyes sickened Millicent Carlyle. The Hewetts had been there for her when her brother's name had been scandalized. It seemed inconceivable to her that she could be the one to destroy the life of her dear friend. All the hatred she had harbored for so long was gone. Now, there was only shame and deep regret.

# CHAPTER FIFTY-TWO

The mood at Chin Wah was boisterous. The Pos were celebrating in grand style. Three days had passed since the assault up in Rhinebeck, and things were beginning to get back to normal. Han Li and Madame Po were working the crowd of Po insiders along with Big Al, Patty and a contingent of Trumentas.

Michael and Cheun Sing were content to sit off alone and observe the festivities. A great disaster had been avoided. Now it was time for thanksgiving and celebration.

"Tell me, my husband, does this celebration mean that all this business is finally behind us?" asked Cheun Sing.

"You know that there is much about the inner workings of our family of which I have no knowledge," said Michael. "But Victor informs me that the Trumentas, and in particular Carmine Cogiulo, have been avenged. We were honor bound to see that they witnessed the execution of Lee Hong. Many innocent people suffered at his hands. You can be sure Victor's methods were long and very painful.

"Cheun Sing placed her hand gently on Michael's "Yes, husband, and you also," she said. "I feel a sense of sadness that it was something so horrible that allowed us to be together. I shall never fail you, Michael, never."

Michael gently wrapped his hands around Cheun Sing's. He carefully measured his words. "I know, my love, and sadly, I do agree with you. All that happened in the past was necessary to bring us to this time. I cherish the memories of Mae Lin and Katherine, because they were wonderful people who gave their love to me. For me, that is the greatest gift anyone can receive. But now, it is obvious that my life, my destiny is with you. And I could not possibly be happier. To be a Po and to share that life with you is all I could ask for.

Michael and Cheun Sing looked lovingly into each other's eyes and shared a long kiss. After a pause Cheun Sing asked, "Do you suppose anyone would mind if we were to leave, Michael? After all, we are still on our honeymoon and there is still much work to be done."

"Work?" said Michael. "What work could there possibly be after all we have been through?" he wanted to know.

Cheun Sing's eyes met his, then ever so softly, she said, "An heir."

Michael smiled and looked over to where Wee was sitting. Suddenly he turned back. I'm sorry, did you just say heir?" asked Michael, completely taken aback.

Cheun Sing simply smiled. Obviously that was a "yes."

"Well, time to leave," exclaimed Michael as he bolted to his feet. He took Cheun Sing's hand and led her up. Once again they kissed, then began making the rounds of goodbyes to begin their quest of a greater cause.

THE END

# EPILOGUE

Michael and Cheun Sing live in New York City. Theirs is a fascinating life as members of one of the wealthiest and most powerful crime families in the world; a world that can be as dangerous as it is glamorous. Michael enjoys a close relationship with a high-ranking police official and is at times, a confidante of the mayor's office. An Italian-American Chinese Grandmaster; Michael wears many hats and is often called upon to operate on all sides without violating any.

His is an American story, for only in America could such a story take place. And yes, that greater quest did bear fruit. Their names are Daniel Manasseh and Isaiah Ephraim.

# ACKNOWLEGEMENTS

With great appreciation and endearing friendship, I would like to thank the following invaluable contributions to this book.

Pat Cucuzza - For keeping me on point.

Tina Laychak - For diligent monitoring of the text.

Arthur Shulz - For constantly building me up and encouraging me on.

Bishop Jay Ramirez - For inspiration and unwavering friendship.

Raquel Torres-Del Monte - My wonderful daughter who never seems to think I can't do it.

Special thanks to Toula Magi without whose help this project would never have gotten off the ground.

To all of the above, I extend my most fervent appreciation for all you have done, valuable time spent and cheering me on.

# About the Author

Alan Del Monte is a successful hairdresser and salon owner in Milford, Connecticut. A former high school history teacher, Alan also spent ten years in New York City recording studios as a musician and sound engineer. Today, Alan spends his time writing novels in many genres. Alan and his wife, Jan live overlooking the waters of Long Island Sound, in the Woodmont section of Milford. Alan has two children and seven grandchildren.

# OTHER BOOKS BY ALAN DEL MONTE

www.ingramcontent.com/pod-product-compliance
Lightning Source LLC
Chambersburg PA
CBHW020829260626
47169CB00003B/905